THE GLASS SLIPPER

G·K
Hall
&Cº

Also by Mignon G. Eberhart
in Large Print:

Alpine Condo Crossfire
Another Woman's House
Casa Madrone
A Fighting Chance
Five Passengers from Lisbon
Hasty Wedding
Murder by an Aristocrat
The Mystery of Hunting's End
Next of Kin
The Patient in Room 18
Three Days for Emeralds
Two Little Rich Girls
Unidentified Woman
The White Cockatoo

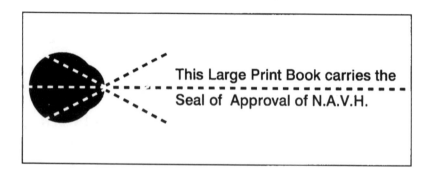

This Large Print Book carries the
Seal of Approval of N.A.V.H.

THE GLASS SLIPPER

Mignon G. Eberhart

G.K. Hall & Co. • Thorndike, Maine

Published in 1998 by arrangement with
Brandt & Brandt Literary Agents, Inc.

G.K. Hall Large Print Romance Series.

The text of this Large Print edition is unabridged.
Other aspects of the book may vary from the original edition.

Set in 16 pt. Plantin by Minnie B. Raven.

Printed in the United States on permanent paper.

Library of Congress Cataloging in Publication Data

Eberhart, Mignon Good, 1899–
    The glass slipper / Mignon G. Eberhart.
      p.   cm.
    ISBN 0-7838-0143-2 (lg. print : hc : alk. paper)
    1. Large type books.   I. Title.
  [PS3509.B453G53   1998]
  813′.52—dc21
                                            98-13746

THE GLASS SLIPPER

CHAPTER I

It was Steven who talked of the glass slipper. That was the night the thing began; the night Rue Hatterick had her first intimation of disaster; the night of November eighteenth. That was the night Flagstad sang Isolde, the night of the Bachelors and Benedicts ball; a cold, drearily rainy night in Chicago, with the pavements slick and shining with reflected lights from the towers of Chicago's near north side.

Rue gave herself a last glance in the mirror and went to the window and pushed aside the gray taffeta curtains which had been selected as everything else in the house had been selected by her predecessor, the first Mrs Hatterick. Brule had not come home to dinner, and she had not yet heard him arrive, and they were going to be late. She looked down into the street below — or tried to look — but the black windowpane only reflected herself in her shimmering silver-shift gown. It was a clouded image, however, darkened by the black backdrop of the night outside, she looked strange to herself standing there, a slender, fair woman with bare, smooth white shoulders and light hair exactly and faultlessly coiled. Her mouth was scarlet, and in that wavering reflection her black eyebrows looked a little heavy and serious and her gentian-blue eyes very brilliant.

How many times had she seen herself reflected just so in the dark glitter of a window against the still night. With startling clearness the composite recollection of many nights came to her; anxious, muted nights in a great hospital; herself raising or lowering a window, pausing to put her cheek for an instant's rest against the cold glass — and to see herself then, as now, as another woman. Then her fair hair was not so faultlessly done but instead was pulled back smoothly to a knot below her starched, trim white cap; her nurse's uniform was white and crisp and trimly tailored, refreshingly astringent in memory and in contrast to the clinging, artful loveliness of the gown she now wore; her face then was scrubbed and bare of any suggestion of make-up. For the chief of staff, the great and famous surgeon, the veritable emperor of that small, intensely circumscribed and terribly important world, Dr Brule Hatterick, had frowned on make-up on the faces of his nurses.

But he liked it on his wife's face — softly and glamorously applied. He didn't like the serious, thoughtful expression her beautifully planed face with its firm generous chin and curving red mouth was all too likely to take on. Moments when her dark-fringed eyes were likely to be intensely blue and straight and keen as a whip and uncomfortably serious. And unfortunately there had been too many times during the short period of Rue's marriage to her emperor when she had

8

looked just like that — as serious, Brule Hatterick would say, as if she were assisting him, as she had done so many times, at a very difficult operation. It annoyed him. He wanted her to be gay and laughing and, though he didn't say it, frivolous. A doll, pleased with the pretty things he gave her instead of love. A person who didn't really matter and thus wouldn't trouble his conscience.

Not that she had any right to expect his love, that had been clearly understood, and it was outside their agreement. But it had been a serious business, stepping into another woman's place, trying to fulfill all the duties that had fallen to the lot of the well-known and socially prominent first Mrs. Hatterick, Crystal Hatterick, whose beautiful portrait still hung in Brule's library.

Rue let the curtains drop into place. By putting her forehead to the cool glass — approaching close to that strange woman who looked back at her — she could perceive street lights and the long black outline of the Hatterick limousine opposite the front door, but Brule's coupé was nowhere to be seen. Perhaps he had arrived while she was dressing.

She was nervous. She went back to the dressing table, touched her hair, which was pulled upward away from her face in the mode and arranged in smooth curls high on her head, hesitated a moment to make sure there was no flaw, no wrinkle in her gown, no detail that was out of place and that Brule's eyes that saw every-

9

thing would see and disapprove. A little gust of impatience touched her, and with one of the impulsive gestures she was learning to control, she picked up long white gloves and small, jeweled bag and turned to leave her room.

The big silken bedroom which had been in its pseudo-Victorian luxuriousness a triumph of the decorator employed and assisted by Crystal Hatterick. Crystal had liked the thin, old French carpet with its faded pastel flowers; the chaise longue heaped in satin and lace pillows; the tiny pink marble mantel with its gilt clock and mirror; the ruffled, elaborate dressing table; the French prints on the soft gray walls; the great swan bed with its crepe de chine sheets and its down puffs; even the adjoining bathroom was done in soft, flattering shades of pink, and the great clothes closets were lined in quilted satin, heavily scented.

The first time Rue had ever entered that room she had hated the soft, enveloping scent of roses that permeated it; she still hated it and could not entirely dispossess it. It clung to the room like a ghostly reminder of Crystal's presence.

A French screen, all cupids and Fragonard-like ladies and gilt, stood before the door.

Rue, pausing, remembered sharply and clearly the first time she'd entered that room; she saw herself standing on the threshold, a little hesitant because it was the great Mrs Brule Hatterick she had come to nurse; because she had been se-

lected (from all the nurses at the hospital) by
Dr Brule Hatterick to care for his wife. She'd
had a panicky instant, standing there in the
shadow of the great screen, her blue nurse's cape
still over her shoulders; her little leather bag in
her hand. What would Mrs Hatterick be like?
Would she be a difficult patient? Would she,
Rue, succeed in the exacting eyes of the great
Brule Hatterick? It had taken all her courage to
step around that screen and go to Crystal, ill,
white, hard to please, waiting for her in that
great soft bed.

She had failed because Crystal Hatterick had
died. Yet she hadn't failed in Brule Hatterick's
eyes; for a short ten months later he had married
her.

Married her and brought her as mistress to
that house she had first entered as a nurse. Crystal's house.

The autumn had not been so difficult; they'd
been at camp; she'd been able to fall in with the
routine of the household even if she had not
quite grasped the reins of it from the capable
and determined hands of the domestic staff
Crystal had hired and trained. Steven had
helped, quietly and kindly. Madge had been her
main problem, but she had known Madge would
be; it was mainly because of Madge, Brule had
told her in that curiously frank interview, that
he wanted her, Rue, for a wife.

But now it was winter; the social season was
beginning; Brule depended upon her to carry on

exactly the same life Crystal had balanced so easily and lightly in her poised and certain hands. But Crystal had been born in that very house; it had been her money and her position that had started Brule on his meteorlike flight upward. She had been considerably older than Brule; she had known all the people who could help him; she had known all the affiliations, all the loyalties, all the age-established feuds; she had known who counted and who didn't; she had made no mistakes. Rue had all that to learn; and she must learn it, for Brule's position demanded it, and Madge, now fifteen, later must be suitably launched.

Well, Alicia would help. Alicia Pelham, who had been Crystal's best friend and was to be married to Steven.

It must be that Brule had arrived without her knowledge and was now dressing in his own rooms at the end of the narrow long hall. This was one of the first big nights of the season; surely he wouldn't be late, certainly he would be there to support Rue in her new, untried role.

Yes, she was nervous.

Only her fellow nurses at the hospital would have guessed that nervousness. It made her eyes a little brighter, her head more erect, her movements a little more deliberately controlled.

In the hall she met Steven, and he paused to look at her.

"Going to the opera?"

"Yes."

"And to the ball later?"

"Yes."

He smiled down at her. Steven Hendrie, tall, dark, with his temples faintly gray, was a distinguished-looking man in his late thirties. And he actually was distinguished, for he was a composer of note in spite of the semi-invalidism which had dogged him for years. His big, time-mellowed Steinway piano was in a sunny corner of the wing on the first floor which had been built for his workroom; the repetitious, clear notes from the piano were so constantly and familiarly a part of the fabric of the household that you were almost unconscious of the sound.

Crystal's brother — or stepbrother, was it? — and Brule's patient, Steven was a fixture in the Hatterick household. He had never married, though his engagement to Alicia Pelham was a long-standing affair. Crystal probably had liked having him there, especially when he became famous. And after Crystal's death he had stayed on with them, for it was his home as much as it was Brule's, since Crystal had willed it to them jointly. He bore his share of the expenses, so he was in no way a pensioner on Brule's bounty. Rue liked him, for he'd been from the first her friend. She never knew exactly how much he knew of her curious relationship with Brule, but she thought he guessed a great deal, for he was extremely sensitive. And, especially lately, he had befriended her in many small ways. Steven, indeed, made her life bearable. And Steven

13

could always manage Madge. She answered the smile in his deep-set, strangely luminous brown eyes with cheerful friendliness.

"You are very splendid," he said. "Schiaparelli?"

"Yes. My first." Rue looked down at the expertly suave lines of her gown.

It was then that quite suddenly Steven's eyes sobered. He touched the dress lightly with his strong, musician's fingers. And he said rather gently: "Little Cinderella. I wonder — does the glass slipper ever pinch your little foot?"

Cinderella. It was an apt analogy of course, so far as it went.

She was mistress of that house and all its luxury and beauty. In the hall below a maid waited with a dark sable wrap of incredible softness to place around Rue's shoulders. Outside a motor was waiting, long and shining, with a uniformed chauffeur at the wheel.

A year ago, thought Rue with a strange little clutch at her heart, she had scrambled for a place on the crowded elevated; had clung to a swaying strap, had fought her way through crowded streets. Curiously there was a touch of sadness in the thought. She ought to be happy. Married to the chief of staff; the fashionable young Mrs Hatterick — jewels, gowns with the labels of famous dressmakers, furs — everything a girl could want.

Steven was waiting, looking into her eyes without, now, the faintest glimmer of a smile. It was

14

as if he really wanted to know something that Rue could not tell him. As if he waited for an answer, and the answer was one that Rue could not give.

"No," she said, avoiding his eyes. "It doesn't pinch. Is Madge downstairs, do you know?"

It was a rebuff. Steven's eyes deepened a little. He said coolly: "You would never tell if it did. Yes, Madge is still downstairs, I think. Do you want to see her?"

"I thought I'd show her my dress. But — I'm not sure Brule has come yet."

"He hasn't." Steven looked at his watch. "I'm afraid you're going to be very late. I expect he was detained with a patient. Don't mind being late; it will only give Brule a chance to show you off in all your glory. There's nothing like entering a box in the middle of the overture for getting the concerted gaze of all the opera glasses in the house. And I must say you'll do him credit. It's your first public appearance, isn't it?"

"I — yes."

"Don't worry. You're very beautiful. Here's Madge now."

She came up the stairway, eyes lowered and pretending to be unconscious of Rue and Steven standing at the top of the steps. She was a living, feminine reproduction of Brule; lithe and compact and trim, with ruddy cheeks and wide, ruthless jaws, masked only a little by the youthful roundness of her face. Her thick hair was cut long and fell on her shoulders in a dark mane;

15

her mouth was straight and a little sulky; even her square small hands were suggestive of strength.

She said nothing. Steven spoke, bridging the gap between Rue and Madge as he had done so often in the past two months.

"Isn't she lovely, Madge?"

Madge stopped. She wore a simple, dark silk dinner gown with a little-girl white collar; she looked demure, if sullen; but then she lifted thick long eyelashes and gave Rue an altogether unchildish look.

"It is a beautiful gown," she said coolly and added with studied rudeness, "My father chose it, didn't he, Rue?"

"I chose it," said Rue. "But I hope Brule likes it."

"It must be nice," said Madge, "to have so much money to spend. You never had it before, did you?"

"Madge," said Steven quickly and sharply, "don't be silly and childish." Madge whirled abruptly away and went quickly up the second flight of stairs without another word, and Steven turned hopelessly to Rue. "I'm sorry, Rue," he said. "She's got dreadful manners and a worse disposition. She looks like Brule, but she's exactly like Crystal."

"Hush, she'll hear you. . . . I don't blame the child. It can't be easy to see another woman taking your mother's place. She loved her mother."

Madge's own door closed. Steven said slowly: "Madge is too young and too selfish to love anything. Don't mind her, Rue. She'll come around."

Another door opened and closed heavily. It was the great front door in the hall below, and Rue said: "It's Brule. I'll go down to meet him. Good night, Steven. I wish you were coming."

"I wish so too," said Steven. "Well, my dear, keep your chin up but don't lead with it."

He knew she was nervous. He knew she dreaded the thing that lay before her: the eyes, the leveled opera glasses and lorgnettes, the whispers. That's the new Mrs Hatterick. The nurse he married, you know, after Crystal died. So soon after, too. They say she was the nurse who took care of Crystal when she died. How young she is! Well, you never know.

She wondered if any of them would be kind.

Steven took her hand and in an encouraging gesture touched it gently with his lips, and Rue smiled her gratitude and went down the curving stairway, clinging a little to the polished railing, her short train swishing gently on the steps. Would Brule be pleased with her appearance?

But it wasn't Brule who waited for her in the library.

It was Andy Crittenden. Dr Andrew Crittenden.

She stopped short on the threshold. Expecting Brule, it was disconcerting to see instead a tall, lean figure whose youthfully graceful shoulders

17

and blond hair she instantly recognized. He was standing with his back to the doorway, pouring himself a drink from the bottle and siphon which stood on a tray on a table. But she knew instantly that it was Andy Crittenden, for he was as familiar a figure as was Brule. How many hundreds of times had she bobbed to her feet when he entered a hospital room, swiftly, yet with an appearance of cool leisure and a charming smile as was his way. Brule was reverenced by the nurses, sometimes hated, always feared, instantly obeyed. But Andy was adored; they hung on his words; they invented excuses for seeking those words. He was young, his eyebrows had a humorous lift; his orders were terse and brisk and not pompous. And he had a way with women, a charm that went straight to the nurses' hearts. Except, that is, with Rue. She hated men who had a way with women. She hated men whom nurses from their feminine-burdened world adored. And she hated Andy Crittenden after she had nursed Crystal.

But he was like a son to Brule except in years; he shared Brule's offices; he had been from the first Brule's protégé and friend. Even after Crystal's death and the things Brule must have guessed, Brule still was Andy's best friend. He sent him patients, he permitted Andy to pinch-hit for him when Brule himself had other and more important irons in the fire; if Brule had a confidant, Rue thought, it must be Andy Crittenden. Brule, then, was as sensitive to Andy's charm as any of Andy's fluttering female patients. There was nothing Rue could do about it; and she had been trained in a hard school to keep quiet when she could do nothing. She had to admit — for Rue had the habit of honesty — that Andy was a good doctor, he might even have had the brilliant career that had already begun for him without Brule's help. She had nursed for Andy as she had for Brule, and she gave him grudgingly a professional respect. And because of Brule she'd had to accord him a surface friendliness.

He emptied his glass and poured another, while Rue, a small straight figure, watched him with implacable eyes. Drinking too much, too, she thought; a man as young as Andy Crittenden didn't need two stiff highballs to brace himself for — well, for what? Why was he there? And where was Brule?

He put down the glass and then sensed her presence and turned. He wore tails and a white tie, and all the nurses in the hospital would probably have swooned away from sheer admiration. Rue's mouth tightened. He said: "Ah, there you are. I was waiting for you."

She came into the room toward him. Odd how a beautiful gown gave you poise and an ability to appear gracious whether you felt gracious or not. "For me?"

He was ill at ease. He said: "Yes, of course. Didn't Brule telephone?"

Andy always knew more of Brule's affairs than

she, his wife, knew. Was it possible that she was jealous of Andy? No, certainly not. She had other and fully sufficient reasons for her hatred.

He noted her hesitation. He said quickly: "I expect he didn't have time. He was hurrying off. He said he had a patient. He meant to telephone to you himself. He can't make it tonight. He — he sent me instead. If you don't mind."

"You mean he can't go?" It was a disappointment; she'd been depending upon Brule's assurance and support.

"Brule ought to have telephoned. He — it's one of those things — he said he couldn't help it. He was awfully sorry. Do you mind awfully if I — take you instead?"

"Thank you. It's kind of you. But I think I won't go tonight. I — I didn't really feel up to it anyway. I — was only going because Brule wanted me to go. I —" To her own astonishment and with a slight feeling of shame she resorted to the old and tried excuse. "I've had a headache all day. . . ."

He was watching her, his blue eyes narrowed and keen.

"You look well," he said rather dryly. "I never saw you look better. Or knew you to have a headache."

Before she realized his intention he came to her, touched her cheek with the back of his hand then put cool strong fingers on her pulse. Never lie to a doctor, thought Rue absurdly as she forced herself to meet his eyes openly. For a

20

sharp, still instant they stood there facing each other.

Then Andy released her wrist.

"I want you to go," he said abruptly. "There's a special reason. I've got to talk to you."

CHAPTER II

Later, in the warm motor, purring quietly along Michigan Boulevard, she wondered a little that she had given in so easily. Was it habit, because she had for five years obeyed Brule and obeyed Andy's least and smallest order? Was it because she forgot for the moment that she was now Mrs Brule Hatterick, enviable in her security, in her luxury, in her position?

Her sable wrap was light and warm about her shoulders; she pulled on her long white gloves slowly. The tonneau was warm and deliciously comfortable in contrast to the glimpses of cold, wind-swept streets through which they passed. The Wrigley Building rose white, wraithlike under its floodlights; on the other side was the lighted entrance of Tribune Square below tier after tier of offices, lighted only here and there, which rose into the dark night. There was a bitterly cold wind off the lake, and flurries of snow which looked unutterably desolate swept along empty streets. The bridge was up, and they waited for it.

Andy, beside her, took off his opera hat, smoothed it thoughtfully and replaced it. His white scarf came up to his chin, his profile was clear in the half-light. From the river below, lost in the darkness, a freight boat tooted hoarsely.

Andy leaned over and rolled up the glass between the tonneau and the front seat where Kendal, the chauffeur, sat, straight-necked and imperturbable.

How well Andy knew the car! How instantly his gloved hand had found the correct lever when he closed the window!

Rue wondered what he wanted to say to her. Evidently he didn't want the chauffeur to overhear. It was something about Brule of course. Was Andy intending to take her to task for some unconscious failure in her role?

Even in the car, which Crystal had used almost exclusively, there was a lingering, faint scent of roses. Rue moved restlessly and looked out the window. The scent of roses always reminded her strongly of Crystal; it was almost as if it were intentional on Crystal's part. Crystal, that tall, thin woman with ash-blonde hair, into whose place Rue had stepped.

How many times, Rue wondered, had Andy, top-hatted and white-tied and correct, escorted Crystal? Well, if he had anything to say, let him say it.

The barge, unseen in the shadows below, tooted again. Other cars had halted around them; their motors throbbed, and the medicinal smell of alcohol from radiators drifted upon the cold air.

Andy said suddenly in the semidarkness: "I think we'd better go to the opera, if only for the first act. Then we can leave and go somewhere we can talk. Unheard."

Rue turned with a jerk.

"Why, really, Andy! As if anything you have to tell me can't be said openly."

Andy interrupted her.

"You are quite wrong. You don't seem to understand . . . The bridge is going down again. We'll not be late."

Rue gave a small, rather nervous laugh.

"What is wrong, Andy? You sound quite forbidding. Is it — have I been neglecting Brule?"

"No," said Andy. "You've not been neglecting Brule. It's just that I think it's best for you to be seen at the opera as if nothing had happened."

"As if —" Again Rue turned abruptly toward him. "What on earth do you mean? What has happened? Brule —"

"Oh, Brule's all right. Nothing has happened. It was just a chance expression. Don't pay any attention to what I say."

Incoherence was not one of Andy Crittenden's traits. He had as a rule wit and decision. But he was also obstinate; as obstinate as Brule but not in Brule's unpleasant manner.

It meant now that whatever he had to say he found difficult and that he would take his own good time about saying it. Well, then she could be as obstinate.

Besides, he could have nothing very serious to say; she hastily canvassed the possibilities; he might have a message from Brule to her, and that held unpredictable potentiality. Otherwise there was nothing.

The bridge went down, and the stream of motors moved smoothly forward across the bridge, with the huge, lighted bulk of the merchandise mart glowing above the river at their right. Into the stream of traffic along Michigan with the lighted store windows looking bright and cold. There were few pedestrians, and those they saw were hurrying, bent against the savage wind.

Andy sat frowning, saying nothing. They turned on Randolph Street, passed, now, crowds and lighted moving-picture theaters. There was Henrici's, in a curious way the very heart of Chicago; it had been there and it would be there, catching the flow and pulse of the life of a great city. The theaters were lighted; already girls in fluffy long skirts with their youthful, very dressed-up escorts, were pouring into the Sherman Hotel on their way to the College Inn. They crossed under the stark, dark beams of the elevated, and a string of lighted cars rumbled and rattled swiftly over their heads. Kendal turned again on Wacker Drive; cars were thicker here, and became increasingly numerous until as they crossed Washington Boulevard they were obliged to crawl along, a foot at a time, in a flood of other long, chauffeur-driven cars, which gave glimpses of women, furred and jeweled, unassailable in their security against the cold, against the traffic hazards, against anything that was unsafe.

Well, she was safe. Cinderella. Married to the king of her world. Who could be safer?

She saw herself, suddenly, scurrying along Randolph, almost exactly a year ago now; taking the streetcar, transferring to a bus, clutching her little leather bag, aware that her nurse's cape gave her a kind of immunity. She had gone that way the day she went from the hospital to nurse Crystal.

Now she was riding so softly, so safely; so warmed and protected and secure, in her own car.

They were almost there. She fumbled with the fastening of her glove, and Andy saw it and turned, taking off his own gloves.

"Let me," he said and fastened the glove swiftly and with the certain deftness of his surgeon's fingers.

The car drew up at last before the entrance to the Civic Opera. Women, their gowns shimmering in all colors below their furs, were crossing the wide walk quickly, so the wind would not disturb their elaborately coifed hair. Men were assisting their ladies' progress with one hand and clutching their top hats with the other. The walk before the Civic Opera entrance was always windy, always cold.

An attendant opened the car door. The cold wind struck against her silk-clad ankles and thin little silver sandals. Andy paused to speak to Kendal. A newsboy was near, shouting his wares above the din of motors and cars and the

26

shouted orders of the mounted policemen. Andy turned, saw the newsboy and lingered to buy a paper and, in the cold and wind and under the great lights, to glance quickly and anxiously along the headlines. He frowned and threw the paper down and led her into the warm, bright confusion of the lobby.

He knew, even, the number of the box which the Hattericks shared and had shared for years with two other families, and established Rue in her pink plush chair expertly. No one else was in the box that night, and Rue was glad. The overture had begun; the rustle and murmur was dying down, although new arrivals constantly drew the attention of the battery of opera glasses and delicate small lorgnettes.

In Chicago, and in spite of sundry vicissitudes, the opera is still fashionable. Below the great, modernly rectangular proscenium, the orchestra seats were ablaze with color and jewels; behind them and above, the boxes were like velvet jewel cases themselves, flatteringly in the softest pink, only a little shaded by Chicago's soot. And, like jewel cases, they set off beauty and color and glitter.

"Everyone is here," said Andy. "Hello — there's Alicia." There was a note of surprise in his voice which Rue was aware of even as she turned to follow his look.

"Over there," he said. "With the Streeters."

"Oh, I see. How lovely she is."

Alicia Pelham was lovely; Rue thought she was

the loveliest woman she had ever seen, so utterly beautiful that it was actually difficult to talk to her — you were so transfixed with admiration. Alicia was probably in her late thirties and certainly more beautiful than she had been at any time, for her beauty was the kind that richens and glows with maturity. Her black hair was shot with unashamed gray, triumphant because of her small, unlined and classically beautiful face. Her eyes were deep, brilliant gray like jewels, except that only an emerald approached their brilliancy and hardness, and an emerald is green. She was tall and white-skinned, with jet-black eyelashes which accented and never veiled the brilliancy of her eyes. Her face was pointed and small; her lips deeply crimson over incredibly white and perfect teeth. She smiled seldom and faintly; yet she was a brilliant conversationalist.

She had been for years Crystal's best friend. She had no money in later years, and Crystal had calmly supplied her with a sum which met Alicia's living expenses, and Alicia as calmly had accepted it, as well as a substantial legacy at the time of Crystal's death. They had been schoolmates; they had gone to debut parties together; Alicia had been Crystal's bridesmaid at her wedding, but Alicia had never married. Not, Rue knew, for lack of offers. Alicia Pelham could have had almost any man she wanted by lifting one of her slender, long, white fingers.

She had never married; she lived in her own small, perfectly furnished apartment; she had many friends; she went constantly; her name was almost never out of the society columns. Somehow she managed, with no visible source of income, to clothe herself beautifully; probably the dressmakers were glad to have Miss Alicia Pelham's patronage. She wore jewels too; emeralds as a rule, which were supposed to have come from the wreck of the Pelham fortune. She opened bazaars; she greeted distinguished guests; her small, perfectly cooked dinners were famous among a chosen few. Somehow she managed to have pictures done by the very latest and most fashionable painter; the cleverest writers, visiting the city, somehow turned up to lunch with her at the Foreign Club; the best-known actresses and singers and playwrights appeared at her small after-the-theater suppers.

Always an intimate of the Hatterick household, she had at last become engaged to Steven Hendrie. The engagement had lasted for two years. Rue thought, privately, that Alicia was not too anxious to give up her own independent, utterly free life; her little trips abroad with friends who, Rue imagined, obligingly paid the expenses; her own desirability as a single, unattached woman guest at those dinners where a single woman is so urgently needed to fill in. Perhaps, after all those years, Alicia was simply and comprehensibly loath to give up her own manner of life. Certainly there was no rift between her and Steven. Certainly Steven was a man any woman would have been proud to marry. Rue's heart warmed at the thought of Steven.

She looked at Andy. He was still frowning at Alicia. And he looked, she realized suddenly, terribly worried. In the shadow of the motor she had not perceived that. Now, in the light, she saw the tenseness of his mouth, the small sharp line between his eyebrows that, in the old days, had meant he was frightened about a patient. Something quick and cold and uneasy clutched at her. All his talk in the car, then, had not been just talk. There really was something troublesome that he knew and wanted to tell her. She had been wrong to permit herself to be confused or annoyed. She said suddenly, reversing unconsciously to her old manner of address:

"Doctor Crittenden —"

She had not called him that since her marriage.

He turned quickly.

"Andy, I mean. I — there is something wrong. I didn't understand. You must tell me."

He hesitated and glanced over his shoulder at the pink curtains over the door into the box.

"All right," he said. "If you must have it. No one can hear; it's as good a place as any. Something pretty awful has happened. I — I don't know how to tell you. I've been trying to find some way. I —"

Waves of music crashed around them. Rue put her hands on the railing of the box. He said unexpectedly:

"It's about Crystal."

"Crystal?"

"Yes. It's — God, Rue, I hate to tell you this. But you've got to know. You see, they've been inquiring. They came to see me. Because I was her doctor, you see. I was the attendant physician."

"I don't understand you." It was herself, but her voice sounded strange and muted by the music.

"Of course you don't. You see — well, it's the police. They came to my office this afternoon. Rue, don't scream — don't faint — you look so white. I oughtn't to have told you here. But there's not much time —"

Rue gripped the railing with gloved, numb hands. What monstrous thing was he trying to tell her? She heard him say, clear and close to her ear:

"They say Crystal was murdered. And you see, you were her nurse. And you married Brule."

It was sheer luck, though Rue was quite unconscious of it, that the lights were lowered just then. Vaguely she knew that Andy had taken her hand; had moved his chair closer to her, was trying to tell her more, was warning her, was saying low and urgently:

"Rue, be careful. Don't say anything. What a fool I am! I oughtn't to have told you here. Rue, Rue —"

"I was with her when she died." Her own

31

words were dragged from some enormous, diz-zying cavern.

"Look here. We've made an appearance here. The house is dark. No one will notice. Let's go. Come —"

He was propelling her to her feet, quietly to the rear of the box; the curtain was up, and a tremendous, lovely wave of sound swept the house. No one would see. No one would notice their departure. They were outside the box. They were walking swiftly along the heavily car-peted floors. Here was the elevator. The atten-dant looked at them curiously. Andy said tersely, as if his voice were a wire stretched tight:

"There's a drugstore somewhere near, isn't there?"

The boy said yes, and gestured.

Bright lights and the cold wind sweeping her skirt tight against her body, entangling her feet in her own train. Andy had a tight grip on her arm. How cold and sharp the wind was! How bright and exposed the long, platformlike walk seemed.

Then they reached the drugstore, bright and shining and smelling of food. It was warm there; too warm. The heat and the lights were unut-terably confusing. She was sitting at a small, white-topped table. A boy came to ask for their order, and his face swam hazily against the warmth and lightness.

Andy must have given an order, for all at once there was a white, steaming cup at her hand.

"It's black coffee," said Andy. "Maybe you ought to have brandy. But I — you've got to listen. Drink it."

The cup shook in her hand and spilled, and she thought, It's ruining my glove. Andy's been drinking too much. He's had some terrible thing happen — he doesn't know what he's saying — it is not true.

The hot liquid all but burned her tongue.

"Better?" said Andy. The boy had gone to the front of the store and turned on the little radio; there was dance music; and the boy looked out at the cold, wind-swept street and whistled, keeping time and tune with the music from the radio.

"He can't hear," said Andy. "You've got to listen, Rue. You've got to do as I tell you."

"When —" whispered Rue stiffly and stopped.

"You mean when did I hear it? Tonight. Just after the office closed. The police — two detectives — came to me."

She had to moisten her lips.

"Does Brule know?"

Andy looked away from her; he took a long time about drinking something in a glass. He said then:

"Yes, he knows. He — couldn't come himself. He — Rue, listen. You don't realize what it's going to be. You see, I think — God, Rue, don't look like that."

In a split second of terrifying prescience she knew what he was going to say.

"You —"

"I think they are right. I think she was murdered." He said it almost defiantly.

Yes, he was mad. He'd been Crystal's doctor. He'd signed the death certificate. Someone's — her own — cup clattered loudly against the table, and Andy glanced sharply at the boy, still oblivious to them, and back at Rue.

"And," said Andy with paralyzing unexpectedness, "I want you to come away with me. Away from Chicago, I mean. Now. It's the only way." He leaned across the table, the lean angle of his jaw sharp against the bright orange of an advertising placard behind him. He said urgently: "You're in danger, Rue. It's worse than anything you ever dreamed of. You must come with me."

"With . . . you . . ." said Rue's voice again out of a vast distance.

And Andy said curtly, as if he were angry:

"With me. Now. You see, I love you."

CHAPTER III

Somebody began to sing over the radio — huskily, with heavily accented beats; the boy at the window accelerated his whistle. All her life afterward Rue was to remember the lilting tune. "Have you got — any castles — that you want — me to build —"

Andy heard it, too, and smiled in the strangest, tight way that had no mirth in it. He said:

"It's true. You've got to believe it, Rue. There isn't time for — for talk. Will you come?"

"But —"

She couldn't believe him when he said he loved her, either; it was as unexpected, as nightmarishly fantastic just then, as the other incredible things he had said. It was as if it all blurred together, dreadfully confusing her.

He leaned forward again, speaking slowly and very earnestly as if he must make her understand. "Listen, Rue. I know this is a — a blow. But you've got to listen and you've got to believe me." He pushed back his sleeve to look at his watch in a habitual gesture; it wasn't there, and he seemed to remember with a frown that he was in evening dress and reached for a thin, elegant-looking watch which was in his pocket. His initials were engraved on it, and Crystal had given him the watch; Rue remembered it sharply and with curious bitterness. She'd given it to him during the last week of her life; it was Andy's birthday; Rue herself had seen the presentation and the way Crystal had looked at him. Brule had been in the room too; he had watched and smiled below his short black mustache, but it had seemed to Rue that there was knowledge in his eyes.

Andy shoved the watch into his pocket again. "I've got it planned. We'll go back to the house and get some clothes for you; there'll be time. Then we'll take a midnight train north. Canada, I suppose . . ."

She simply couldn't sit there quietly and listen to so mad and fantastic a plan.

"Andy, don't. This — this isn't possible: I'm not going with you. I've done nothing. Crystal wasn't murdered. I was her nurse. I know —"

"I was her doctor," said Andy.

"But you said nothing. You didn't notify the police: you didn't question. You signed the certificate; you didn't even seem surprised. You — you accepted it. If you knew it was murder —"

"I didn't know then," said Andy. "I do know now."

"How do you know? You can't know. And if she was —" Her throat closed.

Andy looked ashen.

"I can't tell you, Rue. Isn't it enough to convince you of my sincerity when I tell you that I'm — giving up everything I've worked to make secure? My profession, all my connections. I'll give it up gladly to take you away."

"You can't do that. And anyway, I am not going with you. What right have you to suppose —"

"To suppose you would go away with me? No right. Except that I love you, whether you believe me or not, and I want to save you. That's all."

"But you must tell me. Tell me everything you know. I've got to know."

"You've got to believe me, Rue," he repeated. "I can't tell you everything — there's so little I know. But . . . Very well; you'll understand better if I — begin at the beginning. You see, when Crystal died, she had been for two weeks actually on the mend; you knew that."

"Yes. I didn't expect her death just then. But it seemed so natural. There was nothing — Andy, how could she have been murdered? There was no way. There were no symptoms of anything. She — was it poison?"

"So the police say. It had to be that."

"Do you mean they've found poison?"

"No. They have to get Brule's consent to make an exhumation. But he'll have to give it. Otherwise it would look bad for him. After all, he inherited most of Crystal's property. But it probably was poison. There were no symptoms. I remember when you called me that night and said she was worse, I couldn't believe it; she'd seemed so well. And I got there just after she died. You said she'd gone into a coma; you said that over the telephone. I remember that. And I told you to call Brule, and to hell with professional ethics about a doctor's attending his own family, didn't I?"

"Yes. And I called Brule. But we couldn't do anything. She died without returning to consciousness at all. It was about eleven o'clock. I thought she was in a natural sleep until I took her pulse for my chart. She was dead when you arrived. She died naturally; she couldn't have been — murdered," whispered Rue all at once, as if it was a word she could not speak aloud.

"I thought it was natural then," said Andy.

"If you think she was murdered you must know who did it. Who —" Again a wave of complete disbelief came over her. She said: "It isn't true! It can't be!"

"It is, Rue." It was like a groan. He brushed his hands over his eyes. His gloves lay on the table: he picked them up with a tight, nervous grip, and said quickly as if to get a bad job over: "I'm as sure of it as — Listen. Tonight when the police came I was closing the office, the office girl and nurse had gone, and Brule had gone to see a patient at the hospital. They came — a little fellow by the name of Funk and another one. I knew they were detectives, but I didn't guess what they wanted. At any rate they came in and insisted on talking to me privately. Asked particularly to make sure Brule was not in the office and there was no way he could hear them.

"They said — it's a crazy thing, Rue; they said

38

they'd been getting letters; letters urging them to look into the matter of Crystal's death — and the manner of it. Letters that said she'd been murdered. They didn't show me the letters; I had to believe them. They said they finally had to take some notice of the things; even the district attorney had received one or two. So they looked up the records and found I was the attending physician and had signed the death certificate. And they came to question me. They'd already talked to other people, too; had inquired into the circumstances of Crystal's life — her relations with her family, everything. It — it's only a question of time till it reaches the newspapers; I suppose there are whispers already. They can't go about enquiring like that, no matter how carefully, without somebody getting wind of it, and the moment anybody guesses the truth it'll be all over town.

"Well, the main point of evidence was that one of the servants had told them that she was definitely better and that everyone was surprised when she took so sudden a turn for the worse and died. I was surprised when she died that night; but Brule — Brule wasn't. Naturally I reproached myself; I didn't know where or how I'd made a mistake, but I reproached myself bitterly for not handling the case right. My patient died, and she was Brule's wife. And Brule's been — so much to me."

So was Brule's wife, thought Rue.

"I was — horribly upset. You remember that."

"Yes, I remember. I remember that you and Brule talked of it. And that Brule reassured you."

"Yes, he did, didn't he? He said she'd never been strong; had never had much resistance. Well — then this afternoon, when they questioned me, I — oh, there's no time for all this talk. You must come."

"Why do you think she was murdered?"

"Because — because that accounts for it, Rue. Poison. That accounts for her death. As nothing else ever did."

"You were not satisfied then that her death was what Brule said it was."

"No," admitted Andy. "No, not entirely. But I wanted to be. Anyway, she was dead. It wouldn't help to make a fuss, demand a post-mortem, stir up a lot of talk. I blamed myself: I thought I had missed something important, something organic. Sometimes symptoms do deceive a doctor; you know that, Rue." There was a look of pleading in his eyes.

"I accused myself of everything; I told myself that I had let myself be swayed by Brule's diagnosis when I ought to have sought further myself. Oh, don't misunderstand me: I'm not trying to alibi myself; I'm not blaming Brule. And God knows I didn't suspect murder. . . . Oh, I blame myself. Now. I've always let Brule influence me; he's done so much for me. I owe him loyalty."

"I am Brule's wife," said Rue. "I can't go away with you. And — and even if this is true,

40

if Crystal was murdered, I still can't go. I didn't murder her."

"Listen, Rue." Andy was white and tense. He said rapidly: "You are Brule's wife and you may think I'm failing in loyalty when I tell you I love you and when I ask you to go away with me. But there are greater loyalties than those of friendship and of obligation. And as for this — Crystal's murder — oh, my God, Rue, don't you understand? You were alone with her when she went into that coma; you said then, as you said just now, that you thought it was a natural sleep; that you only discovered it was not when you went to take her pulse for the ten o'clock chart note. You were alone with her; she was all right and better when I saw her at six and when the day nurse left at seven. Brule said he came in about nine and you told him she was asleep. At something after ten you called him, and she died shortly after. You had been alone with her all that time; she would have taken anything you might have chosen to give her, thinking it was medicine. And then you see, in the eyes of the police you had a motive. You married Brule."

"I gave her nothing. I didn't —"

"I know you didn't, Rue. I believe you; if — if I had seen you do it with my own eyes I'd still believe you. But that's the situation."

"I must go home. I must see Brule. Where is he?"

A shadow like a veil dropped into Andy's eyes.

"I'm not sure. I think he'll be home later."

"Why didn't he come to tell me?"

"Because — there were things Brule had to do."

"What?"

"I — I don't know exactly. It's an ugly situation any way you look at it. I got hold of Brule right away; as soon as I could get rid of the police. I told him all about it; if he can pull any wires he's going to. But I think it's gone too far. The district attorney himself can't stop it now without exhumation; if nothing shows up then, things are all right and we're safe."

"You're afraid something will be found," said Rue in the strangest voice.

Andy hesitated; one hand tightened around the glass; after a moment he lifted his eyes and looked straight at Rue.

"Yes," he said. "I'm afraid. Will you trust me, Rue?"

His eyes plunged deeply into her own; for a moment it was as if all the world had fallen away into limbo and only the two of them, Andy Crittenden and Rue Hatterick, were left. As if, thus, they were all important to each other. Yet dimly she was aware of the blare of the radio; of the boy's shrill, constant whistle.

The door of the drugstore opened sharply, and a cold blast of air swept in upon them, and the boy stopped whistling and went to greet a man who lounged toward the soda fountain and gave them a quick, oddly observant look which seemed to take in every detail. The coffee cup

42

and Andy's gloves and Rue's little silver-and-blue train looking so out of place on the bare, white-tiled floor. Andy saw that look too; his eyes jerked away from Rue to watch; the man at the soda fountain turned harmlessly enough to order something to drink; Andy said quietly: "Come. I told Kendal to come for us in about half an hour. He'll be at the door soon."

His question went unanswered. All at once it seemed to Rue that the music from the radio and the heat in the drugstore were unbearable. She pushed back her chair with a clatter of scraping metal, and Andy sprang to help her; he paused to pay the boy at the cash register, and Rue, walking ahead toward the door, caught her own reflection, garish and bright, in the mirror behind the soda fountain. A slender woman in sables and a silver-blue evening gown; a woman with a paper-white face and great terrified dark eyes and a red, meaningless mark for a mouth; a woman with a white kid glove that was stained with coffee. Did the man leaning on his elbow there at the soda fountain actually turn to observe her covertly as she passed? Or did she only imagine it?

Andy came quickly after her, his footsteps hard and reassuring on the bare floor. The music flared all around them with a ghastly falseness, to Rue, in its gaiety, and Andy opened the door and she passed ahead of him again into the night-lighted, cold street with the wind seizing viciously upon them.

"Was that a — detective?" The wind snatched her words and hurled them eerily into the shadows, but Andy heard.

"No. Why should he be a detective?" But it was too quick a denial; she knew she had voiced his own thought.

The wind hurled her blue-and-silver train around her ankles. She grasped the soft furs closer about her throat. Andy, holding his hat against the onslaught of the wind, said something unintelligible but with a surprised note that caught Rue's ears.

"What —"

"Nothing. I thought it was Alicia Pelham. There ahead, getting into a motor."

She followed his look. Half a block ahead a car had stopped just before the lighted entrance to the opera proper; she had the barest glimpse of a woman's trailing skirts as she got into the car; the attendant closed the door; the shadows from the tall pillars obscured the little scene, but as the car swept away from the curb Rue said:

"It's Brule —" and stopped.

Andy did not reply. Rue added quickly: "It looked like Brule's coupé. It couldn't be, of course. I'm going home, Andy."

He was looking up and down the street, with its slanting subway entrance.

"Kendal ought to be here soon. Ah, there he is now."

Andy, of course, would recognize the car before she did. They reached the broad space opposite the green-room, and an attendant recognized Andy and said: "The Hatterick car, sir? Here it comes now."

"Thank you."

The attendant hadn't called Andy by name; he had only associated him with the Hatterick car. Rue said rather crisply: "The car that just now drove away — wasn't that Doctor Hatterick?"

The attendant, cold and pinched-looking in spite of his greatcoat, glanced at her and at Andy and said: "I don't know, madam," politely, and the limousine paused quietly beside them. Andy opened the door and gave the attendant a tip.

The door closed behind them and the car moved off slowly. Andy said: "You're cold. You're shivering," and reached ahead for the thick soft robe and put it over her, leaning down to tuck it gently around her feet. His black shoulder and the edge of the white scarf about his chin were very close to her. He said, pulling the robe around her, "You're shivering. You are trembling," and took her suddenly in his arms.

His warm cheek was against her cold one. He said against her mouth, "I love you. Rue, Rue . . ." and kissed her.

Kissed her long and hard and drew away to look into her face through the dark and then kissed her again.

When Brule kissed her he did it swiftly, formally, when others were watching and he had to — a mere brush against her cheek.

Brule. She moved to escape Andy's arms and he held her.

"Nothing matters now, Rue, but you. Don't think of Brule. Think of yourself. I love you so, dear. You — you were married to Brule so suddenly, no one knew. I didn't know anything of it until he told me — and then it was too late; it was the day before your marriage. What could I do? . . . You must have known I loved you, Rue."

Unwillingly, irresistibly, she replied.

"No . . ."

"Back in the days when you were at the hospital — remember? I used to watch for you when I went along the halls and sat at the chart desk. Among all the white uniforms and white caps I always knew the little square set of your shoulders; the smooth knot of gold hair under your perky little cap. I used to make excuses to talk to you; I would complain a little of this or that — and hope the other nurses would leave so I could talk to you alone. I — I didn't know for a long time that I was in love with you. Not till just before Crystal's illness."

"Crystal . . ." said Rue. Crystal, Crystal; Crystal's car that he knew so well; the scent of roses that still clung to it; Crystal.

He relinquished her slowly. For a moment he said nothing; his profile was a clear silhouette against the area of light under a street lamp outside the window. They passed on into shadow, and he said: "Crystal. So that was it. How can I convince you? And there's so little time. You

46

must go with me, Rue. At once. There's no other way."

She felt all at once quite cool and collected; frightened, conscious of catastrophe, but conscious also of the need to gird herself to meet it. She said:

"That would be running away. Leaving Brule when he needs me."

"Brule!" cried Andy. "Rue, you don't understand —"

"We can't leave, Andy. I understand that. It would be mad. It would be — would be like a confession of guilt."

Afterwards she remembered those moments, though at the time they were disjointed, confused, full of incoherent, futile argument. They plunged through darkened streets, they glided along lighted theaters, they paused for traffic lights; she was clearly conscious of only one thing out of the turmoil, and that was the necessity to resist Andy, to go home, to wait for Brule. Brule was never at a loss for expedient; Brule always knew what to do. Brule had the sharpest, shrewdest worldly wisdom, and he had, too, a certain ruthlessness which would stand them all in hand now. Besides, Brule was her husband.

Andy was at last beaten down, sullen, silent. They reached the Hatterick house, and Brule's coupé was not in front of the door.

"For the last time, Rue," began Andy. "Believe me, I'm only thinking of you."

"But it's the wrong way, Andy. We've got to face the thing. If it's true — if she was really murdered —"

The car had stopped, and Kendal opened the door. She said to him: "Will you take Doctor Crittenden to his apartment, Kendal, please."

But Andy was already out of the car and putting up his hands to assist her. Through her gloves she was absurdly conscious of the warmth and strength of his hands and the way he held her own a second too long.

"Don't bother, Kendal," he said. "Thank you. I'll walk." He went up the steps with Rue and rang the bell.

She would not ask him to come in and to wait for Brule if he were not yet there. There was some obscure but important reason for not doing so.

Kendal, a stolid, silent figure, got into the car again, and it moved away. Andy said:

"Perhaps I was wrong, Rue; I suppose the thing to do is stay here and face it. Flight — does seem melodramatic. Crazy. But — but you don't know —" He stopped short. "All right, Rue. I'll go. But remember what I've said tonight. Remember I love you. And I'll do anything in God's world to help you. Will you remember that?"

His voice was serious, weighted with awareness of the horror that lay before her. She shivered a little, not from cold.

"Yes, Andy," she said and the door opened.

Light from the hall streamed out. Gross, the dourly efficient German butler, dating from Crystal's regime, stood in the doorway with an expression of painfully withheld but painfully curious disapproval. He did not wait for Andy's departure. He said as Rue entered:

"Two persons are waiting to see Madam. They insisted on waiting. I told them Madam was at the opera —"

Rue's heart gave a heavy throb in her throat. She turned slowly toward the butler.

"Who?"

She was aware that Andy had come into the hall too. Gross closed the door, shutting off escape.

"They say they are from police headquarters, madam."

CHAPTER IV

"This is preposterous," said Andy. "Mrs Hatterick can't possibly see them tonight, Gross. Tell them—"

They were all aware of the man who stood suddenly in the doorway opposite them. Although he was actually only a symbol, impersonal, commonplace, completely, utterly ordinary. He was mediumly tall, mediumly bulky, his face was full, and his cheeks puffed below small, cold eyes; he was partially bald, and the most minute description of him would equally well have described a hundred other men you'd encounter in the Loop, say at Madison and State streets on a busy noon hour. His name was Oliver Miller; he was important then and always to Rue merely as a symbol, as a mouthpiece, as a voice through which a hidden, massive, utterly forbidding power expressed itself.

"Mrs Hatterick," he said. "We are waiting for you. I am Oliver Miller of the police. Will you be so good as to give me a few moments? The district attorney sent me here." He had actually, in the most ordinary way in the world, a card in his hand. One that, apparently, he had not chosen to relinquish to Gross. Gross murmured and was still.

Andy said: "By what authority —"

"Good evening, Doctor Crittenden. By the authority of police headquarters, as you know. It's only a short interview; if you wish anyone else to be present, Mrs Hatterick, it's quite all right."

Rue turned swiftly to Gross: "Has Doctor Hatterick returned?"

"No, madam."

"Rue, there's no need for you to see them now. We'll get Guy —"

Guy — that was Guy Cole, their next-door neighbor and one of the best criminal lawyers in Chicago. Something stiffened and tightened about Rue's throat.

Miller said easily: "Only a few questions, Mrs Hatterick. It won't take long. I assure you we'll not distress you. You can be present, Doctor Crittenden, if Mrs Hatterick wishes it. It isn't important."

Not important!

Rue nodded dismissal to Gross. She walked into her own drawing room, followed by Miller and Andy. Another man was waiting there; his name was Funk, said Oliver Miller in the most polite way, like an introduction. She found herself acknowledging the mousy, thin, gray little man; he looked like a rabbit, and scared, as if he might pop under the Louis Quatorze sofa at any moment. Yet in his way he was as commonplace and as ordinary and as unthreatening as Miller.

She sat down, trying to appear self-possessed

and calm. Andy, still in his black overcoat and white scarf, took up a position near her.

"Won't you sit down," she said, and Miller did so — in a fragile French armchair which looked as if it might collapse at any moment under the man's bulk. Funk discovered himself in the shadow of the stiffly draped, pale green satin curtains, and no one knew how he'd got there.

That drawing room, too, had been Crystal's; she had decorated it. Its pastels, its French chairs, its gilded mirrors and crystal-hung lamps had been Crystal's selection. Rue had never liked the room; now it seemed garish and full of a grisly contrast. Crystal's room; Crystal's white hands touching and selecting those soft fabrics; and now the two men in the room had come, businesslike, to investigate Crystal's murder.

Murder. The word caught at her again, squeezed her heart, sickened her.

"What do you want to ask me?" she said.

"I expect Doctor Crittenden has told you why we are here," said Miller, while the little Funk watched with frightened, nervous eyes under thick black eyebrows that had a worried-looking slant. Miller waited for her answer.

Andy said: "I told her something of it, yes. That you had got the idea from a series of mischievous letters saying that the former Mrs Hatterick's death ought to be investigated."

"Yes. Now if you'll be good enough to answer

my questions yourself, Mrs Hatterick. You are Doctor Hatterick's second wife?"

"Yes."

"You were married two months ago in the vestry of the Third Presbyterian Church —"

"Yes."

"Before your marriage you were a nurse?"

"Yes," said Rue again and named the hospital. Her hands were shaking. She stripped off her gloves slowly, trying to control her trembling fingers.

"Exactly. In fact you were the nurse who took care of the first Mrs Hatterick at the time of her fatal illness?"

"Yes. That is, I was the night nurse; there was also a day nurse."

"Miss Juliet Garder. Yes. We've already talked to her."

Talked to Julie. What had they said? What had Julie said? What had Julie thought?

"She says on the night Mrs Hatterick died she left the house at seven. She went off duty, then, she said, and you arrived at that time."

"That is right."

"She says that at that time Mrs Hatterick seemed much better; she had been improving for some days and was definitely better."

It wasn't a question, and Rue waited.

The little man in the shadow of the window curtain discovered a heavy gold tassel which seemed greatly to interest and astonish him; he touched it with thin, not too clean hands, like little claws. Miller went on: "But at eleven o'clock that night Mrs Hatterick died. Is that true, Mrs Hatterick?"

He took, thought Rue, extra pains to roll Mrs Hatterick repeatedly over his tongue, as if the name alone had some significance. As, perhaps, to him it did.

She didn't dare think of that significance. She said:

"Yes, that's true. She fell into a coma shortly after I came on duty; I thought it was a natural sleep until I went to her about ten, I think it must have been, to take her pulse."

"Why did you do that?"

"Take her pulse, you mean? I took it several times each night and made the entry on my chart; as a rule I did it, if she was asleep, without waking her."

"Chart. Do you have those charts?"

Rue thought back.

"I don't know. In the hospital your charts are kept on file, but when on private duty I've never made it a custom to keep my charts. Someone may have kept them; I don't know."

"You mean someone in the household? A maid?"

"Perhaps. Perhaps Doctor Hatterick has them."

"Doctor Crittenden was the attending physician. Do you happen to have the charts, Doctor Crittenden?"

"No. I looked at them every day when I came

to see — to see my patient."

The little Funk relinquished the gold tassel. Miller said: "Well, well — that will come later. Now don't misunderstand me, Mrs Hatterick; I don't want to exceed my duty; none of us want to do that; but as much for your protection and Doctor Hatterick's protection as anyone's, it is our duty to prove that there's no truth in these letters. If there's any rumors going about it's our duty to prove those rumors wrong and slanderous. We feel you'll want to help us do that."

"Yes, certainly."

"Therefore we feel you'll do everything in your power to help us."

"Yes."

"Then you'll forgive me if my questions seem to — seem to touch on your personal and family affairs."

"What do you want to say?"

"Now, now don't get upset, Mrs Hatterick. I only want to know if — well, if you were very much surprised when the first Mrs Hatterick died?"

Steady, thought Rue. Andy was as still as a graven image.

"I hadn't expected it. But unpredictable things like that do happen sometimes; a nurse and doctor can do their very best with a patient and still lose the patient."

"Did your husband — that is, Doctor Hatterick himself — attend his wife when she was ill?"

55

"No. A doctor never attends members of his own family."

"But I expect the attending physician enjoys the complete confidence of the, say, physician in the family. In other words, did Doctor Crittenden ever consult Doctor Hatterick about Mrs Hatterick's illness?"

"I'll answer that for you," said Andy. "Yes, certainly. He knew and approved of my treatment and diagnosis."

"Did he suggest any part of that diagnosis?"

After a second Andy said: "No. It was my case."

"I see. Mrs Hatterick, was the first Mrs Hatterick altogether happy in her family relations?"

"I can't possibly answer that question," said Rue. "I was her nurse, not her confidante. There was no reason to suppose she was not happy."

"Your marriage to your patient's husband took place not more than ten months after Mrs Hatterick's death? Now I don't want you to misunderstand me; you must realize that when so short a period elapses between the death of a man's first wife and his remarriage, people are bound to ask questions."

"There were reasons; my husband will tell you what they were. Is there anything else you wish to know?" Rue was suddenly, furiously angry; but she was frightened, too.

The little man, Funk, discovered a bronze figure on the table near him, touched it with an exploring, dirty little claw and said in a morose and scared voice: "Home. Daughter . . ."

"Exactly," said Miller. "Quite comprehensible, I'm sure."

". . . How long," finished the little Funk, and shrank behind the table and wouldn't look at anyone.

"How long have you known Doctor Hatterick?" asked Miller.

"I trained in the hospital where he was chief of staff. That's been eight years; I was eighteen when — I was obliged to find a profession for myself so as to earn my own living."

"Eight years ago; you've known him for eight years then?"

"Certainly."

"Knew him well, I expect."

"That's enough of that line, Miller," said Andy. "Have you any real evidence that Mrs Hatterick — Crystal Hatterick, that is — was murdered?"

"We've put the cards on the table, Doctor. You know exactly what our position is."

"Mrs Hatterick has answered everything you've asked her. She'll be right here in case you have any further inquiries —"

"Going," murmured a small voice at the door, and Funk scuttled out of sight into the hall.

Miller, unperturbed, said: "All right, Doctor Crittenden. The body's to be exhumed as soon as we get Doctor Hatterick's consent. Then there'll be an autopsy. But if we had some notion of what to look for it'd be a quicker and easier job for the chemists. You don't happen to know, do you, Mrs Hatterick, whether or not the first Mrs Hatterick took any kind of drugs — I mean, medicinally or otherwise? It's a help, you know, to know what to eliminate when you're searching for an unknown drug."

"Naturally she was given medicines," said Rue. "Nothing else."

"Medicines. Did you give her medicine the night she died?"

"She doesn't need to answer that," said Andy quickly. "You're exceeding your duty, Miller."

"She will answer though," said Miller.

Medicine. Yes, she had. She remembered it so clearly; the small glass with the prescribed medicine, diluted with water, already prepared. Julie had prepared and left it on the little table by the screen. Rue herself gave it to Crystal at eight. Crystal had taken it and . . .

The marquetry floor with its soft rugs wavered and rocked under Rue's silver slippers; the lights trembled and blurred; the whole world as she knew it spun around and changed its order. For they were right. Crystal had been murdered.

And she, Rue, had murdered her.

Not intentionally; but actually, physically it had been Rue's hand that finally accomplished Crystal's death.

She'd given Crystal the little glass, prepared, waiting on the table. And now suddenly she remembered; Crystal had taken it and had complained of its taste; had said, "It's bitter. Andy must have changed the medicine today," and then she drank it. Drank it while Rue stood beside her, crisp, efficient in her white uniform. A travesty of her own ideals, for her own hand, trained and dedicated to mercy, had given Crystal poison.

Andy's voice was speaking, sharply, with a warning note in it. He was saying: "Certainly she gave her medicine, and I prescribed it. Why not? Anything else would be most unusual."

Somehow Andy was getting Miller into the hall. She heard them talking; she made some motion of recognition when Miller appeared, a shabby felt hat in his hand, and said good night and thanked her. His eyes said, I'll question you again, my fine lady; this is not our last meeting. So you gave her medicine, did you? And she took it and died. And you married her husband.

Andy came back into the room.

"They've gone. You weathered that. Rue, what was it you remembered? I knew by your look there was something."

"The medicine. I gave it to her; Julie had prepared it and left it in a glass on the table where we kept her medicines and water. I gave it to Crystal, and I remember that she tasted it and looked at me and said it tasted bitter; she laughed a little and said, 'Andy must have changed my medicine today,' and then she drank it, while I stood there watching her."

Up to that time, up to the very moment when that small, clear memory arose so sharply and

59

unexpectedly from the faraway night of Crystal's death and presented itself to her, the whole thing had seemed unreal. Every word Andy said to her might have been said through veils, on a stage, in a curious and fantastic dream. Everything else was poignantly real — the coldness of the wind, the swish of her skirt around her ankles, the heat of the coffee he had made her drink. It was as if all material things had taken on an extra and peculiar clarity. But not the thing they talked of.

And then all at once, while Miller questioned phlegmatically and the little Funk examined the satinwood table, memory had supplied that clear, small picture.

She could see the glass in Crystal's hand, the way Crystal had looked up at her, her face pink and her lips crimson and her blonde hair carefully dressed. She had made a little face as she tasted it. And then, her eyes shut tight, had gulped it down. Because it was Andy's medicine. Because she did not dream that there was poison in that little glass.

As there must have been.

Up to the onslaught of that memory the thing had been unreal. Rue had been shocked — and she'd been frightened and she'd had a paralyzing sense of catastrophe. But there hadn't been cold, certain conviction. There hadn't been, in the wake of knowledge, terror.

And some extra sense, some natural, primitive sense that went below all surface laws of comprehension, convinced her of the presence of truth. Crystal had really, actually, been murdered.

And in her heart, horribly, instantly convinced, she was sure that she herself, schooled and trained to save life, had literally taken it.

And Andy knew it. Andy had known it.

He stood now watching her, his face drawn and gray-looking, older suddenly and stern, his eyes blazing with knowledge.

"You say Julie had prepared it? Before she went off duty?"

"Yes."

He rubbed his hands through his hair.

"Oh, God," he said. "If it was in the medicine anybody could have put it there. Who was in the house — But it doesn't matter. There's no use in our asking questions, inquiring, trying to run the thing down now. The thing is to admit nothing. Tell them nothing — and hope that nothing will show up in the autopsy. After a year —"

"It's been a year," she said slowly. "If she was poisoned, would it be traced? Could it be traced? Oh, I know arsenic would remain, but it wasn't arsenic, Andy. There were no symptoms of that."

"Any organic poison can be traced — or almost any organic poison. The symptoms — coma and all that — suggest morphine, opium, possibly luminal in sufficient quantity. If I'd thought of murder . . . But Brule —"

61

Brule had been there when she died. Brule had bent over the bed, had had his wise and expert fingers on her faint pulse; had lifted her eyelids and looked, there at the last. Rue wrenched herself back to that night, she tried to recall details of that scene; Andy, too, was trying to remember. He said, low so Gross if he were in the hall could not hear:

"Do you remember her eyes, Rue? Were the pupils either enlarged or small? Was there anything —"

Rue shook her head slowly.

"There was nothing, Andy. Nothing I can remember. Brule was there, and you know how it is with him. Nobody ever questions him. He is so strong, so sure of himself; so certain; he said she was dead. He — I think you came just then. And I remember Brule sent me to see to Madge. Madge was hysterical; Steven and I tried to quiet her, but Steven was almost as bad as Madge. Someone sent for the undertaker — I think Brule told Gross to telephone. There was nothing. Andy, where are you going?"

He was buttoning the overcoat he had not removed.

"I'm going to find Brule. If anyone telephones, if anyone comes, don't say anything."

He had gone before it occurred to her that he must know where Brule was.

The house was silent. The narrow, five-storied brownstone house where Crystal had lived and married and died at last.

It was cold in the French drawing room; the gilded mirrors looked indescribably vacant and cold and shallow, yet they had seen so much. She shivered under the furs she still wore, rose and went through the narrow hall, which ran along the length of the house, to the library. There was a sullen cannel-coal fire there in the small marble grate.

She took off her furs and knelt to poke the coals to a brighter blaze. She would wait for Brule.

She had never waited for him in their brief married life. Instinctively she knew he would not like her waiting; would not like her to assume any air of possession.

She pushed a deep, leather-cushioned chair closer to the fire and sat down, stretching out her silver sandals.

From a modern light wood frame above the mantel Crystal stared enigmatically down at her, a half smile on her thin, painted lips, her eyes secret, cool, uncannily observant, and the pearls she wore glowing. Madge was to have those pearls.

It was half-past one when Brule came.

The heavy jar of the front door roused her. She was chilled and too much aware of the house and its silence. The fire had gone out long before. She had curled up in the great chair and put her head upon her arms and pulled her furs over her bare, slim shoulders as the house grew colder. But she had not slept. Once she wondered, in the waiting, night silence, if ever again anyone could sleep in that house where Crystal's sleep had been too deep.

Brule saw the light in the library and came in, and Rue stirred and moved cramped muscles.

"Rue!" he said. He was in evening dress and carried gloves and a hat in one hand. He put them down on a table. She saw at once that he was angry. His usually ruddy face was pale, and there were lines in it which only showed under extreme fatigue. His bright, black eyes had points of light, and his straight black eyebrows were frowning. His black, short mustache made a straight, displeased line, too. He was built like a soldier; there was about him a rigidity and compactness that actually meant a trim hard body, always in good condition. He frowned at her questioningly, hesitated and then went to a small cellarette.

"Waiting, Rue?" he said over his smoothly tailored shoulder and bent to take out glasses and a tall brandy bottle.

Her voice stuck in her throat. Of all the things those hours of thought had stirred in her mind to say to him, nothing seemed poised and able to cut through the hard and brilliant shell which always, as long as she had known him, encased the great and clever Brule Hatterick.

As she did not reply he shot a quick, dark look at her.

"Will you join me?" he said and, taking her acquiescence for granted, poured golden-brown liquid into two small glasses.

She was icy cold. Or was it that the questions she had to ask frightened her, stiffened her tongue, made her hands cold and unsteady?

He turned and put a small glass in her hand.

"Drink that," he said. "I see you know. Who told you — Andy? Well, you may as well know what has happened. I . . ." He paused, swallowed the brandy and went on: "I signed a consent for the exhumation of Crystal's body. We'll soon know the truth."

CHAPTER V

In the end all the questions boiled down to one. She put the small glass on the table beside her and leaned forward. He met her eyes directly, but she had never been able to understand him, to penetrate past the guarded regularity of his face. He went to stand before the fire, his erect, soldierly figure blocking itself strongly against the marble behind him. Crystal looked down, watching them.

Rue said: "Is it true? Was she — murdered?"

Brule could be either brutally direct or neatly, coolly evasive; she had seen him in both moods. He looked at her, now, speculatively.

"What did Andy tell you?"

"Andy didn't find you, then? When he left here he said he was going to see you."

Brule looked at the glass he held, tipped it a little and said: "I haven't seen Andy since about six. I take it he told you the main points."

"He told me about the letters, about the police coming to your office. They were here tonight."

"Tonight!" It startled him; she could see that by the way his eyes narrowed and lighted and the way his mouth straightened itself under his mustache. He added after a moment: "What did they want? Did they question you? What did they ask you?"

66

She told him swiftly, word for word as near as she could remember them. When she came to her memory of the medicine she faltered. But Brule extracted it quickly.

"Did you tell them you had given her the last dose of medicine?"

"No — that is, Andy said that naturally I had given it to her and that he had prescribed it."

"And did you give it to her?"

"Yes."

"You remember it distinctly?"

"Yes. Yes, I do."

"Why?"

"Because — because she said it was bitter. And then she drank it." She had meant to question him. She still meant to. But he was questioning her.

"Did you tell the police that?"

"No. No, I didn't."

"Why?" he asked again, watching her.

"Because I — Brule, you must tell me, was she murdered?"

For a moment she thought he intended to evade again, but he didn't. Instead he put the small glass deliberately down on the mantel and turned slowly back to her again.

"You want the truth, don't you Rue? Well then — I don't know."

"But — but what do you think? What are we going to do? What —"

"Nothing. There's nothing we can do now."

"Do you mean —"

"I mean only that. There's nothing we can do. These things take time; perhaps they'll never discover anything that — lends credence to their notion. Any kind of chemical analysis after so long a time has passed is difficult. Unless, of course, they know what to look for; but you can't just fumble in the dark; different poisons show their presence by different and varying tests. Unless the police doctors know what to look for, and I take it so far they do not know, it will be difficult — it may even prove impossible to find and prove the presence of any particular chemical in a lethal quantity. The thing to do is sit tight. Go on with your usual routine. I won't say forget it —"

"Andy thinks she was murdered."

Brule's eyes were bright, dark, altogether enigmatic.

"Yes, I know."

"Do you think so?"

"I don't know, Rue. I've told you that. When she died I did think once of suicide. But I saw no reason for publicizing that — speculation. And I had no very good reasons for it. Except — well, you were there when she died. You know how unexpected it was."

"Who could have killed her?"

"Again, I don't know. It doesn't seem very likely that she was murdered. I don't think the police will ever be able to prove anything."

"Who wrote these letters? It must be someone who knows something of her death — and the truth of it."

Brule lifted his eyebrows.

"Or someone who wants to make trouble. I don't know who wrote them. But when the tumult and shouting have died down for lack of evidence, I intend to find out."

When that look was in Brule's face the nurses at the hospital cowered. It was only something cold and dark in his eyes and a kind of tight look around the clean line of his jaw. But Rue knew it well. She said: "There must be something we can do —"

"Believe me, my dear, there's nothing. Did Andy take you to the opera?"

"I — couldn't stay. He told me after we arrived. We went away. Alicia was there. She left just before we got in the car. We went into a drugstore, and when we came out we saw her leaving."

"Did you? Well, Rue — I'm off to bed."

"But . . ." His assurance baffled her; yet he was right, too. What could they do that night?

"Andy said you were trying to pull wires."

"Oh. I'll do what I can. Guy's coming in tomorrow. I'll talk to him just in case. Don't let this worry you too much, Rue. I'll see to it the police don't bother you; Guy will cook up some kind of protection for you. After all, they have no proof of anything. And they'll probably never have proof."

"But if she was murdered —"

"Well?"

69

"Oughtn't we — do something? Tell the police —"

"Why?"

"Why, because it's right. Because —"

"Crystal's dead. Madge is very much alive and
young. You are, too, Rue, and you are my wife.
Steven is frail and horribly sensitive, and his music is of no small value. I myself have my —
small importance in the world. Andy was her
attending physician, and he's just entered upon
what promises to be a brilliant career. Why ruin
five lives? . . . You don't know, Rue, what a
murder inquiry is. . . . Now, my child, go to
bed."

He went to her and put his hand for a moment
under her chin and looked down at her, smiling
a little. "You'll have weathered many things by
the time you reach my age. How old are you,
Rue? Twenty-five . . ."

"Twenty-six."

"I'm close to forty. I've worked hard. I've
learned, I think, in a hard school to control emotions —"

"You —" She stopped abruptly, checked by
the hard directness of his eyes.

"You were about to say I have no emotions.
Wasn't that it? Well, that is as may be. Go to
bed. It's cold here. I'll have another drink before
I go up."

She went. Wearily up the stairs through the
chill and quiet house. Into the room that had
been Crystal's.

Because Rue had been a nurse she had known many nights when she must stay awake, therefore she knew familiarly the hours of the night. She knew their slowness and their silence, and the curious, terrifying isolation of the gray hours of the dawn. So that night was not unfamiliar to her except that, before, there had been only the need to perform skilled and expert duties; there had been no terrifying questions to haunt her, no tormenting pictures erecting themselves against the curtain of the night. No horror.

And Andy had said he loved her, had urged her to leave with him, had begged for her to let him rescue her. He knew, then, things that Brule would not tell her. Brule with his strength, his worldly shrewdness, his self-control. What did Brule know? What did he think behind that well-schooled mask that was his face?

It was the next day that Juliet Garder came.

Rue did not see Brule when he left the next morning; Madge left the house early, too, to go to the private day school she attended. Madge, who did not know the storm that was about to burst.

And when Rue went downstairs just before lunch she heard Steven's piano. Steven knew nothing of it, then; otherwise that music would not have been tranquil glissades of sound from the distant wing.

If Brule had told neither Madge nor Steven, then there was a reason for not doing so. Rue would have liked to talk to Steven; he was always kind, and it would have been a help, that dark and anxious day, merely to talk to him, but she did not. She snatched the papers from the table in the hall and scanned them feverishly, at first; more calmly as she found no mention of the Hatterick name. When the news broke there would be headlines. The thought actually and literally sickened her.

Steven, in a working frenzy, had lunch sent to his studio, and Madge lunched at school, so Rue ate alone in the narrow long dining room at the back of the house. Gross stood at the buffet and watched morosely while the waitress served her. She wondered what Gross thought, what he knew, how Brule had insured the butler's silence, as he must have done. Otherwise the whole house would have been alive and whispering with the thing.

The day darkened with afternoon, became all in a moment one of Chicago's dark days. It is a curious thing, this sudden shifting of air currents (affected somehow but mysteriously by the lake), which combine themselves with a pall of smoke and fog and settle down like a blanket upon Chicago. Perhaps the extreme concentration of Chicago's business area has something to do with it; perhaps Lake Michigan, stretching north and east into dull grays, enormous, incalculable, is the sole cause; however that may be, it is so accustomed an occurrence that Chicagoans accept it without comment, turn on lights and go about their business quite as if daylight

72

instead of twilight mantles the streets.

Sometimes this pall of abnormal night holds itself upon the Loop district alone; sometimes it spreads beyond the Loop; sometimes it leaves the Loop altogether and travels north or west or south, and plunges some outlying suburb in gloom which necessitates street lights for a day, an hour, before it dissipates itself as mysteriously as it arrives.

That day the black pall held itself close over the Loop and adjacent sections and thus completely blanketed the Hatterick house, for it was in that section of the early hundreds not far from the lake and the river which is called the near-north side. There are in that section many tall new hotels and shining, modern apartment houses. But there are also several streets of houses which are narrow, long and wedged together, built shortly before or shortly after the fire, and too well built to be wrecked, except in some instances, in order to give place to more modern buildings.

The house that had been Crystal Hatterick's was one of those houses. It was brownstone in front, with a wide, carved mahogany door, and plate-glass windows with beveled edges which caught light in slivers that were all the colors of the rainbow. There was a basement entrance down a short flight of steps. The basement floor was actually the kitchen floor and still remained so despite more modern ideas of comfort. There were pantries there, and storerooms and a laundry and drying room, and the furnace rooms. A huge, creaking dumbwaiter carried food, in course after course, to the dining room, which was at the back of the long house and had windows overlooking a small back yard which they shared with their neighbor, Guy Cole. It was enclosed by a high brick fence and had sparse grass and shrubs. From the dining room you also overlooked other houses' back yards, other houses' stained and dark brick walls, other windows blank and shining.

There were, including the basement, five stories; the front and the back rooms of each story were naturally the desired rooms because of the light; in any of the other rooms (opening on each floor from a long narrow hall jutting around the stairwell) you needed artificial light even on a sunny day, for there was almost no space between the lateral walls of the house and those of the houses on either side of it. Heavy curtains masked the depressing, close view of other walls and other windows, but also shut out all the light.

Steven's music room had been added; squeezed into the back where the hall left off, and projecting outward into the narrow back yard; it was a long room, extremely narrow, lighted by deep bay windows, heavily curtained, and was entered from the hall by a door at right angles to the dining-room door. Here were Steven's large concert piano, his long writing table; his radio, his Victrola, his cabinets of records and of sheet music.

Altogether it was not a cheerful house, but it was well and conveniently located and had been kept in extremely good condition ever since it was built. And it had been one of Crystal's main interests; the house, its decoration and redecoration; the pictures, the rugs, the authentic and carefully chosen objects of art had all been an important pattern in Crystal's life.

That day, wandering from one room to another, Rue hated the house.

And hated more than any of its many rooms her own that had been Crystal's, where she sat at last and waited. Waited for news, waited for further catastrophe; waited for Andy to telephone, waited for Brule to come home; waited, though she did not know it, for Juliet Garder.

It was late in the afternoon when Juliet arrived. Coughing a little from the smoke in the laden air, asking for Mrs Hatterick.

"Miss Juliet Garder," said Gross at Rue's bedroom door. "She gave me no card."

"I'll come down," said Rue and then changed her mind. The house was quiet except for the distant faint tinkle of the piano in Steven's studio below. It seemed too quiet and too empty and thus too full of a listening quality which only a silent and empty house, cavernous just then with that abnormal twilight, may possess. "Show Miss Garder up here, please," said Rue. "And order tea. Bring it up when it is ready."

He went away. Juliet. Why had she come? But

it was obvious: she and Juliet had nursed Crystal: obviously between them they might be able to piece out a portion of the truth. All at once Rue wondered why she had not thought of going to Juliet. If she had not been so curiously paralyzed with waiting she would have done so; would have gone to the hospital to see Juliet during the nurse's hours off. Her spirits lifted a little.

She had not seen Juliet since her marriage. They had trained together — Juliet a spare, homely girl with broad, hard-working hands; slow of thought, wiry, lonely, always pressed for money, squeezing through her examinations by a hair's breadth.

They'd nursed together, had gone to hurried matinees and cinemas together. Had borrowed each other's stockings and hats; had jointly hated the head nurse and jointly hero-worshiped Brule Hatterick. Propinquity and shared experience was the basis for their friendship, but it was a real friendship. That is until Rue's marriage, when Juliet had quietly but quite definitely withdrawn. Rue had always felt that Juliet did not approve of her marriage.

But at any rate Juliet had come now. Rue moved about the room, pulled a chair nearer the fireplace, saw that cigarettes were at hand. It was the first time, really, that Juliet had seen her in her new role.

"Miss Garder," said Gross and disappeared.

"Juliet."

"Hello, Rue."

She shook hands. She was as spare, as plain as ever, with the lines on her thin face as sharply carved. Her brown topcoat was a little shabby, her hat at an unfashionable angle, her pale friendly brown eyes looked tired and were rimmed in pink. She looked at Rue and blinked slowly and said again: "Hello — Rue —"

"Why, Juliet! What's the matter?"

"N-nothing," said Juliet and went to a chair. She sat down a little unsteadily, fumbling for the arms of the chair.

"Let me take your coat."

"Coat's — all right," said Juliet, staring straight at Rue and making an obvious effort to speak.

"Julie —" Rue checked herself. She went to the girl and took her gloves and the worn purse which seemed about to drop from Julie's shiny, bony fingers. Julie lifted one hand and pushed her hat back on her head and stared glassily at Rue, and Rue caught a whiff of alcohol and cried: "Julie, you're drunk!"

Julie never drank; she was a militant teetotaller, and Rue knew it.

"Just a cocktail," said Juliet, her thin lips pulled apart in a grin that was like a grimace. "Just a little tiny cocktail. Pink. Say, Rue — there was something I came to see you about. This — you know . . ." She turned and waved a hand at the bed. "Crystal Hatterick. You know — murdered — I know — I know something about that. You know it too. I came to tell you,

77

but now I'm not going to tell. Understand, Julie — I mean, Rue. You're not to tell a thing. Besides, memory is always false. Remember that, Julie — I mean Rue. Rue Hatterick, married to Brule Hatterick. Crystal Hatterick murdered. Memory always false. Tricks you. I was here — in this very room. Remember that screen," said Juliet and closed her eyes; her head fell forward sleepily.

"Remember — what do you mean? Julie. What do I know? Juliet, wake up. Tell me —"

"Sleepy," muttered Julie. "Changed my mind. Don't trust . . . memory . . ."

"Julie!"

Rue hesitated, went across the room and touched the bell twice. Tea would be up. Strong black tea was what Julie needed.

It came almost at once. Gross carried the tray, and Rue, not wanting him to see Juliet, took the tray at the door herself and brought it to the low table before the fireplace. Julie did not look up or rouse, and Rue went back to the door behind the screen and closed it, shutting out the distant sound of the piano — a phrase had reached her ears and she recognized it; it was from the piano score of a modern piece of Steven's own composition, full of violent dissonance. She returned. She didn't know she was excited until she lifted the teapot and tried to pour the tea and her hand shook so she spilled it. It was hot and strong, and she waited for it to cool a little, stirring it, watching the nurse.

At last she took the cup to Julie and lifted her head.

"Listen. Listen, Julie. Wake up. Drink this."

Julie opened her eyes. "Had cocktail," she said fuzzily and with great effort. "Don't want tea. . . ."

"Drink it," said Rue and held it to her lips. The girl gulped but did not wince at the hot liquid, and drank as if she did not know what she was doing.

Perhaps she drank half a cup before she choked and slumped sidewise in her chair. Her plain little hat dropped off; her hair was flat and not very tidy and gave her a defenseless look. Rue got a cushion and tried to prop Julie's head comfortably with it.

But something was wrong. She couldn't make Julie's head stay on the pillow. She couldn't hold Julie upright. Something was terribly wrong in that rose-scented room where Crystal Hatterick had died.

From habit her fingers went to Julie's pulse. Went and sought along the white, thin wrist and sought feverishly, terrified, for a flutter that was not there.

"Julie . . . Julie . . ."

It wasn't a scream, for her voice had gone. And Julie's shabby, thin little body slid slowly out of the chair, hesitated in a queer kneeling position for a grisly instant and then went down on the rug.

Rue couldn't kneel beside her. She couldn't

get down on that French rug and try to find Julie's strangely quiet pulse. She couldn't.

She did.

Oddly her muscles obeyed her will. But there was no pulse on Julie's bony wrist; no heart beat below her worn sweater. No life in her eyes when Rue made her fingers remember their training and pull those thin eyelids upward.

There was a sound somewhere, but Rue did not hear it.

She did not know Alicia Pelham was in the room until a voice spoke to her and said coolly: "Why really — what's all this? One of your friends, Rue? She looks as if you've given her too much to drink."

Rue looked up then. Alicia, coated and hatted and furred, was smiling down at her and at Julie as if amused. Rue heard herself say: "She's dead. Julie . . . dead . . ."

It did not seem strange to her that Alicia was there. Nothing would have seemed strange to her at that moment because all her consciousness was stunned by the one enormous strangeness of Julie's death. She said again with crazy, jerky loudness: "She's dead. She's been murdered. Alicia, what shall we do?"

It was completely still. All the house around them was quiet except for the sound of Steven's piano, distant, still crashing out dissonant chords. Going on, uninterrupted, with that music just as if Julie had not died tragically, in all the pathos of a starved, meager little life — at Rue's feet.

They must do something. Call doctors. What did one do? Julie was dead; Rue recognized death.

Alicia, beautiful in her trim black street suit, suave and elegant with her sable scarf flung around her shoulders and her small black hat set expertly upon the black and silver waves of her hair, was bending over the shabby little heap on the rug. She pulled a loose beige glove from one hand and touched Julie's cheek with long white fingers, rosy-tipped and flashing with a huge emerald. Her fingers shrank and hovered. Then she rose and looked at Rue.

Alicia was no longer beautiful, her face was drawn and gray, and her lips had drawn back from her shining teeth. She cried shrilly and pointed at the rug and the limp thing upon it:

"She — the nurse — she's dead! Dead! So — you've done it again!"

CHAPTER VI

There was no mistaking her meaning. It cut as sharply clear through the fog of horror and bewilderment as the thrust of a knife. But Alicia repeated it:

"You've done it again. It's the way Crystal died. Poison. I suppose the nurse knew and threatened you. She knew it and came here and — Where are you going?"

Rue's feet were taking her across the room; she felt disembodied and light and had no consciousness of moving.

"Stop. What are you doing?" Alicia was following her, her small face thrust forward, her eyes so bright and hard they were feral; the savagery of her attack was at sharp variance to her civilized, sophisticated appearance.

"I'm sending for the police," said Rue, too bewildered to reason. She rang the bell.

Alicia cried: "The police! Are you going to give yourself up?"

"I didn't murder her. I didn't murder Crystal."

Alicia's eyes were very bright and watchful: Rue had an untraceable impression that there was a suggestion of triumph and eager certainty — as if chance had put some weapon in Alicia's lovely white hands.

Alicia said, more thoughtfully, watching Rue:

"You were here when Crystal died. She was better; she ought not to have died. She was in your care when her — extremely unexpected death took place. And you married Brule."

"If Brule were here —"

"If Brule were here he'd know."

"Yes, madam," said Gross, opening the door. "You rang —" he began and saw Julie.

Alicia was breathing quickly, thin red lips drawn back a little from perfect teeth; in the sudden silence Rue could hear that and could hear the way Gross's breathing seemed to stop short and then suck inward sharply. He turned quite gray and became instantly helpless, turning blank pale eyes to Alicia for direction.

"What . . ." he wavered, and Alicia said quickly:

"The lady is dead. She's been murdered. In this room."

How Alicia must hate her, thought Rue swiftly. And how well, up to now, she had hidden that hatred. There was no time to think of that; not with Julie lying dead.

Yet, if Alicia had been a dozen Alicias, Rue was still Mrs Hatterick.

"Gross. Look at me."

"Y-yes, madam." He did so with reluctance. Obviously he preferred to take orders from Alicia. Rue said stiffly:

"Get Doctor Hatterick on the phone. He should be in the office now. I'll talk to him."

He blinked, and she said sharply: "Gross, do you hear me?"

"Yes. Yes, madam."

He took the telephone on the bed table. Both she and Alicia could hear in that quiet room the vibration of the office girl's voice.

"He's not in, madam," said Gross helplessly, looking over the ivory telephone at the little heap on the rug. "He's not in —"

"Ask where he can be found."

"She says try the hospital —"

Rue had remembered Steven.

"Very well. Do so. But first call Mr Steven."

"Yes, madam." He put down the telephone quickly, with obvious relief, and vanished.

"Steven?" said Alicia. "Why not the police?"

Rug did not reply; she went to Julie again. It wasn't possible Julie was really dead. She'd been excited, she told herself; frightened. She forced herself for a second time to bend over Julie.

But there was nothing she could do.

She was again conscious of Alicia's bright, oddly triumphant eyes watching her. She must pull herself together, think clearly, make no mistakes. If they couldn't find Brule, then she herself must act; not Alicia, not Steven. It had been a mistake to say they would call the police; there was no reason — no real reason — to believe that Julie had been murdered. First they must have a doctor; it would be his place to say why Julie had died. And if he said murder, then the police.

Julie. Rapidly Rue went back to the years of their acquaintance. Julie never drank — yet she'd been drinking then. And Julie, inexperienced, would have been so easy to poison in that way because she wouldn't have been able to distinguish the taste of the poison. A strong hypnotic, say, with no nausea.

"Well," said Alicia coolly, leaning against the back of the chair, "I thought you were going to call the police. Why don't you do it?"

Again Rue refused to reply to the taunt in Alicia's voice; that suddenly unveiled enmity mattered, it seemed to Rue then, so little.

And Steven Hendrie, taking three steps at a time, reached the top of the stairway and flung himself through the doorway.

"Gross said —" began Steven and saw Julie and stopped as Gross had done. "Good God! Is she really — dead? What happened? Rue, tell me —"

"We've got to have a doctor. If we can't find Brule, then someone else," said Rue.

Alicia smiled the faintest, thinnest little smile and said: "Why not get Andy? He'll say anything you want him to say. He did before."

Steven flashed a troubled look at Alicia. He was kneeling beside Rue, his face pale and his eyes two bright sharp pin points.

"Andy," he said, failing to perceive or at least to give attention to Alicia's implication. "Certainly. If we can't find Brule we'll call Andy. Though if the girl is dead . . . Gross —"

The butler was in the doorway. "I've already taken the liberty, sir," he said. "Doctor Hatterick was not at the hospital. So I left word at the hospital and then telephoned for Doctor Crittenden. He'll be here in a few moments. Is there — anything else?"

"Wait," said Steven. "You're sure she's dead, Rue?"

"Yes. There's nothing we can do."

"What happened?"

"Nothing. She — just drank her tea and — and died."

"Her tea," said Gross from the doorway in a strangled way. Alicia looked at him and back at Rue.

"Steven," she said, "thank God you are here. Look, Steven. There's the tea tray. There's the cup the poor girl drank from — half emptied. Look carefully, so you'll remember."

"What do you mean, Alicia? Surely you aren't trying to say that —"

Alicia's eyes flashed impatiently.

"Have you forgotten how Crystal died?"

There was a gurgle from the doorway where Gross stood as if transfixed.

Steven got up.

"Look here, Alicia. You can't go around saying things like that. Crystal wasn't murdered. What do you mean?"

"Can't you see for yourself, Steven? Have you never questioned Crystal's death? Or the circumstances of it? Because if you haven't, you may as well know right now that the police have. They think she was murdered."

"Alicia, what are you saying! You are mad. Nobody thinks Crystal was murdered. Who would have murdered her?"

Alicia's clear voice went on; she was still altogether collected and, obscurely, triumphant. Her cheeks were not flushed; she stood in a quiet and graceful pose. Not a hair was out of place, and her white fingers were gentle and detached-looking against the huge black bag she carried.

"Ask yourself questions, Steven. Who was with Crystal when she died? Who knew how to give her poison so you wouldn't think of it being poison? So Crystal would die like that — in a coma without active symptoms of having been poisoned. Who profited by Crystal's death? Who — Good God, Steven, are you as blind as Brule?"

"Do you mean — Rue?" said Steven slowly.

Alicia smiled, a little scornfully as a teacher might with a backward pupil.

"The nurse, Julie Garder, must have asked those questions too," she said with a curious effect of lightness. "Now she's dead. As Crystal died."

There was a slight, muffled motion from the doorway, and some surface sense of Rue's discovered that Gross had forsaken all training and dissolved dazedly into a sitting position on the edge of a chair as if his hitherto rigid knees had

87

failed him. This, said Gross's attitude, was catastrophe.

"Rue, you hear what Alicia said. Of course it isn't true." Steven's deep-set eyes, though, questioned her, begged for reassurance.

"No, Steven. It isn't true. I don't know why she accuses me."

Alicia caught it up neatly and replied with an adroit touch of wistfulness. "I was Crystal's best friend. And I'm engaged to marry you, Steven; I love you. How can I remain quiet and see you taken in by —" She checked herself too obviously. "I make no accusation at all."

Steven rubbed his hands through his hair, already disheveled. He wore a brown sweater instead of a coat and his tie and collar were loosened, and he had on soft wooden slippers.

"I don't know what to do." He turned. "Gross."

The butler jerked himself upward but could not resume his usual rigid exterior. He looked slack and old and said waveringly: "Yes sir."

"Did you let in this — Miss Garder?" His hand indicated Julie, and Gross said, understanding him:

"No sir. If you mean to say did I let the young lady into the house, I didn't."

"But you announced her," said Rue. "You told me she had come to see me."

"And so she said, madam. But she was — already in the house. It — I — I hope it wasn't wrong. I hope the police . . . . I didn't mean any harm. It was unusual, but I saw no reason to tell Madam —"

"What do you mean?" asked Steven.

"I mean, sir, the nurse was already in the house. I came into the drawing room to turn on lights and she was there. Sitting in the dark. She — she seemed to be waiting. She said she'd come to see Mrs Hatterick and would I please let Madam know. So I — I did," said Gross helplessly.

Alicia was listening intently, her small, classically beautiful face like porcelain and as brittle. She said: "Who let her in, then? She couldn't have entered unless someone opened the door."

"I don't know, miss. She — I was taken aback as it were. I didn't ask. But I — I know nothing of this. If it is murder —"

Julie in that silent house; waiting in that shadowy French drawing room. Rue thought back to the silence of the day; the quiet and apparently empty house. She'd heard no sound of Julie's arrival. She'd heard no one moving about.

But then, the house hadn't been empty. Had Julie had that cocktail in the French drawing room while she waited? Then if so, who had given it to her? Only Rue and Steven were at home. Only she and Steven and . . . How had Alicia got there? When had she come? Who had let her into the house?

Rue said: "Gross, when did Miss Alicia arrive?"

The butler opened his mouth to speak, but

Alicia quickly interrupted.

"Why really, Rue," she said, "what a question. I came to see Madge, of course. After all, Rue, this house is almost my home and has been for years. I've always come and gone as I chose. I have always been like a member of the family." Her look said, You are the interloper here; you are the stranger; your time is short. She continued in silky, cool reproof: "At any rate, Rue, this is scarcely the time and place to attempt to quarrel with me."

Steven did not appear to note what she said or what Rue had said; he was staring downward at the little heap on the rug. He said: "Can't we move her to the bed? Or — or cover her. Or wait in another room. If we can't do anything for her . . ."

Again a small voice in Rue spoke almost without Rue's own volition.

"You can't move her; if she was murdered —"

"You see," said Alicia to Steven, "how well informed she is! She's trying to tell us that the body ought not to be moved until the police have come! Oh, Steven." She crossed to him suddenly, beautiful and svelte and slender with her lovely face close to Steven and her lovely hands on his arm. "Oh, Steven, I realize I ought not to have let my feelings get the better of me just now! But how could I help it! I've stood by so long, telling myself that my suspicions must have been wrong. I've told myself that over and over; I've forced myself to be as friendly as I

90

could be with Rue. I've tried to help her. I've felt it was due my friendship to Brule and my love for you to conquer my doubts, to help so that life will go as smoothly as possible for both of you. I've made friends for Rue; I've given hints to the servants, I've tried to help Madge; I've done everything possible. Truly I have, Steven. But this — this proves how futile it's been. It's no use, Steven, I can't keep quiet any longer. How do I know that you are safe? Or Brule! Or Madge! You are my only family; the only people I love in the world. Don't you understand, Steven?"

How beautiful she is, thought Rue with a kind of stab; how can any man resist her beauty? Steven, white, perplexed, was looking down into Alicia's perfect small face. He put his hand upon Alicia's hand.

"I know how you feel, dear," he said. "I suppose it's only natural to resent Crystal's place being filled. But you mustn't let your feelings —" He broke off abruptly.

Brule and Andy were in the doorway. Rue didn't know how long they'd been there, but she thought it had been long enough for them to hear Alicia's words — that or her distinct clear voice had met them on the stairway and in the hall.

"Where is she?" said Brule and looked past Alicia and Steven and saw.

Brule would know what to do. He didn't look at Rue as he went to Julie. Andy followed him.

The room was so still you could hear a faint small hissing in the old-fashioned radiators, concealed below the windows. Neither Andy nor Brule spoke for a moment. Then Brule said in a preoccupied voice:

"No chance."

"She'd been drinking," said Andy.

"Yes, I know. But — I'd say a strong hypnotic; look at her eyes."

"Yes, I see."

Andy rose and his eyes sought out Rue anxiously. Brule got up, too, and looked deliberately at all of them, but his glance when it met Rue's eyes held no special message for her. His eyes were bright and dark and preoccupied. He took off his overcoat and dropped it on a chair.

"Gross."

"Yes sir." The butler sprang forward from the doorway.

"Get a sheet. What happened, Rue? Tell me exactly —"

"Brule," said Alicia. "It's the way Crystal —"

"Wait, Alicia, please. Tell me, Rue."

"She came to see me," said Rue. "She said she'd had a cocktail, and I thought she was drunk. Julie never drank. I ordered tea and gave her some hot tea and — then she died."

"How did she die?"

Rue swallowed heavily. Her hands were pressed against her throat, though she didn't know it; her figure, slim and taut under her green wool frock, was pressed against the chair before her. "She — seemed to become uncon-scious; it was as if she'd been drinking a lot; she talked some —"

Brule's eyes sharpened.

"Oh, she talked?"

"Yes. Some. In a wandering way — not very sensible."

"Why had she come? Were you expecting her?"

"No. I think she came about — about Crystal. There was — she knew something. I think the police inquiry had alarmed her —"

Steven looked up quickly.

"Police?" he said. "Then Alicia was right —"

"Steven, if you'd only believe me," cried Alicia. "Brule, how can you question her like that? As if you believe — with that girl dead exactly as Crystal —"

Brule swerved around with a quick compact motion to look at Alicia.

"You are talking to my wife," he said.

In the little silence Alicia laughed a very small, faint laugh which managed to be unutterably scornful.

"Your wife," she said and laughed. And then as Brule turned purposefully toward the table near the bed she said sharply: "What are you going to do?"

"Get the police, of course," said Brule and took up the telephone. He knew the dial number, and they listened while the dial mur-mured and while he spoke; Andy moved out of

the way as Gross tiptoed into the room with a
sheet and spread it gingerly over the little shabby
heap on the rug before the fireplace. A maid,
two maids were in the hall, peering with frightened faces through the doorway. They heard
Brule give the address. "I think it's murder," he
said. "Yes . . . All right. We won't touch anything."

He hung up.

And dialed again. This time for Guy Cole.

"Guy, can you come right away? Before the
police get here. . . . Yes, it's the thing I talked
to you about but a — bad development. The
nurse — the day nurse, I mean — who took
care of Crystal, has been murdered. Here, in the
house —"

They could hear Guy's exclamation and the
sharp click of his telephone. Brule put down
the instrument and sat for a moment looking
at it; his face was as always impenetrable except
that there was a tight, hard look about his jaw
and his eyes were very bright. He'd been operating that day, probably, thought Rue; for he
looked tired, and there was about him a look
of weary but satisfied accomplishment — something almost intangible, yet to Rue's eyes obvious enough. He was planning now; sitting at
the table in complete silence while his mind
leaped ahead, arranged, considered. They all
waited. Andy removed his overcoat quietly and
put it down on a chair. Steven watched Brule.
Gross hovered, his face sagged and gray, about

the door. Alicia was like a fashionable statue with a face done in alabaster, and jewels for eyes.

Brule said: "Go downstairs to the library. All of you. Guy will be here in a moment. He'll be present while the police question you. He won't let you make any damaging admissions; but of course you'll have to tell the truth. Exactly what happened but that's all. Don't volunteer any information. Stick to the simple facts as you know them. If Guy tells you not to answer, don't answer. Do exactly what Guy says."

"Brule, what's this about Crystal's having been murdered?" asked Steven abruptly. "Has there actually been an inquiry?"

"Yes. But I don't think the police have any direct evidence. Don't answer any questions at all about that. Now then . . ."

He stopped thoughtfully. Andy said slowly:

"Well, that ties it. We're in for it now. But I don't see Brule, why you told the police it was murder. I mean, the nurse. It seems to me it could be either accident or suicide."

"The girl came here to see Rue; she'd probably been questioned by the police sometime yesterday about Crystal's death. Whatever she told them, the inquiry seems to have aroused her suspicions or reminded her of something she knew and wanted to tell Rue —"

"Yes. Yes, that's what she —" Brule's glance stopped Rue; she didn't know what it meant, she only felt that something in that swift look compelled her silence. Brule went on in terse sentences:

"If she really knew anything, if Crystal was murdered, if the murderer knew Julie Garder had any knowledge of it, then Julie was stopped. Before she could tell it. It's obvious — as the police will see it."

"But — but it isn't conclusive, Brule. You know that. That's assuming that Crystal was murdered," said Andy, troubled. "That's assuming the girl actually knew something that would lead to the murderer. That's assuming that even if she knew it she would come here to tell Rue. Wouldn't she have been more likely to tell the police —"

"I said, that's as the police will certainly see the case. Call it murder then, for they will. If it proves to be accident, or if it proves to have been suicide — though God knows why she would have come here to kill herself — let the police discover it. Don't try to dodge their own certain and obvious conclusion; tell them straight off that it's murder."

Steven said slowly: "Of course Brule's right. I wouldn't have seen it myself, but I do now."

"If you please, sir." It was Gross.

"Yes, Gross?"

"I think Mr Cole has arrived."

Brule got up swiftly, with the compact elasticity of motion that characterized him.

"Go downstairs. All of you. I'll stay here. Except — Rue, I want to talk to you."

Alicia gave Rue a swift look, and Steven put his arm lightly about Alicia's waist, and together they left the room. Rue moved uncertainly toward Brule. It was easier to breathe somehow since Brule and Andy had come. Was it because Brule had taken control of the situation from her own frightened, faltering hands? Or was it because Brule had looked at Julie and if there had been anything at all that could have been done to save her Brule would have done it?

"Tell me, Rue, exactly what happened. Quickly. Don't leave out anything." He paused and then said more kindly: "Don't tremble like that, Rue. But tell me. Everything. What time did she arrive? Where did she sit? Where did you sit? Above all, what did she tell you? Did she —" He glanced at the door but the others had gone. His voice lowered, however, and he put his hands on Rue's shoulders and drew her nearer him so he could look directly down into her eyes. "Did Julie know anything of Crystal's death? For you see, if she did, if she told you, if you share her knowledge you — share her danger."

Rue's heart was like a bird caught in her throat. "Her . . . danger . . ." she said stiffly.

Brule's eyes were suddenly a little less hard and bright. He said:

"Don't be afraid. You are my wife, and I'll try to take care of you."

She looked up into his eyes for an instant; but in that stillness they both were aware of a sound growing out of the deepening dusk away off in the distance. A sound that swelled and diminished and swelled shrilly again and grew ever nearer and all at once became horribly eerie and paralyzing in its intent. It was the police siren swooping upon them like a bird of prey, shrieking its triumph through twilight streets.

There was no escaping it. Brule listened, and his hands on Rue's shoulders became tighter. He said: "Hurry. Tell me what Julie told you."

CHAPTER VII

She told him hastily against the eerie background of that nearing siren. Brule's bright, searching gaze seemed to draw from her every smallest phrase Julie had uttered as if she, Rue, were mesmerized. She told of the girl's wavering entrance; of what she had said; of how Julie had seemed confused, as if she'd been drinking; of how she confused names calling Rue, Julie; of her repeated warning that memory wasn't to be trusted, of how she had said that she knew something of Crystal's murder and that Rue knew it too.

"What did she know?"

"I don't know. I can't think — it's all so horribly sudden. I don't know what it is. She thought I knew, too, but there's nothing." Rue's voice wavered upward; there was a bewildering crescendo of sound from below the house, and then all at once complete, shattering silence as someone turned off the siren. A silence which was in its way as threatening as the siren.

"All right. You'll have to go down. Listen, Rue, and obey me. Don't tell the police what Julie said. It would be advertising your own danger. I'm being blunt with you because you've got to know. Remember Julie was almost certainly murdered because she knew too much;

99

she was the day nurse, you were the night nurse; and she was murdered on her way to you."

"You speak as if you know it was murder," cried Rue.

"There's not much doubt of it," said Brule tersely. "We'll make the most of what loopholes we can find — but there may be none. It's murder; I'm afraid there's no reasonable doubt."

He relinquished her shoulders, strode to the window, looked down through the gathering dusk of the dark day and abruptly turned toward her again.

"They're coming in. All of them. God . . . Well, Rue. Remember not to tell exactly what Julie said; say she seemed confused and didn't say anything that made sense; insist upon it. I can't make it too strong a warning. Do you understand?"

"I — yes. I'm to tell them nothing that she said. I'm to tell them I know nothing of Crystal's death that suggests murder."

"That's right. And listen, Rue —"

Feet were on the stairs. People and voices and movement had quite suddenly flooded the house. Brule took her hand.

"Listen! We've stood shoulder to shoulder before this. When life was the stake as it is now. We can do it again."

"Yes, Brule."

He looked at her for a second or two without speaking; then quite suddenly took her in his arms. She felt briefly the pressure of his shoulder

100

and the hard warmth of his face against her own. Then he released her.

"All right, Rue. Go downstairs with the others. Follow Guy's lead in everything and remember what I've told you. . . . I'll stay here and see the police."

They were in the hall when she reached it. She shrank back into the shadow beyond the stairway and watched them flood its narrow width. Gross led them into the bedroom. Her own bedroom that had been Crystal's. Where Julie lay now and the scent of roses drifted from the silken curtains. She heard Brule's voice; she heard other voices. Men in ordinary, everyday business suits carried strange boxes and paraphernalia up the stairs. Here and there were policemen, looming huge and bulky in their blue winter uniforms with the stars and buttons on their chests winking and catching lights.

When they had flooded into the bedroom, she crept along the hall and down the stairs. There were policemen in the hall below, too, but they didn't question her, just looked after her, their eyes all but boring into her back, as she went down the hall, past doors into the drawing rooms and reached the library.

They were all there. Alicia and Steven and Andy and Guy Cole. And Madge was there too; still in her coat and hat as if she had just arrived from school, sobbing hysterically in Alicia's arms, while Crystal's painted face, detached and beautiful in its own curious pallid beauty, stared

101

down at them mockingly from above the mantel. And ten minutes later two policemen walked into the room and remained there, so they had to talk cautiously, aware of listening, official ears.

Madge lifted her head as Rue entered, she stared at Rue with implacable, hating eyes and wiped tears from her face with the back of her hand. Alicia had removed her coat and furs and sat erect and graceful in her suave black street gown with pearls — real pearls — at her throat. She had in that moment an odd affinity with the Crystal above the mantel in that she was, as ever, like a portrait of a lady.

Andy came at once to meet Rue.

"Sit here, Rue. I'll get you a drink. Guy's telling us what to do."

The police inquiry, or at least her initial experience of it as it took place then and there, that night, was like nothing Rue had ever imagined. Mainly she would not have imagined that so many men took an active part in the inquiry. Previous to that she had thought, vaguely, that police inquiry concerning any one crime was in the hands of one police officer, designated so by whatever powers there were. Now she found that instead of one officer directing and sifting and taking entire responsibility for the inquiry, there were at least a dozen. That every department and every angle of invention was to have its own special direct contact with suspects; that there was no opportunity actually for brilliant individual action to be publicized, for instead the whole aim of every bureau and every department was to pool whatever knowledge they rooted out. That a man who kept knowledge he discovered to himself in the hope of a brilliant coup and personal triumph would have been booted out of the police department in a fortnight. There was only concerted knowledge, concerted and pooled action and conclusions; concerted inquiry and effort.

That night, however, the police, the detectives, the preliminary inquiry, the casual-seeming questions was, the whole of it, like a wave that had unexpectedly submerged them; it was exactly as if they were all battling to keep their heads above an unutterably confusing and engulfing flood.

Hours, it seemed to Rue, passed while the police and Brule remained for the most part in the second floor room where Julie had died. Andy and Guy Cole during the waiting made occasional scouting trips into the hall, Andy coming back with a grave face.

After a while they removed Julie's body; Andy pulled the old-fashioned sliding doors of the library together, but it was so quiet in the room that they could hear the heavy tread of the men carrying the girl away. There is only one occasion in the world when the tread of men sounds just like that. Rue stifled a childish impulse to cover her ears. Alicia sat like a still, pale model of fashion; Madge put up her face and listened and gave Rue a long, unchildish look.

It must have been about then that the first reporters reached the house, for next morning there were pictures of the long police ambulance and a basketlike shape, dim in the flare of lights, being carried down the steps. Guy saw the reporters.

"Tell 'em we don't know yet whether it was suicide or — or what," said Andy. "Don't say any more than you can help."

Guy looked at him rather pityingly and went away. He came back with news.

"They're going to have an autopsy done right away. Tonight. Meantime they'll question you. They can't make a definite murder charge yet. But they'll proceed as if they knew it to be murder," said Guy rather dryly. "Remember, when they question you, everything I've told you."

He had warned them and he repeated it, undeterred by the stolidly listening ears of the two policemen.

"Chances are the girl simply took an overdose of some medicine. Nurses are always prescribing for themselves. But in view of this stink they tried to raise about Crystal, you'd better be prepared. Stay on the safe side. You never know what kind of admission, no matter how innocent it is, is going to be turned around by later evidence into something — incriminating," said Guy, pausing and looking at them with large, humid blue eyes. He was a balloon of a man, short, glistening, round, with a fringe of fluffy light hair around an expanse of pink blandness and fat red cheeks. He had the round face of a baby, and the friendliest smile in his watery-looking blue eyes, and was one of the finest criminal lawyers in the country. So far as Rue knew he had no conscience in his professional life; his side won (frequently enough to be notable) be it guilty or innocent; yet in private life he was a good and loyal friend. So Brule had told her, and so she believed, for Brule had known Guy since they were boys in school, and they had been neighbors since Brule's marriage to Crystal, sixteen years ago.

His matter-of-fact way was subtly sustaining. Guy knew about these things; they happened all the time; their own special nightmare was a labyrinth whose twisting paths Guy could follow.

"I'll stay with you," he said. "Anything they ask that I think might be damaging in the event they prove the girl was murdered, I'll object to. They can't force you to answer anything. Unless, of course, they get enough evidence to justify an arrest; if so they are likely to take anybody arrested off to jail in the County Court Building and — keep 'em there a few days while they question."

His eyes remained blue, humid, wide open and ingenuous. The vista his words opened was inexpressibly chilling. Andy stirred restlessly, gave Rue an anxious look and said in a voice that failed to disguise that anxiety:

"You don't think they're likely to do that, do

you? Right now? I mean — well, do you think there's enough evidence against — against anybody to justify an arrest?"

He meant against Rue, of course; everyone knew it.

Guy lighted a cigarette and said he didn't think so.

"Not unless you tell them something you haven't told me. And I wouldn't advise that, Rue."

It was like Guy to address Rue nonchalantly and directly. But it made still clearer her position of prime suspect.

"See here," said Andy, glancing at the policeman uneasily but continuing. "Does she have to tell them about — well, I mean, the tea . . ."

"Why not? Gross knows he brought up the tea tray; the kitchen girl knows it was ordered and prepared. Besides, the fingerprints will be on the cup, and there's no other explanation for Rue's fingerprints being there and not the girl's. Julie's. But if Julie was poisoned and the poison's been in her stomach long enough to show it was given her before she arrived here, Rue will be in the clear."

Madge, huddled at Alicia's feet with her arm across Alicia's knees, looked up quickly again, her small dark face with its strong jaw looking as yellow as a candle. She'd heard them talking of Crystal's death; there was no way to keep the barely started investigation of the previous day from her ears, so Steven had told her of it; kindly and briefly in the ten minutes before the police came into the room. And to do the child justice, thought Rue, watching her, she'd taken it well. She'd turned very pale and stopped sobbing and had clung closer to Alicia. And Alicia had given Rue a queer, brief look above the child's head which had in it a suggestion of complacence. You see, the look had said, how Madge turns to me — not to you, who stand legally in the place of her dead mother.

A small thought flashed across Rue's mind; sometime she must discover why Alicia so hated her, how long she had hated her and yet veiled that hatred in a semblance of kindness and friendliness. And above all, why?

But not then.

And it was then that Brule came in, his face like a mask, and said there was nothing new and that the police wanted to question Rue and would she come into the dining room.

"And Guy," said Brule.

Guy bounced up; he had the incredible elasticity of motion some fat men have and just then it gave an effect of cheerful alacrity which was almost inhuman. Andy rose, too, as if he wanted to accompany her, seemed to realize he could not and stood there watching as Rue rose and went to the door. Queer how much willpower that slight effort of muscles took.

"Don't be afraid," said Brule, and Andy gave her a look of almost anguished encouragement. Alicia watched and Madge, and only Steven remained sunk miserably in his chair, his head in his hands.

"Brace up, Rue," said Guy cheerily. "This won't be bad. They've not had time yet to get the autopsy report."

Eight or ten men were in the dining room; they were talking, and one of them was writing on a report blank, and another held shorthand tablets in his hand. They paid no attention to Rue's entrance although all of them saw her; she stood, waiting, and Guy beside her waited also, while a tall thin man with pale blue eyes as remote as ice and deep lines like scars in his cheeks (Lieutenant Angel, he proved to be) finished what he had to say to a brother detective. The face of Oliver Miller appeared in what was to Rue a blur of faces. Then Lieutenant Angel looked directly at her and said: "All right, Mrs Hatterick. Sit down. Where's that statement, Murphy?"

The man with the shorthand tablet flipped back a few pages and began to read rapidly and in a singsong voice while Rue sat at her own table and listened — a table that was long and stately and polished so beautifully that it gave reflections of the light from the chandelier above and, more dimly, blotches that were faces. Light poured down upon Rue — a light they never used, for it was hard and bright, and Rue preferred candles in the great silver candelabra on the buffet opposite. Guy made himself extremely comfortable in a chair near her and nodded to

108

Lieutenant Angel and spoke to him by name, and glanced recognizingly at one or two other men sitting and standing about them. Rue realized with a start that the man Murphy was reading a statement that Brule must have made. She listened.

" '. . . and I was reached at the hospital by the message from Mrs Hatterick. I hurried home and met Doctor Crittenden at the doorstep; he had got the message too. But the girl was dead, and we could do nothing. I called the police because it was obviously a violent death. Question: You knew it was murder? Answer —' "

Lieutenant Angel stirred and murmured: "Just read the answers."

"Yes sir. 'Answer: I didn't know. My wife said the girl came unexpectedly and asked for her and was shown up to her room. When Miss Garder entered she seemed confused and said she'd had a cocktail. Mrs Hatterick thought the cocktail had affected her and ordered tea and gave the girl a cup of tea. She was trying to make her swallow the tea when the girl became unconscious and died. She telephoned at once for me —' "

"That'll do, Murphy. You subscribe to all that, Mrs Hatterick?"

"Yes." How small and faint her voice sounded; she must speak in a more assured, less frightened way.

"I understand Julie Garder was a friend of yours."

109

"We trained as nurses together."

"Yes, I know all about that. She was one of the nurses on the case when the first Mrs Hatterick died. You were the night nurse."

He didn't seem to expect a reply, but Rue heard herself saying yes. Guy was watching Murphy write, with as detached and unconcerned an air as if he'd been in a theater.

Angel leaned forward. "Mrs Hatterick, your husband says, and you agree that you told him Julie Garder was confused and said she'd had a cocktail. What else did she say?"

Rue swallowed hard, and Guy said nothing. Rue replied: "She was confused; she talked a little in a rambling way; nothing that made sense."

"What'd she talk of?"

"She — she repeated my name and her own; she mumbled something abut a cocktail — pink; something about coming to see me — oh, there was nothing sensible and clear."

"Had you invited her to come to see you? I mean to come today specifically? Had you an engagement with her?"

"No."

"You were on sufficiently friendly terms for her to call without an invitation?"

"Yes, certainly."

"Did she come here often?"

"No."

"Why not?"

"Julie was busy." He seemed to wait for her

to amplify it, but something very quiet about Guy seemed to warn her to say no more than was necessary.

"Then you and Miss Garder were still on good terms?"

"Yes, certainly."

"Can you think of anything else she said?"

Guy stirred. "She's told you everything she knows. It's been a shock for Mrs Hatterick. She's doing well to let you question her at all. Later, if you find the girl's been murdered, Mrs Hatterick can be questioned more at length."

The lieutenant looked at Guy, and Guy looked blandly back at him.

"All right, Mrs Hatterick, I appreciate your willingness to be of help," said Angel. "But there's one or two points that I'd like to know more about right now. Whatever the autopsy proves, we'd like to know how she got in the house and how long she was here before she was announced. Your butler says he didn't let her in. That he found her waiting in the drawing room, having evidently been admitted to the house some time previous. Who let her into the house and when?"

"I don't know. I didn't know she was in the house. I heard nothing."

"You didn't see her downstairs?"

"No."

"You didn't know she was in the house at all?"

"No."

"Think carefully, Mrs Hatterick. Did she take anything while in your room — any capsule or pill?"

"No. I'm sure of that," said Rue and was instantly aware of Guy's disapproval.

He stirred and said: "That all, Lieutenant? Mrs Hatterick's told you all she knows; of course if the girl does prove to have been murdered Mrs Hatterick's willing to be questioned at length."

The lines in Angel's thin long face deepened.

"There's one more question just now, Cole." He leaned back a little in his chair, holding Rue's gaze with his chill blue own; all at once the room held only silence and watchfulness. This was the real question; this was the sum, the crux of the whole inquiry.

Guy shared Rue's intuition, for he was suddenly as deadly still as a crouching animal. And the question came:

"Tell me this, Mrs Hatterick. What did Julie Garder know of the death of the first Mrs Hatterick?"

Guy got to his feet.

"She doesn't need to reply to that, Lieutenant. She doesn't —"

"Let the lady speak, Cole. How about it, Mrs Hatterick?"

Guy said: "She doesn't have to reply; but I will for her. The girl told her nothing, of course. She told her absolutely nothing of the facts of Crystal Hatterick's death."

"Do you subscribe to that, Mrs Hatterick?"

"I —"

Guy answered again. "Look here, Angel; you've had your answer. Tell him, Rue, that I answered correctly. It may as well go on the record."

"Y-yes," faltered Rue, confused by Guy's demand; clinging to the letter of the truth.

A telephone rang in the hall; Angel, disbelief in his cold eyes and another question on his tongue, stopped to listen. They heard the murmur of a voice from the telephone, which was in the recess near the dining room door. It was one of the detectives; he said yes, and no, and after a pause: "You don't say! . . . Okay!"

He appeared at the doorway, eyes seeking Angel's. "It's the doc," he said. "Says it's poison all right. Lethal quantity of some synthetic poison, he doesn't know what yet. Probably a barbituric acid derivative. Can't tell till he runs some more tests. Says it looks to him like murder, all right. But he says there's an awful funny thing. The girl's hands have turned green, bright green on the —"

"*Cary! That'll do!* All right, Cole, you and Mrs Hatterick can go. That's all except hold yourself ready for further inquiry. Now then, Cary. Her hands — Close that door."

The door closed behind them. Someone had hung up the telephone. Rue turned, bewildered, to Guy.

"What do they mean? *Julie's* hands?"

His eyes met her own; they were wide, blue, dewy-looking. "I don't know what they meant," he said slowly.

The door of the music room opened, and they both looked that way. Alicia and Brule appeared in the doorway, outlined clearly against the lighted long room behind them. Brule apparently had opened the door, and as he did so both appeared to pause for another word. They didn't note the presence of Guy Cole and of Rue in the hall. For Alicia turned suddenly to face Brule, said something low and put her head in an affectionate gesture against Brule's shoulder. It was a small gesture, barely sketched, so brief was it. But there was the most definite air of accustomedness about it.

Guy cleared his throat abruptly.

"Come along, Rue," he said. "Green hands — want to know what Brule thinks."

Andy was waiting in the library. Andy, who had said he loved her. She followed Guy toward the library, and the couple at the door of the music room saw them and came toward them.

CHAPTER VIII

"Green hands!" said Brule. "Did you say green?"

Guy shrugged his bulging shoulders. "That's what the fellow said. Then Angel shushed him and put us out and had the door closed so we couldn't hear any more. Green hands."

"But that isn't so," said Brule. "When I looked at the girl there was nothing like that." He turned to Andy. "Did you see anything of the kind?"

Andy shook his head.

"No. It sounds — fantastic. Is there any poison, Brule, that could have such an effect?"

"If an internal poison had the effect of color on the skin after death, it wouldn't confine itself to the hands, the whole circulatory system would have been affected; and that certainly not after death, but before. Anyway . . ." Brule walked over to the mantel and stood with his back to it. "I'm inclined to think it's something the fellows in the laboratory have done — accidentally, like as not; they are no more immune to mistakes than the rest of us. It does sound fantastic. But there are chemicals . . ." he left it at that.

And as always, they accepted Brule's word as final.

Alicia rose and went to the telephone on the long desk.

"How much longer will it be, do you suppose?" she said to Brule. "I had promised the Sidneys —"

"Better telephone and tell them you can't make it. Be careful though —"

"Good heavens, Brule, you needn't tell me to be careful what I say! Do you suppose for one instant all this inquiry is going to be pleasant for me?" She took the telephone and dialed. A maid came into the room with a tray and was followed by the upstairs girl with another; the trays contained coffee and sandwiches, and both girls were pale, with excited eyes, and cast rapid, curious glances about them.

"That's right," said Brule. "No use trying to have dinner when everything's so upset, but you've got to eat." The maids, faces avid with curiosity, went away, and Brule poured coffee, and Andy brought a cup of it to Rue. Alicia was talking over the telephone, and Steven had asked Brule some question and Brule was replying. Andy spoke in a low voice, inaudible to the others.

"I've got to see you alone, Rue," he said. His fingers touched her own as she took the cup. His eyes warmed. "I love you," he whispered. "Remember . . ."

No one could possibly have heard. He turned away. It was several moments before Rue became conscious of Madge's oddly fixed and

116

thoughtful regard. She looked at Madge, and Madge stared back at her, steadily and inimically. But she couldn't have heard what Andy said. And suppose she had, what of it? If there was no affection between Rue and Brule, there could, at least, be honesty. But nevertheless that cold stare in Madge's dark eyes made her uneasy.

They could all hear Alicia's silken excuses over the telephone. She put it down at last. "She'll never believe me again," she observed to no one but so they could all hear it. "I felt perfectly well when I left her house this afternoon — just before I came here — and Winifred Sidney knows it."

It was said a little too carefully. Brule glanced at her quickly, and Andy said:

"Oh, you came straight on here from Sidneys'?"

Alicia nodded. "I arrived just at the time the thing occurred. I came to see Madge. She hadn't got home yet, and as I settled down to wait for her I heard something like a scream. So naturally I went to see what had happened. The door to Rue's room was open. Rue was bending over the nurse. I thought at first, of course, she'd only fainted."

Andy looked at Rue, and Rue put down her cup. "Yes, I — I think I screamed. And Alicia came in just after Julie died. But I didn't know Alicia was in the house —"

Alicia continued quite as if Rue had not spoken at all.

"I trust this interest in my doings doesn't mean that I am suspected of having anything to do with the death of a girl I never even saw before."

Steven looked up.

"You've seen her, Alicia," he said mildly. "Lots of times. When Crystal was sick."

The jet-and-white line of Alicia's eyelids rose and fell once rapidly.

"Oh yes, I suppose I saw her then. But I wouldn't have remembered the girl. I assure you I didn't put poison in her tea, if that's what you mean. Let me have some coffee, Brule."

"I didn't mean that, Alicia," said Steven apologetically. "You know it wasn't in my thoughts at all."

"A synthetic poison," said Brule thoughtfully, pouring coffee for Alicia. "That can mean anything."

"How can they prove it's murder?" said Andy hopefully. "They can't."

But Brule shook his head. "Those letters, Crystal's death — now this nurse's death the instant police inquiry opened about Crystal. No —"

Andy said: "You think yourself that it's murder. Is that right, Brule?"

"I don't know what to think," said Brule. "But I'd like to know exactly who wrote those letters to the police. I want to know because I'd like to ask why." He said it on the whole rather mildly, looking at a sandwich in his hands. The

mildness seemed out of place; then Rue understood it.

He meant that if anyone in that room had
written letters to the police, telling them Crystal
had been murdered, Brule was giving that person a chance to confess it, to tell him why he'd
urged a police investigation.

And there appeared suddenly two corollaries
to Brule's meaning. One was that all the people
close to Crystal and to Brule were in that room.
And the second corollary was worse. That was,
of course, that if Crystal was murdered, if Julie
was murdered, then someone close to them all
had murdered both women. It had to be someone close to them; casual acquaintances don't
walk up to you and give you poison. And besides, there was opportunity to take into consideration: opportunity and motive.

Murder has to rise from intensely personal and
intensely important motives. It is a last and
dreadful resort of urgent emergency. Who then
had to get rid of Crystal? Who had to kill Julie
before Julie could tell the thing that she'd said
she knew? And had said that Rue knew also.

But Rue knew nothing: she'd searched her
mind and her memory, and there was nothing
that gave her the clue to Crystal's death that
Julie had expected Rue to know.

How could you tell a murderer from other
people? How strange that there was no brand,
no insignia of the barrier he has crossed which
divides him forever from other people, which

makes him a pariah, an outcast, a man who has experienced the unforgivable crime? Who has dipped into the dark and mysterious stream and whose hands will forever bear the stain of it.

Hands made her think of Julie's hands, with a rather sickening twinge of horror. Horror — and below it a deep instinctive question, as if the thing held an obscure but important meaning.

Brule was speaking. He was talking again of the letters. ". . . Because whoever wrote them must have had some reason for believing Crystal was murdered. Therefore if we can discover what that reason was we might go a long way toward getting this thing satisfactorily settled." He didn't say, discovering who murdered Crystal.

It was an odd omission. But Rue did not then scrutinize it. For a detective, one who had not yet questioned them, appeared in the doorway and said they were ready now to take general statements from each person in the house, and they would then call it a day, and Miss Pelham and Dr Crittenden could go home.

The general statements were taken then and there. Rue listened — dull with a kind of emotional fatigue. Each was fairly brief, and there was no inquiry until they came to Madge, although every word was taken in shorthand by the stenographer who appeared on the threshold just as Steven, who was first, began to talk.

Steven said briefly that he'd been working all

day in the studio; he didn't know that Julie Garder had arrived at all; the first he knew of the murder was when Gross came to tell him; and that he knew nothing at all about it. Mrs Hatterick and Miss Pelham had been in the room when he reached it. The body had been on the rug before the hearth; a tea tray was on a small table. Yes, he remembered the dead girl but only vaguely. No, he knew of no reason for her suicide or murder.

Alicia's statement was even briefer, she'd just reached the house and was waiting downstairs for Madge to return from school when she'd heard a scream upstairs; she went upstairs and found Mrs Hatterick bending over her friend (Guy cleared his throat just there, and Alicia flashed a look at him but amended it quickly). "I mean, Julie Garder." She said nothing that openly cast suspicion upon Rue, however; except that her statement was so extremely brief and noncommittal that it could be amplified at any time and as she chose to amplify it later. She did not look at Rue once.

Andy, next, said he'd come at once when Gross told him over the telephone what had happened. The girl was dead when he and Dr Hatterick looked at her. Dr Hatterick had called the police.

"Did you notice anything unusual about the body?"

"Nothing," said Andy. "Except that it seemed a case of violent death. So far as we knew the girl was in good health."

The detective's eyes retreated.

"Miss Madge Hatterick?" he said.

Madge, as if she had been waiting her turn, said instantly:

"I am Madge Hatterick. And I want to tell you something."

She stood up as if to speak with more authority, her face seemed suddenly mature and very determined with its square jaws and bright dark eyes. She pushed her dark hair back and looked straight at the detective in a poised manner that belied her dark blue school uniform with its demure lines. Brule looked startled, he went to her and said to the detective:

"My daughter is barely fifteen. She knows nothing of this, and I would appreciate it if you — question her as little as possible. I cannot imagine her testimony being of any possible value; she's only a child —"

"All right, all right, Doctor," said the detective, watching Madge. "Let the young lady speak. She seems to have something on her chest."

"But you don't understand," said Brule. "She's really a child, she knows nothing of —" He looked at Guy, who strolled nearer.

"Now, now, Madge," said Guy. "Don't let yourself get hysterical."

"I'll say what I have to say," said Madge; "you can't stop me. I may be young, but I have eyes, and there've been things happening in this house. Things you ought to know —"

Brule was white. He put one hand on Madge's shoulder and held it so tightly that Madge winced but stared defiantly back at him, his living counterpart. Except — hadn't Steven said? — she was like Crystal inside.

"You're in love with her," she said to Brule in a furious voice. "You're in love with Rue. You can't see how wicked and cruel she is. Who killed my mother? Tell the police who murdered my mother. Tell them —"

"Madge!"

"I won't listen to you. I'll tell them. I'll tell them who was alone with my mother before she died. I'll tell them everything I know —"

Guy was for the first time concerned. "Stop that, Madge. You don't know what you're saying. You're a silly child. Look at me, Madge, I've known you since you were a baby. I'm your godfather; have I ever been unkind to you, or have I ever lied to you? Answer me. Have I? No, look at me, don't look at Rue or the detective or anyone else. Look at me."

He pushed Brule aside and put one hand under Madge's chin. Unwillingly she met his eyes. Guy smiled.

"There now, my dear. Listen to me; when you say anything you must be sure it is the truth; it must be something you could prove if you have to. You can't accuse anyone of anything at all just because you don't like that person. You —"

"All right, Cole, all right. I've got to have a

123

statement. Now then, Miss Hatterick, go right on talking. What do you know about this? Did you know Miss Garder?"

Madge hesitated. Guy took her hand and linked her arm around his own in a sympathetic way. Madge started to speak, stopped, said sullenly: "Yes. She was my mother's nurse. One of them. The other was Rue."

"What time did you arrive home this afternoon?"

"About five-thirty. I was late; we were rehearsing at school."

"In fact the police were here when you arrived?"

"Yes."

"That's enough," said Brule. "Isn't it? I mean, it's evident that my daughter knows nothing of it. And she — she is under age; I mean you can't accept —"

Guy interrupted quickly. "That's a good girl, Madge. Anything that's the truth, remember." He looked at the detective. "You haven't a statement from me yet. I was here before the police. Doctor Hatterick telephoned to me at once. I came in the side door and —"

"What side door?"

"The door into Steven's studio; I crossed through the back yard from my own house."

"Was that door unlocked?" asked the detective.

Guy blinked. "I — why, yes, as a matter of fact, it was."

The detective looked at Brule.

"Is that door always unlocked?"

"Why, I don't know. The room belongs really to my brother-in-law, Steven Hendrie. How about it, Steve?"

Steven, looking ill and tired and disheveled, still in his sweater with his hair rumpled, looked up wearily and said he didn't know.

"It's usually locked at night. I don't know whether it was unlocked today or not."

The detective looked thoughtful.

"There's a back way into the place. Where were you, Mr Hendrie, when the girl died?"

"In my studio, I suppose. I'd been there all day. Certainly no one came into the house that way; I would have known it."

"Mr Cole, here, came in that way."

"That was afterward," said Steven. "I'd gone upstairs."

"Then while you were out of the room anyone could have left the house?"

Steven's face brightened a little. "Yes. Yes, certainly. Yes, of course."

"And anyone could have got in the same way," said the detective. "However . . . Well, I guess that's all for the moment, Doctor Hatterick."

"You mean," said Alicia suddenly, "I may now go home?"

The detective glanced at her, a glance that took in every detail from her beautifully done gray-streaked hair to her slender black suede pumps, and was apparently unaffected by the beauty of her face, which was unusual.

"If you want to," he said briefly. "Leave your address and hold yourself ready for further inquiry. That goes for all of you and means you're to let the police know exactly where you are and not leave town. That's all," he said and walked briskly out of the room, followed by the stenographer.

Steven broke the little silence their departure left.

"Does that mean they think it really is murder?" he asked Guy.

"They're darn certain of it," said Guy and sighed and drew his thin, colorless eyebrows together. "One good thing, they're not making any arrest tonight; that'll give us time to see where we stand. They want to be pretty sure of themselves before they make it very hot for a man of your position, Brule. So far they've been pretty decent. Didn't even separate you as witnesses; didn't threaten arrest. Only room in the house they've really set off and searched is Rue's room: they practically looted the medicine cupboard in your bathroom, Rue."

Her room! They were looking for poison, of course, in the medicine chest; it wasn't a nice thought. She reviewed rapidly in her mind the little stock of cold preventives and headache tablets that must have been in the cupboard, nothing that wasn't in every medicine cupboard and, as a matter of fact, an extremely small and scant supply. Except — what had she done with her nurse's bag containing a large supply of sedatives, left over from her nursing equipment — large and almost untouched and including almost every sedative procurable at the supply druggists'? What *had* she done with it! She couldn't remember, and Guy must have seen alarmed recollection in her eyes, for he said:

"I'll see you tomorrow, Rue, and talk things over. I'll see you all. But don't worry too much," he added with a cheeriness that rang false in Rue's ears. "I've seen funny breaks before now when everything seemed to be sewed up tight. I gather you want to retain me, Brule!"

"My God, yes."

"Okay. Now then, Alicia . . ."

Alicia rose and stood with her arm around Madge's shoulders. "I'm going home," she said. "They can't stop me."

"Please don't go, Alicia. Stay with me," cried Madge. "Please, Alicia."

Something twisted in Rue's heart, she'd have been so unutterably glad if Madge had turned to her. But Alicia was looking down into the child's adoring face, smiling a little sadly.

"I can't stay, dear; your father's here, and Steven. You needn't be afraid."

"I'm not afraid," said Madge, "but I — I just want you to stay; please, Alicia. You can sleep in my room, and I'll sleep on the couch in my dressing room. Father, ask her to stay with me."

Alicia looked at Brule, and Brule looked at

Alicia: Alicia's glance went almost instantly away again, but Brule's remained steady and impenetrable.

Brule said, addressing Madge: "I'm sure she'd stay if you want her."

And Alicia looked at Madge, hesitated, smiled and shrugged lightly. "If you need me," she agreed. The manner of her agreement hinted that she, Alicia, was always at the beck and call of any of the Hattericks; the family friend, the present help in time of trouble. There was an odd little smile on Brule's lips; Madge said quickly: "Come with me, Alicia. I'll show you —"

It was in the little confusion of Madge and Alicia leaving the room, and of Brule being called to the dining room with Guy bouncing along beside him, and of Steven wearily and quietly disappearing somewhere, that Andy was for a moment alone with Rue. He had been upstairs to get his coat and came back into the room, hat in his hand and coat over his arm.

"Rue," he said, and put down his coat and hat and came to her. "You're alone? God, what a mess. Listen, Rue, tell me quickly; I thought I'd never get to see you alone. Exactly what did happen? Nobody can hear. Brule and Guy are talking to the police, and nobody's in the hall. What did Julie tell you? What happened?"

Rue leaned her head wearily on the back of the chair and looked up at him. It seemed years since the previous night — when he had taken her in his arms and told her he loved her and had loved her for a long time. He was remembering it too; his eyes sought into her own deeply; he took her hand with a boyish, anxious gesture and said, low:

"Poor darling. Oh, my sweet, why didn't you go with me last night? We'd have been far away by this time where none of this — this horrible sordid affair could so much as touch the hem of your skirt. I was afraid it would be bad; but I never thought of anything so bad as this. Rue —"

"Don't, Andy. I'm so — tired."

"I know, darling." He glanced at the door. "Tell me about it; hurry, Rue. What did Julie know?"

"I don't know, Andy. She — what she said was confused, as if she were drunk. I thought she was drunk. She tried to tell me something but kept saying she mustn't, that she couldn't trust her memory, that it was something I knew too. But I don't — at least I can't think, I can't remember. It was something she expected me to know but I — I don't, Andy. Who could have killed Crystal?"

"Do you think Julie knew?"

"I — I'm afraid so," said Rue, almost whispering. "It's — there's no other reason for her death. Julie wasn't the kind to commit suicide; she had too much sense."

Andy pulled up a footstool and sat down near her. "Now, Rue, tell me exactly what she said:

words, phrases, everything. Quick."

She told him, wearily but in detail. It struck Rue as rather curious that when she'd finished he said almost what Brule had said.

"For God's sake, Rue, don't tell anyone what she said. You haven't, have you? I mean, Julie was murdered. We can't escape facts. And if anyone has reason to believe that you know what Julie knew —"

"That's what Brule said. No, I didn't tell the police. I —"

"Brule!" said Andy. The queerest look came into his face; he said after a moment, "You mean you told Brule all this?"

"Why, yes. Yes, of course."

"He — asked you?"

"Yes, naturally. Why not?"

Andy stared at the floor. "No reason," he said finally. "Only — only be careful, Rue. If Julie was murdered to keep her from telling anything she knew, you — Oh, my God, Rue!" He turned swiftly and impulsively and took her hands and held them to his face, caressing them as one would a child. "If I could only be with you. All the time. Every moment. You — you must be protected, Rue. You are so — so sweet," said Andy and kissed her fingers.

It was just then that Brule came to the door. They heard his footsteps, and Andy released her hands but was still sitting at her feet when Brule entered.

He gave them a quick look; it was a look that

revealed nothing. He said quietly: "Your taxi's waiting, Andy. See you in the morning."

"Right," said Andy and rose. "Good night, Rue. 'Night, Brule."

After he'd gone Brule turned to Rue.

"You'd better take the small guest room tonight, the one next to my study; I told Gross to have it made ready for you. Go to bed, Rue. If you want a sedative —"

She shuddered, remembering Julie. Brule said coolly:

"Better lock your door tonight, Rue. A thing like this — there's no telling where it may end."

CHAPTER IX

The queer thing was that in the night she remembered what Brule had said. Quite clearly and sharply, as if he were saying it again, warning her.

The trouble was she hadn't locked the door.

That was quite late, after Brule had been called away to see a patient.

It was the ringing of the telephone that awakened her out of a troubled, haunted sleep that wasn't quite sleep nor was it quite sensible awareness, for all the faces and all the words and all the remembered scenes that kept nagging at her were grotesquely importunate and repetitious. But the telephone brought her instantly over the borderline into real sensibility; she could hear it plainly through the closed door between the small guest room and Brule's own study; could hear the low murmur of Brule's voice in reply.

She heard, too, for the house was quiet, the subsequent closing of the door from Brule's suite into the hall in about the time it would have taken him to dress, and presently another low murmur of voices from somewhere in the hall. She sat up, listening; she didn't know whether there were still policemen in the house or not; had they left a guard in the house to see that none of them tried to escape?

Whether or not that was the case, there was after a while a muffled closing of the heavy front door as if by a cautious hand. She didn't hear — couldn't have heard from that room — the sound of the car. But she knew after two months of marriage what the telephone in the night and the closing of the front door meant.

The house seemed extremely quiet after Brule had gone. Everyone was asleep — or if not asleep, then lying, as she was doing, staring into the dark, thinking and trying not to. Steven in his large room on the second floor; Madge in her front room above — or rather Alicia in the front room and Madge in the tiny dressing room. Queer how the thought of Alicia under that roof troubled her; yet Alicia was actually more familiar with Rue's own home than was Rue. Whoever Brule spoke to in the hall outside might have gone with Brule for all the further sound he made. There was a feeling of emptiness and deep, complete silence.

Once she would have been at the hospital, scrubbing up; waiting for Brule in the bright, ordered hubbub of the operating rooms.

Julie would have been there, too, for Julie had gone back to the surgery after her one essay at private nursing which she'd undertaken only at Brule's request.

Julie.

Lying there in the dark room she began again (as she was to do so many times) to go over in her mind the whole course of events as she knew them.

There wasn't, as Andy had said and the attitude of the others and of the police made all too clear, much use in hoping that Julie's death would prove to be suicide.

There was, of course, a line of specious reasoning they could take: that was that Julie had accidentally given Crystal the drug that killed her and then herself committed suicide when the police inquiry at last opened.

It was specious; Rue knew that Julie hadn't committed suicide; there'd been confusion and bewilderment and fuzzy, fumbling attempts to talk to Rue, but no purpose and no knowledge of her own state. Besides, she knew Julie; Julie would have faced even so tragic a mistake rather than suicide. And Julie would not have come to her, Rue, if she'd intended to escape the consequences of any such mistake by suicide.

Furthermore, knowing Julie and knowing as she did the nursing routine for Crystal, a mistake that would have caused Crystal's death simply wasn't possible. She also knew that there was no drug used in treatment, there was no drug available, that could possibly have been substituted by accident for medicine; such a substitution would have had to be intentional.

But she thought from what she saw of Guy's and Brule's attitude that such a line of defense might be in their minds. Or perhaps in Guy's mind alone. There was no surmising Brule's intentions.

She wondered what time it was and turned to see her small bedside clock. Somebody — Rachel, the upstairs maid, probably — had brought into the guest room the things Rue would need for the night: pajamas and dressing gown and slippers, toothbrush and sponge and cigarettes and the little alligator-covered traveling clock which always stood on her bed table. It was a worn and shabby little clock, how long had she had it, and how many weary night hours had its luminous little face marked for her? She could see it now, a glowing halo across the room on the table by the door. It was too far away for her to discern the exact hour; about three, she thought, trying to see through the darkness.

She lay there watching it merely because its small face was luminous against the blackness all around her.

Watching it and thinking. Gradually becoming aware that her thinking was slower, hoping it meant sleep was approaching.

There wasn't any sound. She was sure of that.

But all at once, quite suddenly the small luminous halo vanished.

She opened her eyes wider with a jerk; she'd slept of course. And closed her eyes and — but her eyes were open now, and the small spot of light wasn't there. It wasn't anywhere in that wall of blackness.

She didn't move. Even her heart seemed to

stop and wait and listen.

Queer that it seemed as if someone was in the room. Where no one could be.

But she hadn't locked the door. Brule said to lock the door, and she hadn't. And he'd said coolly: "A thing like this — there's no telling . . ."

It was just then that, all at once, the little luminous halo of the clock became visible again. As if a hand had passed between her and the clock and blotted out its small light and then been removed.

A hand — or some other moving object. A man, say, passing as silently (literally) as a shadow between her and the clock.

There still wasn't any sound.

But stronger than anything was the sudden conviction that now she was alone in the room.

Alone, yet there had been no tangible evidence of anything else in the room — except the clock.

After a while she forced herself to reach for the bed lamp. Light in the room proved its emptiness. It was a small room, its ceiling too high for its other dimensions, so it was like a little box done in sea-green chintz and a few old, comfortable, mahogany pieces: bed and small dressing table and a chair or two and the table — across the room because there was no space for it beside the bed. There were three doors actually in the room; one leading into a small washroom with a shower because it was too small for a tub, another leading to Brule's study,

136

closed, with a delicate Japanese panel concealing it, and the door into the hall.

A glance convinced her; she rose and locked the door into the hall and pushed aside the silk embroidered panel to try the door to Brule's study which was locked.

She had slept and dreamed. That was the explanation. She turned off the light.

But she didn't sleep again until objects in the room were beginning to have bulky shapes and she heard Brule return. There was again the sound of voices, prolonged this time as if in discussion. But after a while Brule's study door closed softly.

It was when morning came, gray and cold, with Rachel bringing her breakfast tray and Rue hurrying to unlock the door, that the real threat the night had held came to light.

Rue, hair brushed and a warm, woolly bed jacket around her, looked wearily at the tray.

"The mail hasn't come yet," said Rachel. "Shall I throw this out, madam?"

This? thought Rue and looked.

Rachel was standing beside the small table near the door, holding a tray with a thermos and glass on it in her hands and looking dubiously at the empty glass.

Empty?

"What do you mean?"

"This," said the girl. "The powder in the glass. Medicine, I suppose, madam."

The breakfast tray clattered perilously as Rue

pushed it aside and scrambled out of bed.

"Let me see."

She took it in her fingers — as she ought not to have done. She looked incredulously at the small sifting of a kind of gray-white powder in the bottom of the glass.

"What — what is it, madam? You look so — I'd better call Doctor." Rachel started for the door.

Rue was still standing there in white pajamas and white bed jacket like a frightened child when Brule came — hurriedly, half shaven, in his dressing gown. He took the glass and looked and said to the maid: "All right. You can go."

Rachel went, reluctantly. Brule closed the door.

"Good God, Rue, what is this?"

"I don't know. I don't know — except I couldn't see the clock."

She told him, stammering, not quite coherent. When she'd finished he said: "Get back into bed. You're trembling with cold. Here."

He put down the glass and held the tray while she clambered into bed again, and then put it across her lap. He adjusted her pillows and pulled an eiderdown up over her feet.

And went back to look at the glass.

"What is it, Brule?"

"I don't know. But if it's what I think it is . . . Well, we'll soon know. I'll take it to a place I know and find out exactly what's in it. Meantime . . ." He frowned. "Rue, I'd better tell

138

you." He came back to stand beside her. It was cold in the little room; he pulled his dressing gown tighter around him; his hair was wet and ruffled, and the white soap was drying on his face.

"Tell me what?"

"About last night. I was called away on the first phony errand in my experience."

"You — I thought you went to the hospital."

"No, I didn't," said Brule grimly. "They — whoever telephoned said they were afraid to move the fellow; said I'd have to come out there; gave me an address out toward Cicero. I didn't like the sound of it, but I — hell, I never thought of it being a plant. Nothing happened to me; I just found the street finally and went up and down hunting the number that had been given me."

Quickening alarm must have shown in her face, for he interrupted himself to say reassuringly: "I wasn't alone. I got Kendal up to take me; I'm not such a fool as to go to a new patient and an address I never heard before, in the middle of the night. And besides all that, the policeman somebody left here in the house (God knows why!) conceived it to be his duty to go along. Kendal had his revolver. So all three of us chased up and down the street awhile looking for the number with a flashlight, and cursing; finally routed out a cop on his neighborhood beat, and he said there was no such number. Woman on the telephone spoke with a foreign accent; I couldn't understand her very well; talked as if she had mush in her mouth and a clothespin on her nose. May have been a man. Said the nonexistent patient had been hurt in an accident and was having a hemorrhage. Well, we live and learn."

"Brule!" It was a wavering, breathless little sound composed of relief and terror.

He smiled and leaned over to pat her hand as it lay on the white silk-covered eiderdown.

"It's okay. I'll never do it again —" He stopped abruptly. Conjecture was in his eyes. "Good God, Rue, I never thought of that. It was to get me away from the house — me and the cop downstairs. It was while I was gone —"

After a moment she said: "But I don't know anything about Crystal's murder. Julie didn't tell me anything. There's nothing —"

He sat down on the edge of the bed.

"Listen, Rue. It's occurred to you, of course, that you were not supposed to see Julie; if Gross had not happened into the front of the house just when he did, Julie would have died before she spoke to you. Somewhere there's been a careful planning of time — time for the poison to take effect. Time to make sure Julie was definitely removed from whoever murdered her before the poison could kill her. Time to prevent her from reaching you — and she wouldn't have reached you if Gross hadn't found her." He paused and said: "You must know something. Think. Think hard."

"I can't, Brule. There's nothing. I told you

140

exactly what Julie told me —" What was it Andy had said? Something about not telling anyone what Julie had said; something that warned her without warning her. Something that . . .

Had he meant Brule? Had he tried to warn her against Brule, even while Andy himself was still too loyal and too faithful to Brule openly to express his doubts?

Brule had been in the house when Crystal died. Brule had frankly admitted (or was it so frank an admission as it had managed to sound?) that he'd doubted the publicity offered and publicly accepted reason for her death. Brule had coolly and calmly gone about covering up any possible query concerning it.

Brule said slowly:

"It would be an incredibly daring thing to do; and I don't understand . . ." He didn't finish that either. He rose and said instead, crisply: "We'll not tell the police of this, Rue. Or anyone. Not yet. It may prove to be nothing; I'll take the glass. All right, my dear. You'd better stay in the house today. I mean, don't take any chances."

He went away without another word. Half an hour later he knocked and put his head briefly in the doorway to say he was going to the hospital.

"Don't look at the papers, Rue," he said as if they were unimportant. "It's just one of those things; a Roman holiday. I told Gross to throw them out."

That was like Brule; to tell her not to look at the newspapers and in the next breath explain that she had no choice because they'd already been thrown out.

But one was on the hall table when she went downstairs, and she read it, slowly, with cringing recognition. It was a late edition, however, and stated baldly the decisions, such as they were, of the police department.

Juliet Garder had been murdered; they said it flatly, in black and white. And her murder had followed the opening of a police inquiry into the death, a year ago, of Crystal Hatterick. A third statement emerged from the welter of print, and that was that the theory held by the police was that both women had been murdered by the same person and by much the same means, and that by concentrating on the murder of Juliet Garder they would solve also the problem of the murder of Crystal Hatterick.

They gave no specific reason for the theory; they didn't need to. It was almost fatally reasonable; Brule had foreseen it. It was the only workable, practicable, wholly tenable theory.

The poison was named in garbled general terms; there's a well-founded prejudice on the part of the police against announcing to the general public any particularly efficient but not well and familiarly known manner of doing away with your fellow beings.

And an inquest would be held the next day.

Inquest. Rue's breath caught; that meant she

would have to attend as a witness. That meant — or might mean anything.

Andy came about noon; he had news, he told her at once, and closed the door of the library so no one would hear. But Steven had taken refuge in his studio, and Madge and Alicia (whom Rue had not seen that morning) were with him. Madge had refused to speak that morning, childishly but rather dreadfully, if Rue were in the room. Rue had tried to talk to her; had tried, seeing the child's obvious distress, to make at least a friendly gesture. It was instantly, coldly repulsed with the brutal rudeness which only a child can show.

Yet Madge in her very rudeness was pathetic. Steven again had understood.

"Come into the studio, Madge. We'll talk."

"Alone?" said Madge. "Except for Alicia, of course."

"Yes — if you must have it."

"I'll call Alicia. She was tired and slept late." She went away, and Steven gave Rue an apologetic, troubled look. Steven had slept no better than anyone; his eyes had dark pockets around them, and he couldn't eat.

And then Andy came.

And talked to her for a long time while Crystal watched from above the mantel. Watched and listened coldly with the chill, remote smile on her painted face.

"You've read the papers?"

"Yes."

"You read what they say is the reason for Julie's murder? That it was because of the inquiry opened into Crystal's death?"

"Yes, yes, Andy. But —"

"Listen, Rue. I've been at the hospital this morning. Do you know who I saw the moment I got out of my car? A detective. Standing at the door. There were others inside. They'd been at the nurses' dormitory; they'd gone through all of Julie's things; they'd taken letters and papers from her room to be examined. The nurses told me they'd been questioning, questioning. . . . They've been at my place already this morning; they've been at the office talking to the office girl, talking to the office nurse, talking to the elevator boys and doorman. They — God, Rue, it's like a trap — hundreds of traps everywhere. But the whole, horrible meaning is that they're going to arrest you."

"Andy —"

"Yes. They'll have to, there's nothing else to do. It's — why, they've questioned the nurses all about you. It's all over the hospital. They've asked about you and Brule. How well you'd known each other before Crystal's death, about your sudden marriage; they've looked up your record at the hospital from the time you entered it eight years ago. They've pried and questioned and tried to induce people to say damaging things, and, Rue — Rue, my darling, let's leave. Before you're arrested. It's a matter of hours, and I can't stand to see you —" He stopped.

144

She was standing facing him, sickened by the pictures his words put before her. He took her in his arms and pleaded with her. "Come with me, dear. What does any of it matter if we have each other safe? You don't know, Rue, how horrible it'll be for you. The things people will say, the newspapers, the accusations. They'll say — they are saying now that it was because you and Brule wanted to marry that — Crystal was killed."

"Andy. You know that isn't true." Her voice was harsh and strained.

"Good God, of course I know it isn't true! I've known all along."

He pushed his hands worriedly through his hair, it was a boyish gesture. So was the impatient movement with which he flung away from her and then back toward her again. As if torn with inner conflict and indecision, he cried:

"I've got to tell you the whole truth, Rue. For your own sake." His mouth trembled a little as if he hated the thing he was going to do. "You'd have to know sometime. And I've been loyal long enough. It's you, now, I'm going to put first. Listen, Rue, last night — no, night before last when I came to take you to the opera — well, Brule sent me."

"Yes?"

"Well, he used to send me to take his place with Crystal too. To take her to parties and to the opera and —"

All at once the room seemed unbearably hot,

and the dark day spread confusing shadows in the corners. Andy went on jerkily:

"And do you remember when we waited for the car we saw a coupé like Brule's, and a woman —"

"A — woman —"

"He sent me to be with you so as to leave him free to go to her. Exactly as it used to be when Crystal was alive."

"Alicia . . ." whispered Rue.

"Alicia. It's been going on for years."

CHAPTER X

Always conscious of Crystal's portrait, it seemed to Rue that she had never been so strongly aware of it and aware of Crystal's painted look, her enigmatic, knowing eyes and the half smile on her thin lips. The library was quiet for a moment, but it was a charged silence full of meanings and unuttered words. From the studio came a soft tinkling sound of Steven's piano; Steven playing for Alicia while Madge sat and listened and brooded — sullenly, hating Rue.

The dull gray daylight pressed foggily against the windows; the light upon Brule's big desk spread a downward glow which left the corners of the book-lined room in shadow. She knew Andy was waiting for her to speak. She had turned abruptly away from him and walked to the desk where she stood, forcing herself not to look at Crystal's portrait, to overcome that strong awareness of it. She said at last while Andy, with a kind of compunction in his silence, waited:

"I can't believe it."

"It's true," he said gravely.

"But Crystal —"

"I know." She turned again to look at him. "I know, Rue — that was the ugly thing about it. I would do anything for Brule; he's done so much for me. I didn't question him; I've never questioned him about anything. The first few times he sent me to take Crystal somewhere she'd set her heart on going I thought nothing of it. It seemed so — so perfectly comprehensible. Brule is terrifically busy; he's great. He's . . ." He hesitated and said boyishly, "He's not like other men. I've always done what he told me to do; I didn't quite realize — perhaps I didn't want to realize — how things were drifting along and where we were all headed. It wasn't fair to Crystal; it wasn't fair to anybody —"

"Steven," said Rue. "Alicia's engaged to Steven; he's in love with her."

"I know. Look here, Rue. I know I was at fault about Crystal, but what could I do? It all came about so gradually; Crystal was so much older than I that I — it didn't occur to me that she would — oh hell, Rue, I can't say it. Do you understand?"

An older and fading and very vain woman's infatuation for a young and attractive man. And that woman the wife of the man who, of all other people in the world, had his guiding hand upon Andy's career, who, as Andy freely and frankly said, had done "everything" for him.

"Yes," said Rue slowly. "I suppose I understand. You — ought to have had more courage, Andy."

"God, Rue, don't you suppose I know that now? Don't you suppose I tried every way to — to escape the thing when I saw what Brule — I

148

mean what I had let myself in for? I wasn't in love with Crystal; I was tremendously fond of her; we were good friends for a while. Then — well, there's no good talking about it. I had my loyalty to Brule; I had a kind of loyalty to Crystal — she'd been so damn good to me, Rue. I couldn't go to Brule and say, 'See here, I can't take your wife out as you insist on my doing because I think she's — well, fallen in love with me.' I couldn't —"

"What did you expect to do? Eventually, I mean?"

Andy looked tired and white.

"I didn't know," he said. "I kept hoping something would break. Alicia . . . Steven . . . It seemed to me that when they married Brule would go back to Crystal, and I would be — set free. I know it sounds crazy, Rue, but think of my obligation to Brule."

"How long has Alicia been engaged to Steven? Two years or so, isn't it?"

"About that. Alicia keeps putting him off. And Steven's really in love with her. He worships beauty, and she's so beautiful."

So beautiful, thought Rue with a queer little stab in her heart, that Brule is in love with her too; for years, Andy had said. Years . . .

She avoided Andy's anxious, troubled blue eyes; she took up a paper knife on the desk and turned it in her fingers and forced herself to ask the question she must ask.

"When Crystal died, then, and Brule was free

149

to marry, why didn't he marry Alicia?"

Again the library was very still; the music from Steven's studio rose in a crescendo; "Arabesque of Night," he called it, fancifully. It was the thing he'd been playing at the very moment Julie died. Rue recognized its insistent, almost hypnotic rhythmic bass emphasized by the muffling of distance and doors which shut out the treble notes. Andy was finding it difficult to reply, she thought; poor Andy. She'd been unjust. That was because she'd seen the look in Crystal's eyes when Andy entered the room.

At last he said: "Rue, I can't answer that without hurting you. I've got to know first — do you love Brule? Or is it just hero worship? Why did you marry him? I know it gave you money and position and security. I know that almost any woman would have jumped at the chance because of Brule's face as well as because he's such a swell fellow. But you — I — I can't see you marrying anybody for any of those reasons. And yet I don't think you love him."

She turned the paper knife in her fingers, noting with exactness its carved ivory handle. The insistent beat of Steven's playing was the only sound in the room, and it was as ever confusingly hypnotic, dulling thoughts and rationalization, drawing out emotion alone. Why had she married Brule — Brule who was in love with Alicia and had been in love with her for years?

Yet the knowledge wasn't exactly a shock. Or rather the shock was there, but there'd been a faint disturbing warning of the thing. She remembered the night before when she and Guy had seen Alicia brush her cheek affectionately and with that unmistakable air of accustomedness against Brule's shoulder. Guy's expression hadn't changed. He'd said something and attracted the attention of the two in the doorway, but he hadn't looked surprised or in any way affected by the brief little scene. But then Guy must have known. Everyone must have known except herself and Steven. Steven so wrapped in his music and in his dreams of beauty that a flaw in his beloved had never even been suspected. Exactly what, Rue wondered, was the status of the affair? Andy's words had obviously been chosen to give her, Rue, the least possible pain. Andy was waiting now for her reply. Why had she married Brule?

He moved nearer her; she felt his presence and would not, again, turn to meet his eyes. He said: "Won't you look at me, Rue? Won't you answer? You see — I thought, the night we went to the opera, that you loved me. As I love you."

"Don't, Andy."

"If it's because you don't want to hear what I have to say, all right. I'll not harass you. I — I love you too much. But if it's loyalty to Brule, surely you see that that loyalty is a mistaken one."

"You haven't told me why he — married me and not Alicia." If only Steven would stop playing; it would be somehow so much easier to talk

151

coolly and clearly, so there'd be no more mistakes.

"You haven't answered me," said Andy, "or — or perhaps you have. Have you, Rue?"

"No, no, Andy. I . . ." She moved away from him toward the end of the desk. "Don't you see I've got to know!"

"All right," said Andy. "I warned you I didn't want you to be hurt. But if it's only your pride —"

"Whatever it is, tell me."

"He married you because he and Alicia quarreled. After Crystal's death. Now will you go away with me, dear? Before it's too late. I hate telling you this, but it is because I love you so. Rue — they're going to charge you with Crystal's murder and with Julie's."

She said dully: "I didn't kill her."

So that was why Brule had come to her and asked her to marry him; had told her — so frankly, she thought — that it would be a marriage of mutual convenience, a sensible, companionable kind of thing. He'd said no word of loving her or of wanting her to love him. He'd been honest so far as that, at any rate. And if she thought in her heart that sometime, somehow he'd come to love her — well, she'd been foolish to think it. Mad, really. But she hadn't known that Alicia was her rival — Alicia with the kind of beauty that Helen must have had.

"Rue," said Andy impatiently. "Snap out of it. Forget Brule; I had to tell you for your own

152

protection. So you'd realize you were morally free from him. Under no obligation. But forget him. Forget Alicia. Put the whole thing in the past. Let me take you away before — well," he said grimly, "before they fix it so that I can't take you away."

The grim truth of the thing tore through her preoccupation; it was in its way salutary.

"They can't arrest me!"

"But they're going to, Rue. I know you didn't murder Julie. But you see, you gave her the tea. You were the one she came to see. If you come with me now it will give them time to discover the real murderer. At this moment you are the obvious suspect."

She walked around the desk and sat down. She wore a yellow sweater and a blue skirt and looked just then very young and defenseless. She was pale; her hair under the glow of the lamp looked burnished and soft; the night had left smudges around her eyes.

"Obvious suspect," repeated Andy and laughed shortly. "You!"

"Andy," she said slowly. "You said — that first night when you told me about Crystal and the letters to the police — that you thought she was murdered. You said you thought the police were right. Why did you think so?"

"Because of Alicia," said Andy. "There's no sense in beating about the bush any longer. I tried once to tell you some of what I knew without telling too much, and it only made things worse for you. I thought Alicia — well, after all, Alicia was here the afternoon of Crystal's death. And Alicia stood to gain by her death. It would leave Brule free to marry Alicia with no trouble about a divorce and no hint of talk. It was for Alicia the easy way out, and Alicia — somehow I've never thought that Alicia had any scruples in particular when it was something she wanted."

"But Crystal — Crystal practically supported Alicia, didn't she?"

Andy shrugged. "Yes — with Brule's approval. Perhaps at his instigation. Remember the situation between Alicia and Brule is — is a curious kind of thing. Both of them are conventional at heart; both of them hate anything that appears vulgar, common — blatant. And yet they are frantically in love. It was a dreadful thing — Brule marrying you to hurt Alicia. I don't know what it was they quarreled about; I don't know when and how they made up their quarrel except that when they did it was too late. Brule and you were already married. And Brule — to do him justice, Rue, I think he tried to break the thing off; I think as soon as he realized what he'd done (you know his temper; you know how furiously and quickly he reacts to anything), well, I think when he realized what he'd done to you and to Alicia he really tried to break away from Alicia. But it was too strong for him. It —"

"Don't make me talk of it, Andy. The point

is, now, Alicia is too civilized, too sophisticated to think of murder."

"What a baby you are, Rue! Alicia is a polite and polished and beautiful savage. When did she turn up yesterday afternoon?"

"Just after Julie died. She — Alicia came into my room."

"Exactly. Had you known she was in the house?"

"N-no. She said she had come to see Madge. You heard what she said."

"Is there any reason why she shouldn't have given Julie the cocktail? While Julie waited. Or she could have met Julie outside and taken her someplace and tried to persuade the girl not to talk. And perhaps — perhaps Julie wouldn't be persuaded: perhaps Alicia realized she'd have to poison again, and simply, neatly, did so. Called Julie's attention to somebody passing and popped a capsule in the cocktail."

"Don't! Andy — it makes it sound so real!"

"It was real," said Andy. "Perhaps not just as I've described it, but something like that must have happened. It could have been Alicia. Why not?" Andy rubbed his hands through his hair and replied to himself. "Why not? Because we can't prove it. She could have done it. But somebody else could have done it, too. Proof is the thing we've got to have to clear you, and the thing we can't get."

"Alicia could have come to my room last night," said Rue. "But she couldn't have called

Brule away. Well, yes, she could have done that. But she —"

"Your room!" Andy stared at her and leaned his hands on the table to look closely into her face, his eyes were alert and frightened. "What do you mean?"

"I'm not sure it was anything, really," said Rue slowly, but told him.

"First time that has happened to Brule," said Andy. "I mean the phony call. It's one of those things doctors are on their guard against. Brule doesn't know yet what the powder in the glass is?"

"I don't think so. I've not seen him since early morning."

"It means," said Andy slowly, "that whoever did it thinks Julie managed to tell you something before she died. It means — good God, Rue, it means somebody free to come and go in this house! Somebody who knew just how to get Brule (and the policeman who was left here last night) to leave the house. Somebody — See here, Rue. There's no use dodging unpleasant facts. It's occurred to you as it has to me and to everybody concerned in this case that there's — there's damn few suspects."

He stopped abruptly. The strangest, still look came upon his face. "Rue — are you sure Brule actually left the house?"

And as she stared back at him, half afraid, half caught, testing the speculation that hovered almost tangibly in the air between them, he said slowly and strangely: "He's so strong, Rue. And so — so ruthless. You've seen it as I have. But God, Rue — he couldn't have done this. Not to Crystal —"

She wanted to remind him of the things Brule had done; she didn't. She said gropingly:

"There are other people who were in the house or who could have got into the house last night. There's Madge and Alicia and Steven; Guy Cole comes and goes at will and always has. I don't know whether or not the house was locked last night. . . ." She searched her mind for others, and there were none except servants.

Andy said: "Madge is incalculable; she's like Crystal except she's got her father's strength, I think; his own queer ruthlessness. And she's — a child really; she wouldn't realize what she did."

"She didn't poison Crystal. She couldn't have poisoned Julie, for there'd be no motive for it, and anyway — Andy, let's stick to facts."

"All right. Facts, then," said Andy. "Who had an alibi for the time poison must have been given Julie? How did she get into the house? How long had she been here when Gross found her and brought her to you? Whom had she seen here? What did she know?"

"Steven had an alibi," said Rue unexpectedly. "I heard him at the piano. I know he was there in his studio the whole time."

"I'm going to question Gross. May I?"

Gross came instantly.

"Madam rang?" His blank eyes took in every

157

detail of the little scene, the two of them talking earnestly, stopping abruptly when he opened the door.

"Gross, Mrs Hatterick wants to know some things about yesterday. Close the door, please."

"Yes sir." He closed the door quietly and advanced. He looked as always stolidly respectable with his pin-striped trousers neatly brushed, and his black coat just a bit too rotund over his black vest, and his eyes blank and extremely observant below that blank surface. He'd been gray with fright the previous day; gray and shattered and all but jibbering. He was now himself again, correctly imperturbable; correctly and remotely helpful.

"Now then, Gross, we understand that when the young lady arrived yesterday you did not open the door for her?"

"That's right, sir."

Andy got up, moved to take a cigarette from the desk and sat down in another chair. Rue watched, and all at once, sharply, Steven's playing in the studio broke off. It left a blank pit of silence. Andy said:

"You told the police that?"

"Yes sir. They asked. I don't know who let the young lady in; neither of the maids admit to it, sir, and it was the cook's rest period."

"Well, my God, Gross, how did she get in the house then?"

"I don't know, sir. I made sure the front door was locked as usual."

"You made sure?" Andy watched the butler for a moment and then said: "Are you really quite sure of that, Gross?"

"Well . . ." Gross's eyes wavered, went around the room and came back to Andy. "Reasonably so, sir. It is almost always locked. I mean with the night latch. Naturally there was a little confusion following the arrival of the police and all; I can't exactly swear that the front door was locked. But in any case the young lady wouldn't simply have opened the door and walked in."

"No, I suppose not," said Andy. "Although if she were confused, a little muddled in her mind, she might have done just that. Opened the door, failed altogether to ring and simply walked into the house and sat down in the nearest chair. According to Mrs Hatterick, the girl wasn't exactly sensible of what she was doing. You got that impression, too, I imagine, Gross."

"Well, yes sir. Now that you ask me I confess that I thought she was . . ." He coughed delicately with a side glance at Rue and said: "A little under the influence. I — was obliged to tell the police that too."

"Good for you," said Andy. "That helps clear Mrs Hatterick, you see. Stick to your story." Gross gave Rue a somewhat surprised and wondering glance; he hadn't, it was obvious, realized that such a statement had its value as indicating that Julie had been poisoned before she saw Rue. Andy went on: "And be sure you stick to it, up and down, no matter how much the police question you. Don't waver for an instant. She was poisoned already — before she saw Mrs Hatterick?"

"Well, I — I wouldn't go so far —"

"Of course she was. No doubt of that, Gross. She had already been poisoned; entered the house probably without remembering to ring; just had a vague notion of getting inside the house and seeing Mrs Hatterick. How long had she been in the drawing room when you came upon her?"

"I — I wouldn't know."

"Well, how long do you think? You were the only person who saw her there, weren't you?"

"I — oh, I couldn't be sure of that, sir. Anyone might have seen her there. I don't know, you see, how long she was in the house. I don't —"

Andy frowned. "Is that what you told the police?"

"I told them everything they asked — that I knew, of course, sir. They questioned the maids too. Exhaustively, I might add, sir."

"Well now, look here, Gross. If anyone had been with the girl when she arrived or if — say if Mrs Hatterick herself had let the girl into the house, as she didn't — but at any rate if anyone had been with the girl and had talked to her, you would have known it, wouldn't you?"

"I . . ." He looked confused. "I don't know. You mean —"

"I mean if there were voices in the drawing

room, you'd have known it?"

"I — well, I don't know, sir. Unless the bell goes, I'm usually in the back of the house during the midafternoon."

"Well, at any rate when you discovered the girl —"

"When I came to turn on the lights, sir, and pull the curtains and bring in the evening paper —"

"Exactly, when you discovered her sitting there, what did she say?"

"Just that she — she wished to see Mrs Hatterick. It gave me rather a turn finding her just sitting there in the shadow of the curtain. The room was unlighted, and if you'll remember, it was a dark day."

"Yes, of course. There was no glass, no cup, nothing like that —"

"Oh, no sir."

"All right. Now listen, Gross. When you let Miss Pelham into the house —"

Gross looked blanker than ever and rather pale.

"I didn't open the door for Miss Pelham either."

Andy jumped to his feet. "What's that, Gross?"

"No sir. Miss Pelham has a key — has had ever since Mrs Hatterick — that is the late Mrs Hatterick's illness. The — the late Mrs Hatterick gave it to her. So she could come and go at will. They were, as you know very well, sir, the most intimate friends."

Silence again in the library. Rue could not now keep from looking at Crystal's portrait, and the shadowy, half-contemptuous, painted eyes seemed to look at Rue. Andy said at last, slowly: "Then you don't know exactly when Miss Pelham arrived. Do you?"

"No sir."

"Good." Andy had an air of triumph. "That's all, thank you, Gross; be sure to stick to your story when the police return to question further. That's all. Oh yes; wait, there's something else. You remember during Mrs Hatterick's illness a chart the nurses kept, that is, that Miss Garder and —" Gross was already nodding.

"Oh yes, sir. I remember it very well. The chart showing the progress of Madam's — I mean the late Mrs Hatterick's illness. It was kept on the small table by the door along with her medicines."

"Exactly. You've a good memory, Gross. Well then, after Mrs Hatterick died, I expect you removed the chart yourself; when the room was cleaned, I mean."

Doubt was again in Gross's face; doubt and a touch of bewilderment. "I — I can't say I remember seeing it, sir."

"Think hard."

"Yes sir. But unless one of the maids took it . . . No, I'm quite sure I didn't put it away, sir."

"I see. All right, Gross. I don't suppose it's

important anyway. Thank you — that's all."

"Thank you, sir," said Gross and vanished quietly.

The door closed again and Rue said: "The chart. The police asked about it too."

"Yes. That's why I wondered. Funny, where it's got to. If Julie had it —"

"I don't think she had. She wasn't here after Crystal's death. And I haven't got it. Why, Andy?"

"I don't know," said Andy. "It's just that the police want it — so I'd rather get hold of it first."

"It's probably been destroyed long ago."

"Yes. I suppose so. I'll warn Brule. Yet suppose Brule himself —" He gave the oddest little sound that was like a groan. "I can't face that, Rue, I've got to go on the theory that it isn't Brule. He — he couldn't have done this! I know his brilliance, I know he could have conceived and carried out such a plan coolly and as brilliantly as he operates — and as daringly. He's strong and he's ruthless; he's cruel when he has to be cruel — but he couldn't have done this. He couldn't — he didn't — but . . ." He swung desperately toward Rue. "But nevertheless . . . Oh, Rue, my dear, haven't you seen and heard enough to convince you?"

Someone was in the hall. It was Brule, for they heard his quick footsteps and his voice speaking, apparently, to Gross. He opened the door and came into the room.

"Oh, hello there, Andy. Glad you're here; something rather — shocking has happened."

Brule walked with his usual assured air of possession across the room and took a cigarette, pausing while he lighted it. The little flame was perfectly steady in his fine skilled fingers; it touched his cheeks, pink from the cold outside, and reflected itself in tiny points in his brilliant dark eyes. His presence filled the room as it always did.

Rue looked at the man who had married her. Married her because he'd quarreled with the woman he really loved. The beautiful, sophisticated woman who had loved him for years before Rue's timid feet had ever crossed the threshold of the place that was now her home — the only home she'd had for so long. My home? thought Rue and suddenly hated Alicia.

Brule settled himself abruptly in a chair.

"Don't go, Andy. The office girl said she thought you were here. I want you to hear what's happened. We've found some stuff in a glass —"

"I told him," said Rue stiffly.

Brule shot her one dark glance that was instantly arrested and speculative as if the very tones of her voice betrayed something of the thing Andy had told her.

If so, however, he didn't explore then and there but continued:

"Oh. Very well. Then you know the whole thing, Andy. Well, the thing is, it — really was poison. I got a chemical report on it — privately, without letting the police know. It's an amazing combination of a hypnotic drug, some barbituric acid derivative, and morphine. Enough to kill a horse."

CHAPTER XI

"And no symptoms," muttered Andy after a moment. "Not a damn symptom. You'd just die."

"As Crystal died. As the nurse died," said Brule coolly. "Yes, and it's only a question of time until the police isolate and identify the poison in Crystal's body and in Julie Garder's."

"Time," said Andy. "Time — that's what we need, Brule. Time —"

"For what?" said Brule. "There's nothing we can do."

"There might be," said Andy. "It may take them weeks to find exactly what the girl died of; it often takes two or three weeks when the laboratory fellows don't know what they're looking for. And in this case there are a hundred harmless sedatives that are hypnotics. Well, in the length of time it will take to pin down the exact drugs anything can happen. I call it a godsend if you ask me. Arsenic now, or — oh, strychnine or any of a dozen other poisons, would have been so easily detected."

"There'd have been symptoms if it'd been arsenic or strychnine. Or as you say, any of a dozen other drugs in lethal quantity. The beauty of this particular combination — to the murderer's mind — is that an overdose of it would certainly induce just what it did induce: a confused heavy drowsiness growing into a coma and presently death. The hypnotic might check the almost instantaneous action of the morphine — although it might not; they might work simultaneously. And they may have been in a capsule which would delay their action. In Crystal's case, however, the thing was exactly what the murderer wanted. She fell into a heavy sleep and died without showing signs of typical morphine poisoning, which would have given us a clue and allowed us to administer what antidote we could have administered at that stage. With the nurse's case it's different; from what you've told me, Rue, and from what Gross told me, it sounds as if something went wrong. Either the quantities were not as they had been with Crystal, or the nurse reacted altogether differently. She was, at least, able to get upstairs and walk and try to speak and then just all at once died. The question is time; when was she given the poison? Morphine takes effect right away; it's a matter of moments. The other is slower. How long could she have remained sensible enough to walk and speak? A capsule would have added to the time margin by twenty minutes. There's no way of knowing until we know exactly what she died of. And the approximate amounts of each drug. In either case it's the overdose given that caused death; both are really beneficent drugs. At any rate that's for the police to worry about. But I'm going to tell them what to look for."

"You mean — give them that chemist's report? And tell them what happened last night?"

"Yes, certainly. The sooner they know it, now, the better. I didn't want anything said of it until I knew just what it was. Now I — know," said Brule.

Andy cleared his throat and said slowly:

"It didn't take your chemist long to analyze the stuff."

"I told him what to look for," said Brule promptly.

"You — how did you know?"

Brule's eyebrows made a quick, straight line across his face.

"Because that's what I thought it might be, Andy. Any other questions?"

"N-no. Except — are you sure it's a good thing to tell it to the police? You know as well as I how few people could have put that stuff in Rue's room."

"I know. Very few people could have given poison to Crystal too. Any number of people, I suppose, could have murdered the nurse, but who did? Who had motive plus opportunity?"

"But, Brule, you — you were all in favor of keeping the thing quiet," said Rue. "I mean, you said that you thought at the time that Crystal's death was not natural but that you thought it wiser to accept it. You said it was better to think of Madge and of Steven and —"

"And of myself and of Andy. And of you, Rue. Yes, I did think so. Things have changed."

"You — you're going over to the side of the

168

police? Do you mean that, Brule?" said Andy.

"I mean we've got to wade through it now. We can't dodge around it."

"But still there's no use in telling the police all you know. Unless . . . What's your idea of it, Brule? Who — who killed her?"

"I don't know. But I do know — Listen, Andy, do you know why I'm at home at this hour of the day? Well, guess. It's because there's nothing to do. My calendar had a busy day marked. I got there, and old man Gillette had canceled his operation; three patients had telephoned to say they were better and were not coming in to the office; the only telephone calls were cancellations of appointments, and the only thing in the world I had to do was make my sick rounds at the hospital. Until this thing is settled it'll be that way. Look at your own desk calendar, Andy, if you don't believe me. We can't dodge this thing. We're in it up to our necks. We've got to go through it and emerge scoured clean. You're ambitious, Andy; sometimes I've thought too ambitious, but I —"

Brule looked at his cigarette and said with a curious tinge of sadness, "I'm the last who ought to complain of ambition. I only know what — too much of it makes of your life. Well, that's beside the point. You're ambitious and you've got a brilliant start on what's likely to be a brilliant career. Well, you're in this thing along with the rest of us. You can't help yourself. The only thing to do if we want to save anything of our work is to emerge from it as clean as a whistle."

Andy glanced at Rue.

"That sounds fine and heroic, Brule," he said. "Exactly what does it mean?"

"What does it mean!" Brule's eyes flashed dangerously. "It means what I've said. Put our cards on the table. Give the police every possible help."

"I see," said Andy slowly. "Then — you wouldn't say that, Brule, unless you see a way through. Unless you know who murdered her and are willing for whoever did it to be charged with murder — or you know who murdered her and know also how to cover it."

Brule's face turned hard; it was a look Rue knew well; she'd seen that momentary stiffening at crucial moments over an operating table. It was like a mask. He looked at Andy for a moment, eyes bright and hard and scrutinizing. Someone walked along the hall and spoke to someone else who answered — women's voices, Madge and Alicia. There was no mistaking Alicia's clear contralto.

Brule said:

"There is another consideration, Andy. In fact there are two other considerations, one of which is that an attack on Rue's life indicates Rue's — innocence; therefore I want the police to know of it. But I assure you now that I do not know who murdered Julie, and if I did I would go straight to the police with the knowledge. However, whatever my motives are or whatever motives you ascribe to me, this is the course we are going to take. Understand?"

It was like the crack of a whip.

"Yes," said Andy.

"Good. Guy's coming this afternoon. I told him about this stuff in the glass in Rue's room when I talked to him over the telephone, and he agrees with me absolutely about telling the police. Also I rather imagine police will be here. I gathered from a — short conversation I had with Angel this morning that they feel they've been pretty careful and cautious and altogether lenient. So we're in for some bad times now that they've come out with the official statement that it is murder. . . . Staying to lunch?"

"No. Thanks, Brule. I've got a couple of sick calls . . ."

He looked at Rue and said: "Brule may be right. But I think it's a mistake to talk too much. However . . ."

Brule went to the door with him and closed it after him and came back to stand before the hearth — just below Crystal's portrait. His face still wore the mask which Rue recognized but had never penetrated.

"Andy hasn't much regard for any ethical consideration on my part," he said. "The curious and rather alarming thing about it is that he's a product of my own teaching. Except — except Andy has no basic strength."

She thought of Alicia and of Crystal and of

Andy caught between Brule's own selfishness and Crystal's vanity.

"Some people," said Rue, "might call it ruthlessness."

Again he shot her a quick, oddly discerning look.

"Ruthlessness?" he repeated. "Well, perhaps. His strongest characteristic is ambition; you've seen that. And I've taught him that there are times when splitting hairs does nobody any good; yes, I suppose I've taught him that. And that there are times when what some people would consider cruelty is actually mercy. As at the moment."

She fumbled for his meaning and was confused by the hard, knowing brilliance of his gaze.

"I mean," he said coolly, "it may appear cruelty to deliberately help the police discover the identity of whoever murdered Crystal and Julie; cruel only because we all know in our hearts that it means some very public washing of any soiled linen, and — naturally, inevitably, in the end a tragedy." His face for an instant lost its hardness and certainty. If she had not known his innate indestructibility she would have said it became sad and yet strangely compassionate — foreboding yet deeply perplexed. But she couldn't be sure of any of that strangely blended emotion except that it was emotion. And it was like getting the briefest glimpse into sentient, moving depths below the frozen surface of a lake.

He put out his cigarette and looked at her coolly and said, "But I do not consider it a cruelty to stop any further attempts upon your life. . . . Has Andy been making love to you?"

"Andy —" She felt the crimson wave creeping upward over her face. But how dare he ask when Alicia was actually in the house? Rue's house, for she was his wife. He was smiling a little.

"Perhaps I've not much right to ask, considering our agreement. But if he has been — stop it."

Cold rage swept like a wind upon her. She tried to speak, tried to cry out against him and against Alicia, and he said: "Don't let him. Andy's good at love-making. I don't intend to give reasons, however, Rue. That's an order."

"Because you've given me orders for years? Because you —"

"Never mind why. But understand that I mean it. . . . Yes, Gross?"

The butler opened the door wider and entered:

"Lunch is served, madam."

It was, as somehow circumstances so often managed to be, to Brule's advantage to be interrupted just at that point. There was nothing she could say or do; she was obliged to bottle up her fury, to control it and the things she wanted to say, to acknowledge the butler's words, to go to the dining room, to face Alicia with rage and something very like hatred in her heart. Rue, who had never hated anybody before and didn't know the sears and scars that hatred can leave. For an instant flight appealed to her; she could go upstairs, plead — oh, plead anything — refuse to sit at the table along with the others — with an unbidden ghastly presence hovering there, too, and that was murder.

Brule, watching her, said with infuriating amiability: "Ready, my dear? If you don't feel like having lunch Alicia can take your place."

"Thank you, I feel perfectly well," she said icily and preceded Brule along the hall. She was unfolding her napkin when it occurred to her that Brule had bested her again, that there had been a knowledgeable gleam in his eyes that foretold Rue's instant decision.

It was the first but not the last meal they had together in the isolation of those days. For it was, in the most positive way, isolation, and all of them were sensible of it; it was as if they were shut off from the rest of the world, held somewhere in captivity and with invisible but strong bonds. Other people were going about their usual routine, were living their normal contented lives, but not they. It was an isolation which strongly pointed up (as tragedy or misfortune does) the happiness of other times, the great joy of the average, commonplace day and event.

That first meal was none too pleasant; Alicia and Brule talked, for Steven was silent, eating absently as if unconscious of what he did, and Madge was sullen, staring at Rue only to lower her thick eyelashes instantly if Rue returned her look. But Brule talked without hesitancy of the police inquiry, of the inquest next day, and of what line Guy would probably advise them to take. Alicia addressed her remarks altogether to Brule, Madge and Steven, pointedly and markedly ignoring Rue with the cool precision of one who has learned how to snub along with other more felicitous accomplishments.

There was never with Alicia any sense of guest and hostess relation: Rue was always quite subtly but definitely placed in the position of interloper, of intruder. So far, that is, as Alicia was able, with only Madge's sympathy and backing, to indicate such a position.

Alicia's accusation of the previous day had merely marked their relative positions. She had not repeated it in the presence of the police. Brule had said no word of it. Steven, lost in his own abstraction, appeared to have forgotten it.

Rue had not forgotten. Yet was obliged in that rather horrible emergency to accept Alicia's presence. If only she were not so beautiful, thought Rue, and so sure of herself. The older woman's worldly poise was, just then, a weapon. For Rue, too strongly aware of Alicia, had not the experience of dissembling Alicia had had; a word or a look would have betrayed her feelings to Alicia and to the others.

Pride is a hard taskmaster. But it was pride alone that kept Rue, more poised and certain of herself outwardly than she knew, in her rightful place that day at the table. Signaling to Gross and the waitress, giving low orders, replying now and then to Brule. Replies which Alicia apparently never heard. It was a relief when Guy came in, looking as always shiny and scrubbed and pink.

He was, however, too cheerful, so there was a meretricious air about it, as if his sympathy were all on the outside, and actually inside, he was congratulating himself on being definitely and completely an outsider. Or so it seemed to Rue. Brule greeted him with an air of anxiety and relief as if, in spite of Brule's strength and indestructibility, he wanted Guy's help.

"Thanks, yes; I've had lunch, but I'll have coffee," said Guy.

They went into the library for coffee. It was from the first word curiously like a council of state, except that it was so brief. For it lasted only half an hour or so, and the burden of Guy's warnings was simply, silence.

"Don't tell anything you don't have to tell," said Guy as he had said the night before. He looked at Madge over his cup, and his bland eyes had an extraordinarily cold look, and he said: "And that goes for you, too, young lady, and don't forget it. There'll be no more hysterical outbursts such as the one last night."

Alicia permitted herself, then, to look at Rue. Alicia was as always perfectly turned out. Rue felt herself pale and hollow-eyed. Alicia was flawless, except if you looked very closely you might have noted that the fine small lines around her eyes were a little sharper. But Alicia knew things about light and shadows and when they enhance and when they betray. She had chosen a chair removed from the light on the table but facing it so there were no downward rays to discover shadows and hollows and lines. Yet her astounding beauty could have emerged from anything, without detection of flaw. She was wearing green, a moss-green wool which was a marvel of fitting and above which her pale skin was like a gardenia, and her frosted black hair shone, and her eyes were as bright and gleaming as any jewels. Alicia had been wearing black the night before; that meant then — why, it meant she'd sent for clothes! That she intended to stay; that Madge wanted her and would insist upon it.

Brule said, "You were going to talk about alibis, Guy. You said if we all had alibis it would simplify things."

"Well, naturally," said Guy cheerily. "And I think you have. According to your statements at any rate, it seemed to me as I listened last night that you wouldn't be hard put to find alibis. Let me see." He looked at them consideringly; Steven was the nearest, standing at arm's length from Guy before the hearth, drinking his coffee meditatively, and he began with Steven.

"You, now," he said, "were in your studio all day, weren't you?"

Steven swallowed and said, "Yes. Working."

"At the piano, I suppose?"

"Yes. Mostly. I transcribed some notes early in the morning."

Steven showed the effects of nerve strain. There were great dark pockets around his deep-set eyes, and his fine, musician's hand was noticeably unsteady; but then Steven was never particularly well, never had the lean, hard look of good health and iron nerves that Brule had. That day, in deference Rue supposed to Alicia's presence, Steven had discarded his usual sweater for a handsome smoking jacket and looked unwontedly dressed up; his hair (also rather unusual in the daytime) was brushed smoothly back from his narrow, high forehead so the gray at the temples showed clearly and would have charmed his matinee hearers had he been giving that afternoon, as he often did, a concert. His deep brown eyes had as always a tendency to follow Alicia.

"But in the afternoon you were constantly at the piano?"

"I think so. Yes."

"I heard him," said Rue abruptly. "He was playing when Julie came and when Gross brought the tea tray and when — when Alicia came into the room just after Julie — died. It was the same piece. I know it well."

"Exactly," said Guy in a congratulatory way. "There you are. A perfect alibi. How about you, Alicia?"

"You know mine," said Alicia smoothly. "I've

already told you. I was at the Sidneys'; I came directly here from there. Any of them — Mrs Sidney or the maid who let me out the door — will back up my statement."

"You came directly here? That is, you didn't stop to shop or do any errands?"

Alicia's slender eyebrows went up in two black arches.

"Perhaps. I walked from Banks Street. I remember looking in a florist's window; oh yes, and I stopped at a little place near Shubert Street and ordered some handkerchiefs — rather intended to order them, but the girl I always order from was out, so I didn't. I believe I stopped for a moment in a bookstore."

Guy was looking worried.

"Anybody see you who knew you?"

"Why, I — don't know. Does it matter?"

"Well, my dear Alicia, it's not an alibi, so far."

"I don't suppose it is. But after all, I'm not accused of murdering the girl."

"No one is accused yet," said Guy. "Madge? Oh, you were in school."

Rue made a motion to speak, and Guy saw and said quickly: "What is it, Rue?"

"There's some question of how Alicia managed to enter the house," said Rue, holding her fingers tight together on her lap. "Gross says he didn't know Alicia was in the house, either."

Alicia's eyes were lambent. "Rue seems to have been consulting with the servants," she said. "However, if anyone wants to know how I got into the house —"

"I'm afraid we do want to know just that," said Guy. "Or rather the police will ask it."

"Well then," said Alicia, moving her small head contemptuously, "I simply walked in. I've had a key for a long time; Crystal gave it to me. I came into the house and realized Madge wasn't home yet and — waited. But it was only a moment or two before I heard Rue scream. I saw no one while I waited. I think the police will understand my — being as I've been for so long free to come and go in this house; I don't suppose they will take me to be an intruder." She looked at Brule, who said nothing.

Guy cleared his throat and said: "Oh dear me, no, Alicia. Certainly not. Now then, Brule, what's your alibi?"

Brule did not reply at once but seemed intent on the ashes of his cigarette. Finally he said: "I don't have one, Guy. I was in my car at the time the murder seems to have occurred — driving to the hospital as a matter of fact, but I had stopped along the way. Due to the dark day there was a traffic mix-up — trolley car went off there at the bridge, held up a lot of cars for twenty minutes or so. I saw what was happening, managed to park the car and leave it and went into some little bar near there for a drink. I don't know exactly what the place was called but imagine I can find it — if necessary," he added with his eyes on Guy.

Guy wriggled very slightly.

"I'm afraid it will be necessary, Brule," he said. "You know how the police are when they get the bit in their teeth."

If they hadn't known before, thought Rue later, they were soon to know. At two o'clock exactly police arrived again. If they had been lenient the night before when there was a question of whether or not the girl had actually been murdered, then they regretted that leniency. For they were like locusts devouring; no room, no cupboard, no shelf was too insignificant to receive scrutiny; no person above suspicion; no questions too trivial to be asked.

And they did not leave.

They were still there at nine that night when Rue had that unexpected interview with Alicia.

Each witness, that day, had been questioned separately and at length. Rue herself was just emerging from two long hours spent, again, in the dining room with light beating down in her face and a constant bombardment of questions hurled at her. Guy was there, too, mouthing unlighted cigarettes, flashing her warning glances now and then but unable to stem that flood of inquiry. She was trembling when they let her go at last, unutterably tired, her very knees unsteady, her head and eyes aching. But they had not arrested her. They had only shown her the teacup with her own fingerprints on it; had only demanded over and over again what she knew of poisons, what Julie had known of Crystal's death, why Julie had come to see her. How long

181

she had known Brule, and why they had married so soon after Crystal's death, and how long they had planned that marriage. And, again and again, details of Crystal's death. What had Julie told her: had Julie told her anything they hadn't known about Crystal's death?

She didn't tell what Julie had said: didn't say to them: She told me there was something I knew of Crystal's death — *but I don't know: Julie was wrong.*

If only she knew what Julie had meant and could tell them!

The little man called Funk, who had first come to question her, was present too. Skulking behind other and broader shoulders, examining the silver on buffet and serving table. And apparently obsessed with only one thing and that was the green on what he called the "deceased" hands. He kept popping out of obscurity to inquire, Had the deceased worn gloves? No? Well, had there been any kind of stain — not necessarily green but any color on the hands of the deceased? No? Well, did Mrs Hatterick know what caused the green on the deceased hands? Oh, Mrs Hatterick didn't.

The thought of it was as always a little bizarre, a little frightening.

They had questioned no one else so long and so persistently. Yet in all that questioning they made only one or two perfunctory inquiries about the powder in the glass: Brule had told them, as he said he was going to do. Could they consider it a ruse to suggest her own innocence?

But if so, they still did not arrest her.

She encountered Alicia at the door of the small guest room, beside Brule's study.

Alicia was at the door of that study, her lovely hand on the doorknob as if she were just leaving it. She paused and looked at Rue. Below were police, all around them was a fabric of continuous movement and sound. But in the upper hall just then there was no one.

Alicia's bright gray eyes flickered once down the length of the narrow hall and toward the empty stairway and came back to Rue.

"Wait, Rue," she said. "Have they arrested you?"

"No," said Rue and opened the door to the guest room.

"Look here," said Alicia suddenly. "Why don't you confess and have done with it?"

I can't talk to her, thought Rue and entered her room. Alicia's white hand shot out, amazingly strong and wiry, and gripped her wrist.

"So you won't reply," she said. "Very well. But understand this. I'm staying here, you know. It's my right to stay here. It's my right," said Alicia slowly. "Because Brule really wanted me to marry him. He asked me to marry him. He only married you because he knew Crystal had been murdered. He knew that sooner or later the truth would come out. He thought if he married you it would divert any possible suspicion from me. Now" — she relinquished Rue's wrist and stood looking at her with bright, watchful triumph in her eyes — "so now do you understand just what your place is here? Just how much you can expect in the way of protection from Brule?"

CHAPTER XII

The really dreadful thing about it was that Rue knew Alicia's statement to have elements of truth.

It coincided in the most perfect way with what she knew and with what Andy had told her. It dovetailed completely with her own understanding with Brule; with the whole circumstance of their marriage. It fitted perfectly, even, Brule's own admission about Crystal's death.

After a moment she said deliberately:

"Why would you have been suspected — if you had been Brule's wife when Crystal's murder was discovered?"

Alicia blinked, opened her mouth, closed it, opened it again and said:

"I don't — Because there would be talk —"

"Do you mean that you knew when she died that it was murder? How did you know?"

Alicia had recovered: her eyes had a bright hard glaze.

"How could we fail to suspect it? You see now," repeated Alicia with cool brutality, "that you can't count on Brule's protection."

Rue said slowly: "Nevertheless I am Brule's wife." She closed the door.

It gave her the last word, and there was a small element of satisfaction in that.

Except that what Alicia had said sounded true. It explained Brule's course; it explained her own marriage as nothing else had done. Andy hadn't been right in his own surmise, that is, that a quarrel with Alicia, regretted too late, had accounted for Brule's marriage to Rue. But in all probability that had been the answer Alicia or Brule himself had given Andy; if it had been a question of Crystal's murder, and Alicia and Brule both hoping to keep it a secret, taking so drastic a step to protect Alicia in case the truth came out, then they would have told Andy (if they had to tell him anything) some such story.

But why was it necessary to protect Alicia?

And why had they been so certain Crystal was murdered?

After a long time she went to the telephone. She didn't know just where Andy would be at that hour so she called the physicians' exchange which gave her his club, the Town Club; the porter, however, assured her that Andy was not there and hadn't been there since noon of the previous day. She hung up without leaving her name. Perhaps it was better not to talk to him just then.

That night she locked the door. It was when she was trying to sleep that she remembered a curious feeling of something being not quite right about the telephone; something a little different in the listening quality — and thought quite suddenly, Why, of course; the wire leading from the house is tapped.

It was a customary thing, she supposed; but it gave her a somewhat chilling glimpse into the police activity which surrounded them.

That night the house was completely silent except for a quiet, very much subdued game of poker that went on in Crystal's gilt and satin drawing room with the silk curtains pulled; a game that was regularly interrupted for quiet rounds of the house, flashlights piercing the gloom of the butler's pantry and the studio and second-floor stairway.

"I don't like that studio," said one of the policemen, returning to the drawing room. "Looks like a cave under that big piano."

"You mean you don't like murder. . . . It's your deal."

"A machine-gun murder don't bother me." He unstrapped his heavy revolver holster and put it down. "It's these fancy killings that get under my skin. You can't figure ahead." He indulged in a flight of fancy. "An amateur killer's sort of like a lunatic. You don't know where he's going to break out next."

"Go ahead and deal."

Morning came slowly. Morning and the inquest.

It was, however, extraordinarily brief; all the witnesses were there, pale and uneasy in the cold morning light, in that official, barren room, laden with the mingled scents of stale tobacco and sweeping compound.

And almost all the witnesses were asked,

briefly, to testify. It was not as difficult as Rue had feared it would be because of that briefness. Mainly it was a résumé of the circumstances surrounding Julie's death. Rue sat in her turn in the witness's chair and faced the jury and the coroner, who had a cold in his head and questioned her sadly between sneezes. There were other witnesses, but the most important one seemed to be Lieutenant Angel himself, for at the end of his testimony he read a letter.

"Miss Garder's death immediately followed the opening of police inquiry into the death of another person about a year ago," he said.

"Whose death?" said the coroner, knowing full well and sneezing loudly.

"That of Mrs Crystal Hatterick. The first wife of Doctor Hatterick, who is present."

"What brought about this inquiry?"

"A series of typewritten letters addressed to the police and to the district attorney."

"Do you have those letters?"

"Yes."

"Will you read one and show it to the jury?"

He unfolded a sheet of paper and read while the coroner blew his nose.

"This one," he said, "was addressed to the chief of police. It reads as follows: 'This is to call your attention to the death a year ago of Mrs Brule Hatterick; the writer suggests police inquiry into the circumstances of her death.' " He folded up the paper, handed it to a clerk who gave it to the jury.

Angel looked down his nose. "There were a number of other letters," he added thoughtfully. "Some openly stating that the woman was murdered. We have them all. The one I have read is typical."

"How many were there altogether?"

"About eleven or twelve altogether. That is, that we know about. There may have been others to people in authority of which we were not informed."

"Do you know who wrote the letters?"

"So far we have been unable to discover the writer."

"And you have undertaken police inquiry into the death of Mrs Crystal Hatterick?"

"Yes."

"And the results were what?"

"After securing an order for exhumation an autopsy was performed which revealed the presence of a poisonous drug in lethal quantity."

"Your conclusion is that it was a violent death?"

"Yes. Certainly."

"You performed an autopsy also upon the body of Juliet Garder?"

"Yes."

"And the results in that case were what?"

"The presence of a poisonous drug in lethal quantity was also discovered."

"Has the laboratory completed its findings?"

"Not yet; tests to determine the exact analysis of the specimens are in progress."

"But you have definitely determined that there was poison found in both bodies?"

"Yes."

"That is all."

The conclusion was foregone. There were a few questions designed to show that suicide was not a likely theory; this was readily accomplished by the coroner's emphasizing of the fact that Julie's death had almost immediately followed the opening of police inquiry into Crystal's death.

Rue was brought briefly to the stand again in this connection.

"Mrs Hatterick — before your marriage to Doctor Brule Hatterick you were a nurse?"

"Yes."

"You were one of the nurses who took care of the first Mrs Hatterick during her illness?"

"Yes."

"You were, in fact, with her at the time of her death?"

"Yes."

"Was there anything unusual about her death?"

"No. That is, it was unexpected."

"How was it unexpected?"

Rue, feeling Guy's blue, humid gaze, said it was because they had thought she was better.

"But there were no symptoms of anything but a natural death," she said firmly.

"I see. Is there any possibility, Mrs Hatterick, that your close friend Juliet Garder, who also nursed Mrs Crystal Hatterick, had any knowledge of her death that suggested it was murder?"

Rue hesitated. "Will you repeat that, please?"

The coroner sneezed, gave Guy a baleful glance and said:

"I'll put it another way. Did you talk to Miss Garder at any time about Mrs Crystal Hatterick's death?"

"I — I suppose we did in a general way."

"Do you remember what you said?"

"Not the exact words; I'm sure we must have talked of it."

"Mrs Hatterick, did you ever say it was murder?"

"No."

"Did you ever tell Miss Garder you thought it was murder?"

"No."

"Why did she come to see you the day she died?"

"I don't know."

"You didn't expect her?"

"No."

"Mrs Hatterick, think; did Juliet Garder tell you that Crystal Hatterick was murdered?"

Rue was on oath; and the question permitted an honest answer.

"No," she said clearly but held her breath for the next question.

Guy was purple and, at that stage, could do nothing. An inquest is not a trial, and there are leniencies.

"Did she tell you who murdered Crystal Hatterick?"

"No."

"Isn't it possible, judging from your knowledge of the situation, that Juliet Garder had some evidence bearing importantly upon the murder, if it was murder, of Crystal Hatterick?"

Guy got up and sat down again.

Rue said: "I don't know."

But the point had been made.

Rue was dismissed. A nurse from the hospital, trim and scrubbed-looking in tailored street clothes, gave Rue a recognizing little nod as she passed her, and went to the witness chair. She told of seeing Julie at lunch the day of her death and that she was in good spirits and that there had been nothing that she knew of to suggest suicide.

"You talked with her at lunch?"

"Yes."

"Did she mention the police inquiry into the death of Mrs Crystal Hatterick?"

"No."

"Did she — did you have reason to believe that she believed Mrs Hatterick had been murdered?"

"No," said the nurse, Elizabeth Donney, after a moment.

The coroner frowned. "But she did seem to be in good spirits?"

"Yes."

"Nothing at all to suggest suicide?"

"No."

She, too, was dismissed.

After that there were only a few witnesses; the police who had first arrived at the Hatterick house, a man from the laboratory, the medical examiner and a porter who swore that the body upon which the medical examiners had done the autopsy was the body of Juliet Garder and had been brought from the police ambulance directly to the autopsy laboratory.

It was not quite noon when the verdict was returned, and it was that Juliet Garder was the victim of murder at the hands of a person or persons unknown. In the verdict, naturally, nothing was said of Crystal Hatterick. That inquest would come later; that they believed her murdered was an open inference.

That noon the papers made official statements. Both women had been murdered.

But there were as yet no arrests.

Guy talked of it in a matter-of-fact way.

"They don't want to make an arrest until they have absolute jury proof of guilt. In fact they don't dare; not with anybody as well known as Brule. When they do make an arrest it will be when they are willing to gamble on their murder charge holding. And their case has got to be so tight they can resist every possible pressure you can bring to bear upon them." He watched Kendal negotiate a State Street crossing, and leaned to take the automatic lighter in his pink, manicured fingers.

Rue, sitting in the back seat, furs pulled tight

against the cold, wondered what Alicia was saying to Brule, following the big car in Brule's coupé. She wondered just how Alicia had managed to ride with Brule, while she and Madge and Steven and Guy rode in the Cadillac — Crystal's car with the scent of roses, clear and sweet below Guy's cigarette. He puffed smoke and watched uneasily, sitting on the jump seat with his head bent to peer through the windows, while Kendal crept along Randolph, threading his way among the noon-hour crowds and turned, slowly, northward on Michigan. The most beautiful boulevard in the world.

It was again gray and cold with the raw, desolate weather that is typical of late November. The lake was slate gray and met in the near distance a heavy gray sky. Pedestrians were scurrying against the wind; policemen at the traffic lights wore heavy winter uniforms. They passed the great Chrysler clock and the advertisement for a popular public ballroom, a bright facsimile of a ballroom with mechanical figures, looking immensely cheerful, dancing. They went on across the bridge with cold gray water flowing beneath, and lapping the fringe of barges and street abutments; they passed the Drake and were on Lake Shore Drive with the lake, now, beside them. There were waves and small white caps presaging a storm. Guy said at last:

"The point is they've got you exactly where they want you. As good as under arrest right now. Every one of you. Servants included."

Madge stirred at that and said: "I'm missing the school play. But I can't go back to school. That school. Ever. People will never, never forget. . . ."

Rue put her hand lightly on Madge's, and Madge withdrew her own hand instantly.

It was that night that, besides the columns devoted to the inquest, a curious small story found its way to the newspapers.

A bartender in a little restaurant and bar on a back street not far from the Hatterick house claimed that on the day of Julie's death a girl much resembling her pictures and wearing a plain brown hat and coat had come into the restaurant and had had two cocktails. The first one she had poured into the potted palm near her table; it was why he had remembered her. The second one she drank.

The story, it developed, had reached the police and the newspapers by way of an excited bus boy who had telephoned to both, saying that the bartender, seeing a picture of Juliet Garder in the paper, had commented on the likeness. But the bartender's story, amplified under police inquiry, was actually not amplified but the reverse. He wasn't sure it was the girl; the restaurant side had been dark because it was a dark day and, in the slack time between lunch and dinner, not lighted.

And she had been alone.

He told the police that and stuck to it. He

wasn't able, even, to make a definite identification of Julie.

Had he not surrounded his story with so strong an atmosphere of uncertainty it would have lent color to the suicide theory which, at that point, Guy said he intended to build upon when it came to a trial.

It was that night, too, that Rue asked Brule to send Alicia away.

She did more than ask, she demanded it — shaken by her own courage.

It was, really, because of Andy.

That night as she entered the little guest room Brule called to her from his study next door, and she went in. It was a small, shabby room with great fat medical books nudging the old leather couch and the chintz-covered chairs. A room Crystal and her decorator had not touched. Brule's old desk was there, the one he used, worn, with cigarette marks on it.

Guy had just gone away after a long talk with Brule, in that little study, with the door closed.

Brule said abruptly: "Sit down. Rue — you're not forgetting what I told you about not seeing Andy?"

She had not seen Andy, except at the inquest briefly, that day. Brule's straight black eyebrows made a line across his face. He went on brusquely: "Not that Andy isn't all right; he is. But just now —"

Again an unexpected current of rage caught her.

"Don't you think then, just now, it would be better to send Alicia away?"

Instantly that impenetrable mask seemed to slip over Brule's face; there was a moment of silence while he watched her. Then he said: "I see. So that's the way the land lies. Who told you?"

It was like Brule. She would meet his own method of attack.

"You were honest enough about our marriage; I believed you. But you didn't tell me you asked me to marry you because of — Alicia."

His eyes narrowed a little.

"I suppose it was Alicia who told you. Well — you want to know the truth, and I'll tell you the truth. I did marry you because of Alicia." He leaned back in his chair and waited for what she might say.

CHAPTER XIII

And there was enough she wanted to say. A very flood of fury, of accusation, welled up, clamoring to be spoken, to be cried out angrily. Humiliation has its own special cutting power, and she felt that keen edge so acutely that it was like a physical wound.

But there were things Rue had learned about self-control. She was strongly conscious of Brule's steady, watchful look — a look that perceived so many things, was so deeply, habitually observant of the terms of life and living. She said at last, slowly:

"You've not failed in any way to keep the terms of the marriage you offered me. But now that I — know the truth, I cannot have Alicia in the house. If she stays here I must go."

"Where?"

It confused her; brought her up short to regard the practical aspect of it.

"I think I could find work. I've done so before."

"Not if I refused to let you return to the hospital."

"I don't think," said Rue slowly, "that you would be so ungenerous."

"In any case you've forgotten the police and our present situation. You can't go away. Or at

198

least if you did there would be a lot of to-do on the part of the newspapers — comment and speculation. And in all probability a policeman or two would go with you. You wouldn't much like that."

"It can't — last forever."

"Look here, Rue," said Brule suddenly. "Are you in love with Andy? You'd better tell me, you know." He paused and then went on: "He's been making love to you, hasn't he? I asked you that once before. Oh" — he put his hand up toward her in a quick gesture as if to check words of defense he felt were coming — "I know I've not exactly the right to ask you. Except — you are my wife, you know."

"Alicia . . ." said Rue, half whispering.

"All right. I'll — tell you the truth, Rue, so far as I can. Alicia must stay, if for no other reason than that she's Steven's fiancée and we've got to have her friendship."

"Poor Steven," said Rue. "He's in love with her."

"Well," said Brule. "What about it? That's all right. . . . You think I'm inhuman, don't you, Rue? Perhaps I am, but nevertheless, I expect you to go along with me in this emergency."

"Exactly what do you mean?"

There was a sudden, amused sparkle in his eyes.

"You were always like that, Rue," he said. "In the hospital, I remember; all *i*'s dotted and *t*'s crossed."

"You —" she began and stopped, for it would have sounded friendly.

"I demanded it, I suppose you were going to say." A shadow went over his face. "I'm responsible for too much, Rue. 'Things we have done that we ought not to have done,' eh? Funny how the Book of Common Prayer manages to put its finger on so many of humanity's common failures. Well, just now, I mean — do as I say. Remain here yourself, of course, and Alicia will remain in the house. Don't see too much of Andy just now. And be guided by what Guy tells you to do."

Brule was always clever about getting, in one way or another, the thing he wanted. Even the shadow that was like wistfulness, and the trouble and anxiety in his face, might have been intentional — to arouse that sense of loyalty he knew so well how to arouse in his nurses.

"Why don't you want me to see much of Andy?" It wasn't jealousy. Rue knew that, therefore she could ask it.

"Newspapers," said Brule promptly. "Talk. We are very much — too much — in the public eye just now."

"But I should think Alicia's presence here —" She checked herself. She leaned forward, fingers tightly interlocked. "Brule, why did you think Crystal was murdered? You must tell me that much. Why did you think it necessary to — actually to marry someone else in order to protect Alicia in case the inquiry into Crystal's murder ever arose? What happened before Crystal's death? What had Alicia to do with it? Why —"

"Wait a minute. Who told you all this?" He paused, and as she didn't answer, he went on quickly and angrily: "It doesn't really matter, of course, who told you. I can guess. But get these facts straight, Rue. I did not know Crystal was murdered — and thus there would be no reason at all for me to — marry you to prevent talk and suspicion touching Alicia. That's sheer nonsense."

"You went immediately to Alicia the night the inquiry began. The night we were going to the opera and you sent Andy to take me." She said it with a kind of impersonal detachment; a mere stating of facts.

Brule rose, paced impatiently up and down the small rug and paused in front of her to stare angrily down at her.

"Now listen to me, Rue. I did go to see Alicia that night. And we had talked of Crystal's death. But understand this: in the beginning, at the time Crystal died, I really thought she had either killed herself or had made what she intended to be merely an attempt at suicide — and the attempt had turned into the real thing and she died. That's what I really thought."

"Why —"

"Because Crystal — Crystal was extraordinarily determined about anything she wanted. It's not a pleasant thing to say, but it's the truth; if Crystal had decided that by using a threat of suicide she could get something she wanted, she would use it as a threat. Crystal — well, just believe me when I tell you that, for it's the truth. Believe me and be patient with Madge, poor child. . . . At any rate that's what I thought; Alicia kept hinting at murder, but it didn't seem possible — then. So when the police inquiry began and I heard about those confounded letters, naturally I went straight to Alicia to ask her why she had suggested murder when she did — right after Crystal's death. I arranged to meet her about nine-thirty or so; she said she'd leave the opera, and I was to pick her up in the car, and I did. I didn't see you and Andy; and I did send Andy to take you because I thought you'd be disappointed about not going, and yet I had to talk to Alicia — I had to find out why, when Crystal died, as long ago as that, Alicia had thought of murder."

"And did you —"

"No. She — she either knew nothing or wouldn't tell me. She knew — or said she knew — nothing of the letters. If I could only discover who wrote those letters! It's got to be someone close to us: no one else would care. I suppose I have enemies, but I can't think of anyone who would do anything just like that — who would know, even, the circumstances. There's only Madge, Steven, you —"

"But I —"

"Oh, I know it stood to hurt you more than anyone else; and I know you didn't write them.

At first I thought it must be Madge; she's resented your presence here, and she's tried to make things as tough for you as she possibly can — don't think I've not seen that, for I have. But I kept hoping that time and patience would smooth things over. When I talked to Madge about the letters, though, she convinced me that she'd never heard of them. Steven? Well, I can't see Steven doing just that, either. Also it seemed to me he was genuinely astonished to learn of the police inquiry into Crystal's death. There's Andy — but it would hurt Andy. He was the attending physician; he wouldn't stir up trouble for himself, or for me, for that matter. Andy's loyal to me. And he rises or falls with me, and he knows it; he's still dependent in a large measure upon my backing. I don't mean Andy couldn't go out and make a living without me; he could. But nevertheless he needs me. Besides, Andy — well, there it is again. Andy just wouldn't do anything like that. Alicia would have no reason to write the letters. The servants, I think, are altogether out. There only remains, of the people who had opportunity to observe something of Crystal's death and who are in any way close to us and thus might conceivably have a motive, Guy —"

"Guy!"

Brule shrugged.

"Why not? Guy's been a friend of Crystal's all his life. Mine, too, but he lived right next door to Crystal since they were both children. He handled all her business for her — and his father before him for Crystal's people. She was an only child as Guy was. Guy is a good lawyer, but he has no conscience in particular; he's a good friend of mine, I think — but if there was a choice between me and Crystal I think he'd cling to Crystal's interests. But I may be wrong. I can't exactly see Guy bestirring himself for any reason like that; to avenge anybody, I mean. It's — well, in a queer way it's the work of an idealist — letters like that. There might be several motives, but the first one to eliminate would be the desire to avenge Crystal's death. Who then would want to do that — if you rule out some twisted, childish notion on Madge's part? Who has that particular kind of — well, call it idealism? Conscience. Willingness to stir up all kinds of trouble, probably for himself, too, in order to get what he conceives to be the truth out in the open?"

"Steven —" said Rue slowly and then caught it back in horror. "Oh, no, not Steven. Steven's too good —"

"I know. Too kind. Too — well, he's a gentleman. Besides, he's wrapped in his music; he hates anything that threatens to impinge upon him and thus hold up his work. Steven has the affection for laissez faire of any creative worker; he'll do anything, submit to anything, for peace until he's finished whatever he's working on." He paused, went back to the chair by the desk and looked at her thoughtfully.

"Yet," he said unexpectedly, "he wouldn't be likely to carry that desire for peace — into violent action."

"I don't —"

"I mean, he wouldn't have been likely simply to murder Crystal if, in some way we don't know about, she threatened his peace."

"Steven — murder! It's impossible."

"Listen, Rue. After working in a great city hospital for eight years can you honestly say anything's impossible? . . . I thought not. However . . ." He took a cigarette, lighted it slowly and looked at her through the little cloud of smoke. "However, I don't think Steven murdered Crystal, I'm just explaining why I think he didn't. I've had to consider Steven as a suspect — just as I've had to consider others. There's one more person who might have written those letters — Julie Garder."

That wasn't exactly possible either.

"Why?" she said after a moment.

"I don't know," he said rather wearily. "But she'd be in a position to guess that Crystal's death was murder. I knew Julie, really pretty well. All those years in the surgery. She was almost too conscientious. And she was starved for the kind of life that would have given her a real balance; I mean, in her loneliness events that another person could have taken in their stride would have with Julie loomed very large. There might have been an increasing perplexity and worry about having (as her action in coming here would indicate) actually some clue to that murder in her own possession. She might have worried and seethed secretly for months. And finally, as a sop to her conscience, written those letters. She wouldn't have wanted to make a public accusation; she had her own future to consider and I," said Brule rather grimly, "was in a position to make or mar that future. I think Julie wrote those letters. I think she had some definite clue in her possession, I think she came here (when because of her efforts the police inquiry actually opened) to talk to you about that clue. And — I think you have it, too. Except you don't know what it is."

"I don't. There's nothing —"

"There must be. Think well, Rue."

"I have thought."

"It must be some small thing; something that you remember of Crystal's illness and death — or that you could remember. But something that was so natural, so completely a part of the routine of things that it means nothing to you. I mean it — whatever it is — must have no special significance in your mind. Or at least it wouldn't have had until the fact of murder shed the — light of significance."

"But I — Brule, there's nothing."

He watched her anxiously for a moment. He had the faculty for commanding response, for drawing upon inactive reserve. But Rue had already traveled that path many times and found nothing at all at the end of it. He said at last:

"Would it help you remember events of that day if we could find the charts?"

She looked at him doubtfully.

"I don't know. Perhaps. Where are the charts?"

"I don't know. Somehow I don't think they were destroyed. But Gross can remember nothing about them. I certainly didn't take them away from Crystal's room. Madge says she doesn't even remember seeing them; I've even asked Steven about them, and he said, 'Charts? What charts?' I know Crystal's medicines were thrown out; Rachel, I remember — or someone — asked me about them, and I said, naturally, throw them away."

Rue said after a moment: "If you thought of suicide —"

"Crystal wouldn't have put poison in her medicine. She would have taken it alone. . . . And now it seems she didn't do that."

"Brule, who could have put the poison in the glass in my room?"

"Do you mean actually and literally, who *could* have put it there? Anyone in the house, of course; anyone who could have got hold of the stuff. That limits it. Madge, Alicia, Steven and I were in the house — rather I wasn't actually in the house at the time. That's another thing, Rue, that convinces me you must have some extremely important bit of evidence in your possession even if you don't know it. For that attempt on your life — wasn't really an attempt on your life. I mean it wasn't meant to succeed."

"You mean it was a — threat?"

"Exactly. You've thought that yourself, haven't you? You see, even if you had poured water into the glass, you would have known at your first taste that there was something wrong. You'd never have taken enough to kill you."

"It's not been — exactly pleasant, thinking of it," said Rue in a low voice.

"It was a threat. Think of it only as that."

"Who —"

"I don't know. Madge — so far as I know — has had no access at all to the stuff that was found in the glass. Alicia I don't know about, but I'd say offhand she wouldn't have had them with her, that night, for she had no chance to send for her things. Steven, of course, has a supply of practically everything there is."

"Steven!"

"Certainly. He's had neuritis for years; every time he gets an attack he gets scared about his hands. The only thing I can do for him is keep him supplied with all kinds of sedatives."

"Then Steven had the poison that was found . . ." Her voice broke off. Brule nodded coolly.

"Oh yes. The poison found in Crystal's body and in Julie's. None of those drugs is harmful except in excess. As you know. But I had access to them too; and Andy. And you yourself, Rue."

She leaned forward again, anxiously.

"Brule, there's something that's worried me.

I'm afraid the police have found it. Yet if they have I don't see what's keeping them from arresting me at once. I —"

"Arresting you!" He got quickly to his feet and came to stand beside her. "What on earth do you mean?"

"My — I had a lot of medicines. In a little bag. Left over from nursing — you know how a nurse gradually acquires a lot of medicine."

"Where is it?"

"I don't know. I brought it here — in a trunk, I think, along with my other things. It may be in my room; I can't think where else it would be. There are shelves and drawers in the dressing room; it must have been placed there. Rachel might remember; she helped me unpack. But I've been — I haven't wanted to ask her. And the police have closed the room. I've had to ask permission just to go in and get — clothes and things; a policeman watching me all the time. I couldn't search for the bag."

"What was in it?"

"I don't remember exactly: a pretty complete supply, I suppose."

"Nurses," said Brule with a groan. "Good God, Rue, you never need medicine! You're as healthy as a kitten."

"I didn't keep them for myself. You know how it is when you're on private duty. How often something like that is needed and the doctor tells you to give it, and it's a help not to have to send out —"

He interrupted her: "Oh, I know, I know. They all do it! The whole point is, was there morphine in your drug supply?"

"Yes, of course. I don't know how much. I'd never had occasion to draw on my own supply; it had accumulated gradually. There couldn't have been much."

"But enough," said Brule, "enough . . ." The look on his face frightened her. He saw that, too, and said quickly: "Well, when the room is opened we'll have a look. If the police had found it they would have arrested you. Instantly. So almost certainly they didn't. If someone else did — we'd find it. . . . Look here, Rue." He put his hand suddenly under her chin, lifting her face so he could look directly, deeply into it.

"Rue — it's asking a lot, perhaps. It's asking a — a little blindness and a lot of faith on your part. But will you — trust me? And do the things I've asked you to do?"

His hand cradled her chin softly. She had all at once, with breath-taking sharpness, a desire to turn her face, moving it softly against that hand. So her lips touched it.

The unexpectedness, the sheer craziness of the impulse gave her a queer kind of shock.

Trust him, he'd said. Do what he asked. But that meant accept Alicia's presence and all that presence implied.

CHAPTER XIV

Pride is a luxury of price.

She moved her face from the caressing cradle of his hand. She stood up and turned toward the door.

"I can't do anything else," she said clearly but, despite herself, not quite naturally, and went away.

But that night all the things he'd said haunted her. There were at least two things he had not mentioned, neither had the newspapers, in all their long and repetitious accounts, mentioned either of them. One was the matter of the telephone call which had taken Brule and the policeman out of the house that first night after Julie's murder. It had been a false errand. Who did it, and what had been its purpose? Brule had said nothing of it. The police must know of it, since one of them had actually accompanied Brule. This provided, too, an alibi for Brule at the time she herself knew that that intruder had crept, so silently and so knowingly, into her room. If Brule had needed an alibi.

The other omission was, again, the matter of the stain on Julie's hands.

Brule had talked of it once briefly and dismissed it. The police had apparently kept that detail (and how many others, she wondered, of which she knew nothing?) from the newspapers. There was never a word of it in any account she read. And it would have been the kind of thing that lent itself to headlines.

Had it been a stain? A dye? Some curious effect brought about, say, by a change of temperature or a result of the poison that had been given Julie? Yet in all Rue's professional experience she had encountered no one drug and no combination of drugs that would have brought about just that curious and somewhat grisly effect.

Yet Brule did not seem to feel it of importance enough to consider at length. Or was it that he thought it was of so much importance that he wouldn't talk of it? To them, at any rate?

If Alicia, Rue thought once in the silent, dark hours of the night, if Alicia had crept into her room and put the powder in the glass as a threat, then it wasn't Alicia who had put in that telephone call whose only purpose, so far as they knew, was to call Brule away from the house. For Alicia was in the house at the time and couldn't have made the telephone call. Or wait — could she? There was an outside telephone in the kitchen, on a different line than the house telephone, a convenience for household ordering and for the servants. She pursued that thought for a moment and then rejected it; for Alicia to go to the kitchen, downstairs and through halls, escape the policeman on guard and make the telephone call would have been far more difficult than simply to enter Rue's room without going to the elaborate precautions of getting Brule and the policeman (and Kendal, but that was unimportant) out of the house. And she thought, too (and tried not to think), of what Alicia had said of Rue's marriage to Brule — and what Brule had not said.

It was the next day that Rue went to the hospital.

Another brooding, sullen day, with lights on in the narrow long house, and Madge as sullen as the day. Alicia had breakfast in her room — rather Madge's room. Steven looked ill and scarcely spoke. Brule left early.

It was that morning, too, after Rue (without telling anyone what she planned to do) had ordered the car, that her own bedroom was at last opened. Police arrived early as usual; they had grown more accustomed, by that time, to the ubiquity of police. Even to the bouts of constant questioning which, so far, had taken no new turn.

Rue went immediately to the opened room. She stood for a moment at the threshold, thinking of Crystal and thinking of Julie. The room was in slight disorder; and it had evidently been searched minutely.

The stale odor of smoke struggled with the faint scent of roses. The soft pastel colors looked weary, somehow; in fact the whole room had an air of dreariness in spite of its luxury.

She went to the large cupboard-lined dressing room.

She was still searching when Rachel, neat and

efficient in her crisp morning uniform, appeared in the doorway and asked if she could help.

Rue, standing on a footstool in order to search a shelf, sighed and got down.

"I'm looking for a small brown leather bag," she said. "I think it was somewhere here — on a shelf perhaps. Have you seen it?"

Rachel hadn't. Together they looked again, but the little bag, shabby from years of constant use, was not there.

Rachel vaguely remembered it.

"A small bag," she said. "Yes, I remember. I unpacked it myself when I unpacked Madam's trunks. I believe I placed it in a drawer. There were little boxes of medicines and some things that — looked like the doctor's instruments in it."

"Rachel," said Rue on an impulse, "there's something else that's been lost. Perhaps someone has already questioned you."

Rachel's rather broad, dark face was blank.

"Yes, madam?" she said inquiringly. Rue took the plunge.

"When Mrs Hatterick — I mean —"

"The first Mrs Hatterick —"

"Yes. When she was ill we kept what we called charts — sheets of paper, printed forms, on which we wrote the progress of her illness — things like her temperature and the medicine that was given and —"

"Yes, madam."

"You remember?"

"Yes, madam. They were kept on a little table by the door."

"Exactly. Rachel, after she died and when the room was cleaned, do you know what happened to those charts?"

The blankness on Rachel's face had intensified itself.

"No, madam," she said instantly.

It was too prompt.

"You've — already been questioned about it?" said Rue slowly, watching the maid.

"Yes, madam. The police and Doctor Hatterick and also Doctor Crittenden questioned me. I know nothing of the chart."

"But you — it was you who cleaned the room afterward."

"Yes, madam. But I know nothing at all of the chart."

She's lying, thought Rue and attempted persuasion.

"No one would blame you, Rachel, if you had put them away someplace and forgotten them. Or — even if you know what happened to the charts but didn't want to tell the police for fear of getting yourself in any way involved in this — this horrible thing. No one would blame you; you could still tell me."

The very slight hesitation, the swift weighing of what Rue had said and the instant of choice, convinced Rue. For the maid's eyes wavered, then fixed boldly and with determination upon Rue's. She said:

"I know nothing of them, madam. . . . Shall I clean the room now and prepare it for Madam?"

In the car Rue pondered over it.

Kendal had been waiting at the curb. Madge had been in the hall when Rue left, had noted her coat and hat and that the car was waiting, dark eyes observant.

Rue said to Gross: "I'll be home shortly after noon. Not for lunch."

"Yes, madam. If the police ask for you shall I tell them —"

Always the police! "Yes, certainly."

A small car pulled away from the curb a few doors down the street and unobtrusively followed them.

She had taken one of the morning papers from the table in the hall. Kendal's square shoulders were like a black wall in front. The streets were cold, the sky gray and heavy. A cold wind came off the lake.

She unrolled and glanced at the paper. Headlines, of course. A complete résumé of the inquest. Long columns of print, of necessity repetitious. Halfway down one column she found again her own story of the day of Julie's death. And following it she read, for the first time, Gross's and Andy's and the maids' stories of their own activities the day Julie was murdered. There was nothing significant: Gross and the maids had followed their usual routine. She read Andy's statement; he had been at the office all morning except for a brief sick call at the hospital; he had lunched at a little restaurant on Michigan Boulevard, had made three sick calls at homes, had been in the hospital until four-thirty and had just returned to the office when he had Gross's telephone call. He'd arrived at the Hatterick house just as Dr Hatterick had arrived; they had entered together. He had noticed nothing unusual about the body. (It was an oblique allusion to Julie's hands, the first one Rue had seen.) There followed a statement about Crystal's illness; a repetition of the statement Andy had already made to Miller and the rabbity little Funk that first night.

The night they'd gone to the opera together.

The night Andy had told her he loved her and had loved her for a long time. "I used to watch for you in the hospital," he'd said. "Among all the white uniforms and white caps I always knew the little square set of your shoulders; the smooth knot of gold hair under your perky little cap." It was as if he repeated it, word for word. He'd said other things too; and Andy was young and he loved her and she needed — oh, desperately needed that refuge and assurance.

She thought of him all the way to the hospital; through the crowded Loop, almost brutal in its suggestion of power, along the strip of narrow, unknown back streets. Andy was loyal; Andy loved her; with him at least there would be no more heartache, no more Alicia.

The hospital when they reached it looked

enormous, dotted with lights, looming stark and huge against the lowering gray sky. Great bluish windows on the fourth floor told her they were operating that morning. Who, she wondered automatically, was working there?

She had told no one that she was going to the hospital.

It had been an overnight decision. Somewhere in the record of Julie's last day of life lay the secret of her death.

Rue's mind touched again that curious story told by the bartender; curious because *if someone had been with Julie* it would not have been curious.

Well, she would see the girls — nurses who knew them both so well. Tight-lipped from training and habit, reserving their cool, pregnant opinions, they would not, any of them, have been inclined to talk much to the police. Even if they had known anything.

Something about Elizabeth Donney had perhaps suggested that trip — some intangible girding of herself against the questions hurled at her; that and the friendliness in the nod she'd given Rue.

But when she reached the hospital it was a little grim and forbidding.

The doorman didn't remember her. The girl at the desk was new. The smell of ether and antiseptics struck her now-unaccustomed senses like a blow; once she'd loved it. As she had loved the subdued hustle and bustle; the sense of important things being done; the dim long halls; the lights, the flutter of the nurses' white uniforms. She made her way at last to the nurses' dormitory. Elizabeth Donney was on duty. But three nurses of her own graduating class were not on duty; they would tell Elizabeth that Rue had asked for her; they were anxious to talk; they exclaimed, too, over Rue, hailing her back to the fold. There was (which was a tribute to Rue) a kind of extra flippancy and matter-of-fact acceptance of her, as if they wanted to show her that her marriage to the supreme emperor of their world would raise no barrier that their mutual respect and affection could not pass.

And they talked of Julie; soberly, trying not to show the sorrow they felt. The trouble was they knew nothing; Julie by some miracle of secrecy had even kept the fact of the police inquiry from them; they hadn't known Julie had intended to see Rue, much less why.

Rue went away at last; pausing to look through the open door of a room she'd once lived in, the small, clean room with its two white beds, its small dressing table scrupulously divided in halves; even the little row of stockings washed and drying above the radiator was all poignantly familiar to her. The singular thing was, it aroused no nostalgia and it no longer seemed like home.

It was as she went away that she met Andy. He stopped short.

"Rue! What on earth are you doing here? Is Brule with you?"

And when she said no, he insisted on her going to lunch with him.

"I'm ready to go back to the office," he said. "Did Kendal bring you? Dismiss him and I'll take you home in my car after lunch. I've got to talk to you, Rue."

Why not? thought Rue, and went.

His car was parked in the doctors' parking lot near the hospital; they walked along the street, Rue conscious of the red brick wall of the hospital beside her as if it had been a living thing. How many years had she lived under its influence!

Andy placed her in the seat beside him. He smiled at her as he took the wheel.

"How I've wanted to have you just there," he said and put his hand on her own, "all wrapped in your furs with your little hat on one side so I can see your lovely hair and your eyes — Rue, did anybody ever tell you that your eyes really are exactly like stars? Except they're blue."

"No one," said Rue. "You've an Irish tongue, Andy."

But it warmed her, nevertheless. Except . . . She glanced at Andy's profile as he turned into the traffic. Handsome, regular, boyish; queer, thought Rue, how much better she liked Andy when she was away from him.

If the police car followed them, as it must have done, Rue did not know, for she didn't look for it.

They lunched at the Blackstone, in the old, mellowed room overlooking the lake with the flow of traffic directly below their window and the lake stretching away in cold gray to meet an equally cold gray sky.

Crimson-shaded lamps were on the tables, and flowers. Andy was anxious about the lunch, ordering with care, everything was to be just so, he explained to the waiter. And, as it always is, his anxiety for perfection was a subtle compliment to Rue.

In the balcony the Blackstone Ensemble, muted, all strings and piano, played softly. Andy pushed aside silver and plate and leaned across the table and smiled.

"Nice," he said, "isn't it? When have I had you alone! Oh, darling, I've been starving for you."

Rue looked at him with a little dismay; she was inexpressibly grateful for him, but she was unused to speaking in fervencies.

"Starving for lunch, you mean."

He looked wounded and covered it. And melon came, chilled exactly to suit Andy.

It was a safe, a comfortable world. Soft chatter from other tables, women in furs and smart hats with single, discreet rows of pearls at their throats; flowers and the exciting throb of traffic outside the window, and above it all, weaving it into a harmonious, colorful tapestry, the music of violins and piano.

Luckily they saw no one they knew; it would

have reminded them of the ugly thing that, for those moments, Rue was trying instinctively to forget. Andy helped her. He talked of anything and everything; and made love to her gaily, as if there were no obstacles between them, as if they were carefree and young and had all life before them. With nothing tragic to forget.

Or to face.

Coffee came at last; and the things they must talk of could no longer be pushed aside. Andy began it:

"I talked to Brule this morning. Have they found your nursing kit, Rue?"

He didn't need to say who.

She shook her head. "We looked for it this morning, Rachel and I. And I asked Rachel about the charts; I think she knows where they are; the charts for Crystal's illness, I mean."

They talked of it; and of the inquest; and of Rue's trip to the hospital.

"Alicia is still at the house?" asked Andy at last.

She looked at her small coffee cup.

"Yes."

"Oh, Rue — Rue, how much longer —"

"No, Andy. Don't talk of it."

"But I must, Rue. It's so unfair to you. Doesn't Brule even offer to — to explain? To give her up? To —"

Brule. He'd asked her not to see much of Andy. But lunch with Andy was so small a thing; and she'd needed the bolstering that Andy supplied. The friendly reassurance he gave her.

Or was that all? Had she really, deep in her heart, come to a decision of some kind? A decision that was like a fire laid in the hearth, ready for a flame to light it.

There was something obscurely inept about the simile. Fire? Flame?

Her hand lay on the cloth, beside the lamp. No one could see, and Andy again put his own hand over it. He leaned forward, and there was something urgent in his blue eyes, something urgent on his tongue and about to be spoken.

But she never knew what he'd been about to say. For a man stopped beside their table and said, "Well, hello there," and it was Brule.

Speaking with the utmost coolness and nonchalance, except that his eyes were so bright and his face so masklike.

"Do you mind if I join you?" he said.

CHAPTER XV

Andy relinquished Rue's hand. Brule had seen it, of course. A waiter, hovering, brought an extra chair, and Andy had got to his feet. Then both men were seated again, and there was a menu card in Brule's hands. Menu cards, reflected Rue, are such a help; be nonchalant, look at a menu card.

He ordered quickly.

"Have you been at the hospital?" he asked Andy.

"Yes," said Andy, "that's where I picked up Rue. Were you operating this morning? I didn't see you."

Brule shook his head.

"No. I was at the office. Just happened to come in here for lunch and saw you both."

That, thought Rue, is not the truth. Yet there was no way for Brule to know that they were there, they hadn't known themselves that they'd be lunching together or that they would be at the Blackstone. How could he have known it, then?

Andy apparently believed it.

"That Sims woman from downstate is going to make a go of it," he said. "I'm going to feel pretty good about that case. I followed your advice to the letter, Brule, and she's improving."

Rue listened idly while they talked of it, of another case or two, of the cloakroom thefts at the club, of the morning's political news; with a start she remembered the police car that had followed her to the hospital. She'd forgotten it altogether. Had it followed Andy's car from the hospital to the Blackstone? Then had Brule happened past and recognized the car or the policemen in it? That didn't sound right somehow, either; Brule was the kind of person it was difficult to reconcile with coincidence of any kind.

But after his arrival it was different. The music, the flowers, the lights, the soothing little chatter of voices lost their power to lull her into gaiety; became all at once just so many pleasant props to a stage setting. Now that Brule had arrived, the delusion of escape vanished. The orchestra launched just then, very softly, into "Speak to Me of Love," and it sharpened, curiously, the sense of falseness in that hour or so that she and Andy shared. Brule was there; with him intangibly were all those things they couldn't escape, couldn't avoid in any way but by plunging through them.

Brule was as always quietly hurried. He ate with dispatch and a good appetite and ordered brandy afterward.

"I'll take Rue home," he said briskly, while the brandy made a bright hot little lane down Rue's throat. "I'm going that way."

They went together to the door, passing tables

— which seemed quite suddenly silent and observant as they passed as they had not been silent and observant until Brule, whom everybody knew, had joined them. They went past the bowing but reserved headwaiter, who said: "Good afternoon, Doctor Hatterick," and down the broad steps. In the palm-laden lobby Andy said he had to get back to the office and gave Rue a long look that tried to tell her all the things he couldn't say. But the gaiety of their lunch seemed now false and thin.

Brule's coupé was at the curb. The doorman, too, said: "Thank you, Doctor Hatterick. Good afternoon," and watched them with speculative eyes.

Their ride along Michigan Boulevard homeward was silent. Brule didn't say, I told you not to see much of Andy. He didn't say anything.

Gross opened the door for them and took Brule's coat and hat. There was music there too — coming from Steven's studio.

"I wish he wouldn't play that," said Rue sharply and unexpectedly.

"That?" said Brule, glancing quickly at her.

"It's the thing he was playing — when Julie died." She felt a wave of impatient distaste. " 'Arabesque,' he calls it."

"Oh," said Brule, and Gross said:

"The police are here again, sir. Waiting to see Madam."

After a moment Brule said: "About anything in particular, do you think, Gross?"

"I don't know, sir. The little one they call Funk is there too."

"I see." He turned. "Well, Rue. I'll go with you."

"In the library, sir. We were at lunch when they arrived."

But they wanted to see Rue alone, it developed — politely, for Oliver Miller did the talking, and he was always oily with politeness. Brule went away, and Rue, wondering if she would ever grow accustomed to those frequent, unpredictable bouts of questioning, sat down and, as usual, tried to hold herself steady, tried not to show fright and above all, as Guy had coached them all, to think twice about answering anything.

The difficult thing about those interviews was the unexpected way in which the detectives thrust new evidence into them, pouncing at her in the middle of familiar and worn paths of inquiry to ask something totally new and unexpected. Today it was keys.

Keys to the Hatterick house.

Through what long and tedious avenues of inquiry Rue could only guess, they had discovered the locksmith who had made Alicia's key. He had made it at Crystal's order. They knew the date, over a year ago, now, and they knew that it had been given to Alicia promptly on the day the locksmith had delivered it.

But he had made two keys.

Did Rue know anything of an extra key?

Rue didn't.

"Gross would know," she told them.

The little Funk, standing in the shadow of a window curtain, darted forward, looking very grimy and scared, and said Gross didn't know.

"All the members of the household except Miss Madge have keys, and Gross himself has a key. He says that's all there are."

"Perhaps someone lost a key, and the extra one was to replace it," said Rue. It seemed an extraordinarily tenuous kind of clue — if clue they considered it.

She thought there was a kind of doubt on their faces, as if they agreed with her unspoken thought.

"Perhaps," said Miller a little heavily. "But Gross says there's been no key missing."

"But — but there are so many possibilities; an extra key . . ."

"I know," said Miller. "But the maids and the cook insist they have none, that Gross does all the locking and unlocking. He thought you might have had it, Mrs Hatterick. Or know something about it."

"Well, I don't," said Rue a little crisply. "I have —" She searched in her enormous flat bag, and drew out a smoothly worn key. "I have this one. That's all."

They let her go after a few more questions, again about the time and manner of Julie's arrival. They said nothing, that time, of Crystal's death.

Madge and Alicia were in the studio with

Steven, and he was playing the piano. Alicia sat looking like an extremely beautiful portrait in her green gown, watching the fire broodingly, with its soft light putting a pale gold flush on her beautiful face. Madge sat in the deep bay window near the piano, her chin on her hand, staring out at the dreary gray sky, her scarlet sweater in bright contrast to the heavy brown curtains, which were open, in daytime, for light.

Rue hesitated on the threshold. There was no place for her there. She went upstairs and, forgetting that her own room — Crystal's room — had now been opened and cleaned, went to the little guest room beside Brule's study.

She entered it and closed the door, thinking of the police; of Miller and little Funk with his black eyebrows lifted so he looked constantly frightened, and his clawlike hands. She wondered when they would remove the police guard about the house — unobtrusive, by that time a part of those days. A dark, thick bulk moving quietly along the hall; sitting in the butler's pantry drinking coffee, meeting another equally thick and stalwart bulk outside the house, below the door, talking mysteriously, moving away — only to turn up as mysteriously at the back of the house somewhere. There was always someone there.

It ought to have been a kind of guarantee of safety. It wasn't.

The continually recurring interviews with the police always frightened her. She had dropped her soft fur coat and sat down, thinking of that businesslike interview just past, when she realized that someone — a woman — was in Brule's study. And she was crying and Brule was talking to her.

Afterward she sought back into her memory for other and preceding words — words she might have heard through that closed, concealed door, as she entered the room, as she flung down her coat, as she sat lost in thought of that recent bout with the police. But she never could remember anything preceding the thing she did hear.

The woman sobbed again, wretchedly. And a man's voice said: "Give them to me. You're a fool. Bring them at once — and stop that shouting."

"I can't . . . I'm afraid . . . Murder . . ."

"Oh, you fool —"

It was Brule. And he was angry, his voice at its very white heat of anger. She'd seen him that way once, when a surgical nurse forgot a tube and the patient, a boy of fifteen, choked and died before they could do anything.

Brule's voice now brought the tragic, dreadful scene back to Rue.

Yet when he spoke again his voice had changed. It was almost coaxing. He said: "Come now, my dear. You run along and do as I tell you. Nothing's going to hurt you. Nothing at all . . . nothing . . ."

After a moment a door opened and closed,

and there was silence in the study. Whoever had been there had gone. One of the maids? Cook? Who? Alicia and Madge were in the studio. Somehow the voice, sobbing though it was, had suggested Rachel. Brule must have gone with her.

But he hadn't. For the telephone rang in the study, and Brule's voice answered it.

"Yes — (it's all right, Gross, hang up; I'll take it) — yes, this is Doctor Hatterick." Gross has answered simultaneously at the telephone downstairs. Brule's voice came hard and clear through the closed door. "All right. I'll come right away. Get a blood donor ready — I'll operate right away; have the operating room ready. Get permission from his family. I'll be there in fifteen minutes; ready to operate in twenty —" The telephone clicked, and the door to the study slammed. She reached her own door as Brule started down the stairs.

"Brule —"

He jerked back toward her.

"Emergency," he said. "Let you know . . ." He was running downstairs. She heard him in the hall below. "Get my coat quick. Is my car still outside? No, I'll drive myself. Quicker."

He was gone.

She wished she could have gone with him, to play out the drama that would be played that afternoon, under great blue lights, in the heat and silence and suspense of the white operating room.

She went back to the guest room, perceived

its slick emptiness, remembered that her own things had been removed to her room again and went, trailing her coat, into the laced, silk-draped bedroom with its French mirror and great bed.

There on the hearthrug, below that mirror and beside the delicately carved armchair with its pale gray silk upholstery, Julie Garder had died.

She sat there for a while, in the freshly cleaned and aired room, all tidy now with fresh pink roses on the small gray desk, resurrecting in her mind that scene. And the scenes to follow. Steven rushing into the room, eyes distraught. Andy and Brule following him, Brule stooping instantly over the girl, Andy flinging his overcoat upon a chair and kneeling, then, beside Brule.

She was there when Rachel came.

It had been Rachel in Brule's study. Rue was sure of it. The girl's eyes were red and swollen. She said in a subdued way that Gross had said the doctor had left.

"Yes, Rachel. There was an emergency at the hospital. What is it?"

But Rachel wouldn't say. She looked at Rue with dark, haunted eyes and asked when the doctor would be back.

"I don't know. Rachel, what is wrong? What — what is it you are hiding under your apron?"

"Nothing, madam. Nothing —"

"Nonsense. There's something. What?"

"Really there's nothing, madam. It's nothing at all. . . ."

"Let me see your hands. Rachel —"

The little organdy apron concealed only empty hands. Hands that were doubled up into tight fists.

Rue looked at them and said: "What —" and Rachel defiantly opened her hands and held them palm outward toward Rue, staring at her above them with somber, red-rimmed eyes.

"There," said Rachel, "you see —"

Rue saw. Saw and shrank away and yet had to lean nearer to make sure she saw. But there was no mistake. Clear upon the girl's palms were smudges and blotched streaks of green.

"Where . . . ?" breathed Rue at last. "How . . . ?"

"I don't know! I don't know, madam. I — I washed my hands and there it was. I don't know . . . but I know about her," she cried, gasping and flinging out both stained hands toward the hearthrug as if Julie's shabby little figure were still there. And then she looked at Rue again, and gave a strangled, sudden sob and ran out of the room. Hiding her stained hands below the scrap of organdy.

Rue did not follow her.

She didn't know how much later it was that Steven knocked rather diffidently at her half-opened door and came in.

"All alone," he said. "May I come in? . . . Well, how goes it, Rue? We're just going out for a drive. I thought you might like to go along." He was watching her kindly, instantly aware, as

233

Steven was always aware, of some special trouble. He came to her and smiled down. He already had his coat and muffler on, and was carrying his hat. "Poor little Rue. The glass slipper isn't what it's cracked up to be."

The glass slipper. He'd talked of it before, she saw herself in her blue-and-silver Schiaparelli gown, descending to the stairway to meet not Brule but Andy.

"Poor little Rue, caught between them," said Steven soberly. "I know . . ."

"I know," said Steven. And as she met his sober, dark eyes, all at once she saw something deeper than sympathy, something stronger than affection, and that was truth. Steven did know.

But she had to say it, faltering: "You mean — you know all about it, Steven? You know . . . But you can't —"

"I know," he said again. "Alicia and Brule and — I've known for a long time, Rue."

It was very quiet in the rose-scented room. Rue looked up at the sensitive, slender face of the man who stood beside her.

"But you," she said wonderingly. "You still — love her."

He nodded.

"I still love her. I'll always love her, I suppose. I can't help it. That's love, my dear. I suppose, always, there's a hope — like a little, flickering light at the end of a long lane."

"Steven . . ."

"Don't feel sorry for me." He smiled again.

234

"My eyes are open. Listen, Rue, my dear, you are young. I'm — not. Let me tell you something. There's always a time when it's stronger than you are; I've had my moments of rebellion and of struggle and of — well, of hatred. Not — pleasant moments. But it's no good. I've got to accept the whole of it. Do you see?"

"Y-yes."

"No, you don't." He looked at her for a long moment and then unexpectedly bent and kissed her lips lightly. "What a dear child you are, Rue," he said and turned abruptly and went to the door. He paused then.

"You're sure you won't go along?"

She didn't go. Afterward she thought of it, that instant of indecision. But it would have made no difference.

She heard them leave, Alicia's throaty, lovely voice in the hall: "We'll stop at Field's . . ."

Steven murmured something in reply. Steven, who knew about Alicia and Brule; who had known. Poor Steven.

They had barely gone when Andy telephoned. Gross came to tell her, and she took the telephone call in her own room.

But Andy didn't say much. Even when she told him of the girl Rachel and the grisly green smudges on her hands, he said only:

"How . . . ?"

"She doesn't know." It was cheering, in that house that seemed so silent after everyone had gone, to hear Andy's voice, even if it was at the

235

end of a telephone wire. Even if (though there was no indication of it) police were listening to every word she said.

"Well, never mind," he said at last. "Let the police worry about it. I only called to ask if there was anything new."

"Only that — and the police were here when we got home. Asking about keys."

"Keys?"

"There's an extra key somewhere they can't account for. I suppose someone has lost it. It's not important." She wanted to say: I'm alone. Please come. I'm alone and the house is big and it's so empty and silent.

She didn't say it. And Andy talked for a little and hung up.

After that the house was even emptier. She thought of questioning Rachel further and rang the bell, but Gross came presently and, when she inquired, said it was the maid's day out and she had gone.

The afternoon wore on slowly after that. Gross vanished to some quiet downstairs retreat for his afternoon rest period; only the doorbell or telephone or her own bell would lure him out of it.

It grew dark early. Brule did not return; and she wondered about the emergency operation. She couldn't read; she couldn't write letters. She thought of Steven. She thought of Madge. She thought, wishing she wouldn't, of Alicia.

But Steven's whole philosophy was wrong. Rue could not accept it for herself.

She rose at last, driven by restlessness and the early dusk and her own thoughts. There was something oppressive about the silence of the darkening house. Something too poignantly reminiscent about that rose-scented room, as if the ghosts of two dead women lingered there, watching — Crystal with her mocking, secret smile, Julie helpless and trapped in a tragedy that did not concern her.

Rue went downstairs. Gross had not yet lighted the hall, and it was cavernous in the growing dusk. She went back toward the library. It, too, was not lighted, and she paused at the door to seek the electric light switch. And as she did so she glanced on down the hall.

The door to Steven's studio was closed, and there was a thin streak of light below it.

A streak of light which, as she looked, silently disappeared.

As if someone had turned out the light.

But no one was there. The house was completely still. She walked across the hall and opened the studio door.

The first thing she realized was that the curtains must have been pulled, for the room was so dark that the ashes left in the hearth made a faint red glow. The dark cavern of the room was so still she could hear the pounding of her own heart. But someone must be there. She had just seen that light turned off.

There was a master switch there, too, by the door, and she pressed it.

The room sprang into view — long, with the big piano in the corner and the heavy curtains pulled across the bay windows.

And there was someone there. Someone that lay, oddly, across the piano bench.

Rue must have moved. For suddenly she was staring directly down at the thing on the bench, and it wasn't quite recognizable, yet it was the maid, Rachel.

Her heart was pounding so frantically she couldn't have heard small sounds, but she saw the piece of manuscript paper waver, slide slowly off the rack above the keyboard, flutter sluggishly across the huddled figure and fall on the floor at Rue's feet.

It was music manuscript — printed bars filled with hurried, penciled notes. And across it suddenly a bright red smear spread itself. She stared at it stupidly, not realizing why the paper had fallen in just that way.

CHAPTER XVI

She must have seen more than she thought she saw, for later there were definite details she remembered and could tell the police. She remembered that Rachel wore a coat and was flung, twisted, on the long cushioned bench so that Rue saw the back of her coat, with a long slit cut into the dark cloth and a spreading wet patch starting all around that slit. The girl wore no hat, and her dark hair was bare, without her usual cap. She had on high-heeled pumps, and one of them had loosened somehow and dangled from one toe. There was no knife or revolver or any kind of weapon visible.

She must have seen all that.

But then she only thought with appalling slowness as in a nightmare. Rachel was dead. Rachel was murdered. But no one was in the house. And . . . she had seen the light turned out.

Rachel hadn't turned out the light. Therefore . . . someone was there. Someone . . . and then she realized, still stupidly, that only a current of air from somewhere could have made that sheet of manuscript paper move and flutter from the rack, and that meant a door or a window open, and that meant . . .

She was afraid to look behind her, around the room. She was afraid to move, really, yet move she must and did. Perhaps she ran back to the door; she never knew. The next thing she was ever to be able to remember was ringing the bell in the library, pressing the little pearl button so hard it hurt her finger, and then meeting Gross — moments afterward it seemed, in the pantry. So she must have gone through the empty dark dining room to meet Gross. But she couldn't remember that either.

And it must have been Gross who remembered that there usually was a policeman somewhere about the house. Later Rue had hazy memory of herself huddling against the buffet in the dining room and hearing Gross's voice, husky and unnaturally high, shouting at someone who was apparently in the street outside the house. The front door banged, and feet came down the hall.

And it was really then that the deluge began.

It was a repetition of the night following Julie's murder, only it was worse. And it was all unutterably confusing.

But there was another thing Rue was to remember out of the confusion, and that was Brule's return.

For he came before the homicide squad arrived. Came just after Rue had heard them making frenzied telephone calls to the police headquarters. He came and was met in the hall and cried instantly on hearing the news:

"Where's Mrs Hatterick?"

No one knew. Rue cried: "Brule . . . Brule

. . ." and he came and met her there at the door of the dining room. Lights had been turned on by Gross and shone harshly upon Brule.

"Rue — they say you found her!"

"Yes. Oh, Brule —"

"Who did it?"

"I don't know. Someone was in the house. The lights were turned off — Brule —" She was shivering. He put his arms around her and drew her closer to him.

"You're sure you're all right? I've got to go in there —"

"Don't leave me."

It was then she saw it. The infinitely small, infinitely trivial thing that was so difficult to forget. He still wore his overcoat but had tossed hat and gloves down somewhere. She had put one hand on his shoulder, and he put his own hand to cover it, and all around the square clear fingernail of the middle finger there was a faint red line. A line that was — that could be nothing else but dried blood. She had seen it too many times; there was no possible chance of her making a mistake. She must have caught her breath a little, the wet patch on Rachel's coat too fresh in her memory, for Brule looked at her sharply, followed her gaze and released her hand abruptly to look at his own.

He frowned.

"Glove broke while I was operating," he said quickly. "I scrubbed up afterward in a hurry. It was a long operation, and I was anxious to get home." It was dismissed. Forever, so far as Brule was concerned.

"Stay here, Rue. I've got to take a look."

He joined the men in the studio. In another moment they were searching the house.

Yes, it was the same kind of ordered, engulfing deluge that had fallen upon them, had submerged the house and all within it after Julie's death.

Only it was worse.

This time there was no doubt that it was murder. This time there was no doubt that those other deaths had been murders. This time the savagery, the desperate cowardice behind the whole thing was partially unveiled.

At the time of Julie's death there had been enough doubt as to the manner of her death, enough prestige belonging to the Hatterick name, to induce what the newspapers later called a kid-glove handling of the situation.

There was no more of that.

The witnesses were separated immediately, questioned alone and without a chance to make their stories agree.

Lieutenant Angel himself questioned Rue mainly, although Miller and even Funk, as well as several detectives whose faces were known to her, questioned too. Their questions were as always designedly, doggedly repetitious. But gradually, out of them all, two or three questions began to take on more and more significance through constant rewording, constant repetition.

"You were alone in the house?"

"Yes. Except for Gross and —"

"Yes, we know. Yet you saw the light turned out in the studio?"

"But no one was in the studio?"

"Only — Rachel. I saw no one else. But the manuscript fell off the piano. A door or window must have opened — closed — I don't know."

"There was a strong enough current of air to blow that paper off the piano. Yet you don't know whether a door or window was open?"

"No. The curtains had been pulled."

"Do you expect us to believe the murderer actually left that room and you didn't see or hear anybody leave?"

"I don't know. I'm only telling what I saw."

Perhaps they would leave it at that, ask other questions (When had she last seen Rachel? Exactly what had Rachel told her about the streaks of green on her hands? How long had she been alone in the house?), then slyly, unexpectedly, someone would return to it: "You say you saw a light in the studio?"

Rue asked for Guy Cole, but he was not brought. Probably the others asked for him, too, and without success.

Police were all over the house. By midnight, and after hours of inquiry, there emerged certain salient facts.

Rachel had been stabbed and had been stabbed so efficiently that she had died almost at once, if not instantly. Her hat, gloves and pocketbook were in her room, in the servants' wing at the end of the fourth floor, tossed as if hurriedly across the bed. The police deduced, after suitable inquiry of Gross and the other maid and the cook, that Rachel had taken her hours out, returned, gone straight to her room and after hurriedly removing hat and gloves and tossing down her pocketbook, had gone downstairs immediately to the library. Thus, because she was not in her uniform and had no duties in the library, she had gone there to meet someone.

And her hands were stained with those unpleasant, troublesome streaks of green.

Rue told them all she knew about that. The servants knew it too; they were terrified, superstitious. But Rachel herself hadn't known — or had claimed she hadn't known — where the stain came from or how it got on her hands.

"I warned her," said Gross, quavering and eyes as blank as walls of concrete. "I warned her. It was a sign —"

"What had she gone to her room to get? Do you know?"

And Gross did know.

"The charts," he said. "It must have been the charts. I always thought she had removed them herself. The charts for the first Mrs Hatterick . . . when she died . . ."

It was after that, probably, that they questioned Rue again, after letting her rest an hour. She was by that time in her bedroom — Crystal's bedroom — again. Someone had hustled her there and made her stay, with a detective sitting on a chair near the door — drawing a paper bag from his pocket as time went on and eating peanuts methodically. Every time they came to question Rue he would put away his peanuts, listen thoughtfully, sigh when they went away and start eating again.

Rue huddled in the chaise longue; what was going on in the rest of the house? Steven and Madge and Alicia had returned long ago. Once when the door opened she heard Andy's voice in the hall, speaking to one of the police, apparently, saying: "Why can't I see her?"

"Orders."

"All right then, what about the lawyer?"

The door closed on the words. But Guy did not come.

As to the charts, Rue only knew that she had questioned Rachel about the charts, that she'd thought in spite of Rachel's denials that the girl knew something of them.

"Why would she take them from the room?"

"I don't know."

"Gross says she was crying this afternoon. Why?"

"I don't know," said Rue. And suddenly remembered the girl's interview with Brule in his little study. The girl — she'd been sure it was Rachel — sobbing; Brule in a white heat of rage, which he suddenly controlled, so his voice was almost coaxing when he said: "Bring them —

bring them to me at once."

Bring what? The charts? Then Brule knew. And Brule had been furiously angry and trying, which was unusual with Brule, to conceal that anger. Brule — gone all afternoon, returning just after the murder was discovered — with blood around his fingernail.

Even if the rubber glove had broken while he worked, operating, Brule was by nature and habit immaculate and painstaking. He wouldn't normally have walked out of the dressing room after an operation without thoroughly scrubbing and brushing his hands. Yet — if he'd been in a hurry, if the operation had been unexpectedly long!

"So you don't know why she was crying?"

"No," said Rue instantly.

After all, that scene between Rachel and Brule was not evidence. Why tell the police?

But she remembered it. After they'd gone again and the man beside the door had pulled up a footstool. He didn't question her at all; didn't seem, in fact, aware of her presence until she rose once and went to raise the window.

He was beside her instantly.

"Better not make any motions, sister," he said. "Go on back there and take it easy."

"I was only —"

He jerked his head once, suggestively, interrupting her explanation as finally as if he'd spoken, and Rue went back to the chaise longue.

Yet at one o'clock or thereabouts the door

opened, someone outside nodded or spoke, and the man at the door got up, walked out the door, closing it behind him, and didn't come back. At first Rue kept expecting him to return.

After a long time she got up and went cautiously to the door herself and, after listening, opened it. No one stopped her. She opened it wider — and from the shadow near the stairwell a policeman in uniform lounged forward, and she closed the door hastily.

And, lightheaded with weariness, lay without undressing on the bed and pulled a down puff over her. The police cars were still in the street below; there were reporters there too; occasionally as she heard the front door open or close there was a quick fusillade of lights — flashlights from the cameras of the newspaper photographers, which winked rapidly, like tiny flares of lightning, against her own windows.

Brule himself came finally; he knocked and as she answered spoke to someone outside and entered. She sat up, and he came and sat beside her on the bed. He was gray with fatigue; she caught a glimpse of herself in the mirror near by; a white-faced woman with bright, disheveled hair and a pale green silk puff hunched incongruously around the straight black street dress with the white lingerie touches at throat and wrists that she'd put on — how long ago? — to go on her fruitless errand to the hospital.

Brule looked at her, said: "Rue, child . . ." and leaned over to push her hair gently back from her forehead. "I didn't — God knows I never meant to plunge you into anything like this. If I'd known — but how could I!"

"What are they going to do? What have they done? Have they made any arrest?"

They hadn't. Brule explained.

"They've got a police guard all around the place. They've made a minute search. They can't find any knife or instrument that had any bloodstains on it. There are knives in the kitchen — there's a long paper knife in the library that's sharp; but so far they aren't certain. They've got to make an arrest soon."

"Who?"

He looked away from her and said he didn't know. "You see, it's simmered down just now to a question of alibis."

"And I — I was alone —"

"You aren't the only one without an alibi," said Brule quickly. "I was driving home. I could have done it. The door leading from the studio into the back lawn (that goes to the gate in the wall, the tradesmen's entrance) — that door was open, and the gate is always unlatched. Anybody could have escaped that way."

"But Steven and Madge and Alicia —"

"Were not together," said Brule grimly. "Alicia and Madge went into Field's to do some shopping. Steven sat in the car for a while, then told Kendal he was going to the drugstore for something or other and left him. Steven met all three an hour later at one of the Randolph Street doors — but he'd waited, he told them, at the wrong door. Kendal was to pick up Alicia and Madge at the door nearest Wabash; Steven said he'd waited at the Randolph Street door nearest State Street; but nevertheless, though Kendal went around the block a couple or three times, Steven says he didn't see the car. And Alicia and Madge had separated inside Field's; Alicia went to the seventh floor for a fitting; Madge to the fifth for dancing slippers. You see, any of them could have taken a taxi and returned to the house. There'd have been plenty of time. And Guy was in his house next door the whole time," added Brule unexpectedly. "Alone, reading, he says. With access to the back yard and the studio door. And Andy —"

"Andy . . . ?"

"Certainly; why not? Andy was in his office, he says, but the office girl had a headache, and he let her go home early. He was there when I telephoned; the police had him come here. It's pretty evident just whom the police include in their list of suspects," said Brule a trifle wryly. "They waste no time rounding us up."

"And no arrest," said Rue slowly, seeking into Brule's eyes. But if he knew — or feared — more he would not tell her. He said instead with a pretense of briskness: "So you see, it all simmers down to alibis. And since they're pretty certain the same fellow murdered Julie and Rachel (and for the same motive in all likelihood, and that was knowledge of Crystal's death), then the question of alibis for Julie's murder comes into it too. Steven, now, had a perfect alibi for the time of Julie's murder. You gave it to him yourself."

Rue thought of Brule's words the next morning. When the police brought her the curious thing they had found.

But then she suddenly clung to Brule.

"I'm afraid," she said. "I'm afraid of this house. I'm afraid of every — shadow and every sound. I'm afraid when the door opens; I think I'll die during that split second when I see the door's about to open and can't see yet that it's just a policeman. Or someone I know. . . ."

Brule held her for a moment, her cheek pressing against his hard shoulder.

"Someone you know. That's the hellish thing about it," he said in a queer voice.

And then he spoke of the charts. "Rachel had Crystal's charts," he said coolly. "She told me so today. It was a silly thing, her taking them: not intentional on her part. She took some magazines from the room when she cleaned it after Crystal's death and accidentally carried off the charts too. When she discovered them she just put them away somewhere in her room, intending, she said, to destroy them if no one asked for them. And she forgot them. Until police inquiry began; she didn't know what to do then — she was afraid to destroy them and afraid not to. Afraid above all things to admit to the police that she knew anything. She finally came to me and told the truth; I gave her hell; she'd got that damnable green stain on her hands and was terrified. She cried and went to get the charts. Then I had to go to the hospital. Now the charts are gone from her room. Rue, I — didn't tell the police I knew she had them; it would have made no difference, and I — I've got to be free for a few days."

She felt herself stiffening a little in his arms. But she didn't question. And didn't say, I knew; but I didn't tell them either.

He rose.

"Go to bed," he said brusquely. "Tomorrow's another day."

And it was the next day that the police found the thing that destroyed Steven's alibi.

Angel himself brought it to Rue.

She was up and dressed and had had breakfast, brought to her by Gross, who looked like an old man and spilled the coffee, if Rue had known it, for the first time in twenty-one years.

"Police are still in the house," he mumbled, leaving. "Oh, madam — madam — to think of it . . ."

Angel came shortly afterward. They had found, hidden in the garden, a broken Victrola record, and he put together the pieces so Rue could see the red center with the title on it in gilt.

"Arabesque at Night," played by the composer, Steven Hendrie.

Angel questioned her.

"The day Julie Garder died, according to your testimony, Hendrie was at his piano in his studio?"

"Yes."

"Do you know the name of the piece he was playing?"

"Yes —" Words died in her throat, and she pointed to the broken pieces.

"Are you sure he was playing the piano? Might it have been only his Victrola? Could you tell the difference at this distance?"

"I don't know . . ."

"He could have been away from the room as long as five minutes; it's a large record. And still you would have heard the sound of 'Arab—' whatever this piece is called. Isn't that right?"

"Y-yes. Except —"

Except Steven wouldn't have done it. Not Steven.

"These broken pieces were hidden purposely. And there would be only two purposes. One would be an effort to hide the fact that such a record existed. And there's only one reason to wish to hide such a fact from the police." He looked at her out of ice-blue eyes and said: "I may as well tell you the truth, Mrs Hatterick. If we hadn't found this broken record you would have been arrested this morning."

CHAPTER XVII

It left her feeling a little numb; it was something she had so long expected that when it came there was little sense of realization.

"What does Steven say?" she asked.

Angel answered directly and, Rue thought, honestly.

"He says the record's been broken for some time. Says it was in the book of records and he'd forgotten it was broken. Then the question of his alibi came up, and he remembered the broken record and realized that we might find it and believe it had been intentionally broken; it would (instead of proving that, if you heard the piece being played, Hendrie himself was playing it) tend to cast doubt upon it. It would look too pat, in other words, as if he wanted such a proof. So he took it out in the garden and hid it. He confessed to that quite freely," said Angel with a thoughtful look. "Sounded true. Yet — yet suppose the record wasn't actually broken; suppose — look here, Mrs Hatterick, didn't you say that he had been playing that particular piece for quite a long time that day?"

"I — don't remember. I've been questioned so much about it. Perhaps I did say so. At any rate, as I remember it, he did play that particular piece quite a lot that day. But it's nothing unusual. It's one of his favorites."

"I looked at his phonograph. It's a radio attachment; and it's got one of those automatic things on it, so it can play several records without anybody having to change or turn it on and off. Thus for at least twenty minutes or so there could be continued sound of music — piano records — and actually no one near the phonograph. There would have been plenty of time for him to leave the studio, see the girl Julie Garder, induce her to take a drink of something with the poison in it and return to the studio, and no one would be the wiser."

"But Steven — why would he murder Julie?"

"He's engaged to Miss Pelham," said Angel obliquely. "There's another thing, Mrs Hatterick. The bartender who claims that Julie Garder came into his place and had a drink —"

"Yes."

"We've arrested him. He turned out to be a fellow that's wanted for theft. It's the reason why he tried to evade the whole thing: he didn't want any attention from us at all. It was only a chance remark of his to the bus boy that led to our questioning him; he would never have come forward himself. The last thing he's inclined to do is be of any help to us. So far he's not managed to remember who came into the restaurant with the girl. But I think he will remember — soon. We have ways of sharpening memory," said Angel simply.

"He — he said she was alone."

"Would she have ordered a cocktail, poured it into a potted palm and ordered another, if she'd been alone? No, the way we figure is she went there with somebody who insisted on her having a drink. She said all right, just to be agreeable; you — and the nurses who knew her — insist she never drank. Well, then she watched her chance and poured the cocktail into the plant at her elbow. The second cocktail she drank; perhaps her companion actually went to the bar to get it and put poison in it on the way to the table. We've ascertained that there was no waiter at that hour; it's a small place. So far the bartender has admitted nothing of the kind, but it sounds reasonable. Well, her companion could have been Steven Hendrie. That restaurant is exactly two minutes from here by taxi. You wouldn't have noticed a lapse in the sound of the piano."

That wasn't all the detective had to say.

"Then there are the letters," he went on. "Whoever wrote those letters knew something. You've been asked about those letters; we've made every possible inquiry. We may right now be on the right trail; Funk thinks he's getting warm. But I — I want to impress upon you, Mrs Hatterick, the importance of those letters. If you are innocent . . ." He looked at her in silence for a moment. "If you are innocent I can't put too strongly the importance that the discovery of the authorship of those letters might be to you. Do you understand?"

"But I don't know who wrote them. I know nothing of them," said Rue hopelessly.

He looked at her searchingly, then went to the door. "Tell Funk to come in here," he said to someone outside.

And when the little Funk slipped — sideways, scared-looking, none too clean — into the room, Angel said: "Show her the chart."

"Chart!" cried Rue.

"It was in the maid's room, crumpled up in the wastebasket as if she'd torn it off. God knows why. Perhaps she recognized its importance and tried, thus, to preserve it; perhaps she tossed it there merely because it was crumpled. We'll never know."

Funk said: "It's all right to take it in your fingers, Mrs Hatterick. It's already been gone over for fingerprints."

She took the sheet of paper; it was the usual printed form with a few entries in Julie's small, round handwriting. It was probably the last sheet on the pad. The date was November ninth, the exact date of Crystal's death.

"You recognize it?" said Angel. Rue nodded.

"Read the entries."

She was already reading; searching for the thing that chart must disclose.

Angel watched her, and Funk watched — retreated now after his moment of importance to a position slightly behind Angel from which he could peer at Rue.

But there was nothing of any significance at all on the chart. It was all regular, nothing unusual. Meals as usual, two visits from Andy duly noted, one at eleven in the morning and another about six in the evening, temperature slightly below normal, pulse perfectly normal, no special orders. Perhaps that was it.

"Find something, Mrs Hatterick?"

"N-no," said Rue slowly, "unless it's an omission. She, Mrs Hatterick, said that her medicine tasted different; as I remember it she said (I've told you) that Andy — Doctor Crittenden that is — had changed her medicine that day, although she may have said 'he must have' changed it. She may have been referring only to the taste. Without certain knowledge, I mean. She must have been, because if there'd been a change in the medicine Julie would have made a note of it. Julie was extremely conscientious. She wouldn't have omitted to note a change in medicine or orders. And there is no change noted here."

After a moment Angel said: "Is that all?"

She knew he was disappointed. As she was herself; the charts had loomed so large in the thing; unconsciously she had pinned hope to their discovery. And for that day — that tremendously important day — there was nothing.

"Where are the others?" she said.

Angel's long face lengthened further.

"Whoever killed the girl, Rachel, undoubtedly has destroyed them by now," he said. "Do you have any idea, Mrs Hatterick, why Rachel tore out that one sheet and threw it away?"

But Rue had none.

"She may not have known its importance," she hazarded. "It may have been accidentally torn or crumpled."

He looked dissatisfied. And began again: "Last night at the time she was murdered, you say you actually saw a light in the studio. . . ."

It went on until noon.

But during the afternoon, without any explanation, the vigilance of the police appeared to be to some degree relaxed. Rue ventured out of her room, and no one stopped her. She met Madge in the hall. A pale, frightened Madge, with the sullenness gone from her small square face. She paused uncertainly.

"Rue . . ."

"Yes, Madge?"

"Rue . . ." She hesitated again, Rue had an instant's impression of mute appeal for help. And then someone spoke in the library, and Alicia's voice replied, and the fleeting impression was gone.

"Nothing," said Madge and went on.

Rue took a quick step or two after her. "Madge," she said. "Do you — is there something you want?"

The girl whirled around to face her; again Rue had that quick impression of an appeal; then Madge's dark eyes became determined and hard again, and she said: "Nothing." But added:

"Thank you, Rue."

Puzzled, Rue watched her go toward the stairway. It was almost an overture for peace; yet the instant she'd spoken the child had frozen again. Or was it the sound of Alicia's voice that had done it?

Alicia was in the library; Guy was there, too, and was just leaving, he told Rue. Guy was hurried, avoiding her eyes, jumbling instructions together. Clearly Guy felt that they were imposing upon his powers of legal defense.

"Rachel murdered," he said complainingly. "Good God, what next! Well, I'll run along now."

After he'd gone Alicia went coolly to the library door, looked briefly into the hall and closed the door. She turned to Rue then, deliberately and purposefully.

"I'm glad you've come down," she said, looking straight into Rue's eyes with her own bright, jewellike gaze. "I want to talk to you. I think we'd better have a clear understanding. You and I."

She gave Rue no chance to reply. She walked directly toward her, so close that the faint scent of gardenias drifted to Rue, and she could see the quick pulse beating in Alicia's creamy, soft throat — only faintly lined. She said:

"There's something you ought to know. However this thing turns out, Brule loves me and I love him, and it will take more than you to come between us. Do you understand that?"

Rue looked back at her, noting that strongly beating pulse with a kind of detached interest. How it betrayed Alicia's real feelings when Alicia's voice was quite cool and controlled!

"What about Steven?" said Rue with honest curiosity.

The jet-black line of Alicia's beautiful eyelids flickered.

"Steven?" she said. "Steven isn't important. He's been only a pretext, a — blind, if you want to call it that. So Crystal wouldn't guess the truth. It was easy for me to make him love me, and I did; I'm telling you so you can see how important Brule is to me. I wish I could make you see that I am equally important to Brule. But you're in love with Brule; you are trying to deceive yourself; you don't want to acknowledge the truth." She paused, her eyes shining and secret with some deep preoccupation. In a moment she went on with an air of friendly frankness, only belied by that throbbing pulse in her throat.

"There's no use in my trying to tell you that it is, really, a friendly impulse that led me to speak to you. You wouldn't believe me."

"No," said Rue candidly.

"But nevertheless . . . Rue, can't you see for yourself that Brule loves me? That he'll never love you? That there's no use in your trying to hold him because he married you as he did? He regretted it instantly. Ask him if you don't believe me. Ask him to tell you the truth. And he

260

— I can prove to you how much he loves me."

"What do you want me to do?" said Rue, again with that strangely honest curiosity.

Alicia's lovely hands made an impatient movement. She said:

"What do you think? I want to be sure that, when this is over, you'll leave Brule. You'll consent to a divorce — or ask for it, rather; it will make it easier and better all around if you'll ask for a divorce."

She's getting close to the kernel of her motive, thought Rue. She said:

"Why are you saying all this to me now? When things are as they are here?"

Alicia hesitated. She turned suddenly and went to the door and listened and came back to Rue and told her, deliberately as if she'd planned it, yet with a queer kind of anxiety, too.

"Because there's something I know that, if the police knew, would cause your arrest. But it's something I can keep them from discovering."

"What?"

"Will you —"

"Will I bargain with you? Promise to divorce Brule for your silence? How childish you are, Alicia!"

"Childish!" Alicia's eyes widened like a cat's.

"Alicia — tell me something else. Why did you think Crystal was murdered?"

She could hear Alicia's quick breathing; she could see the heavy throb of that pulse along her white throat. Alicia whispered suddenly, a little breathlessly:

"Because Brule did it. For me. I've always been certain of it. Do you understand now?"

The scene all at once stopped being tawdry and theatrical. It took on in an instant the poignant terror of a nightmare. Rue forced herself to look away from Alicia's small, beautiful face with its blazing eyes and lovely red mouth. She forced herself to shrug and walk across the room. This is not real, she told herself; it isn't happening. Things like this — and remembered Rachel flung across the bench. Remembered the patch of red upon the sheet of manuscript. Things like that didn't happen either — and yet had happened. She said in a tight, strained voice:

"You can't expect me to believe that. Brule —"

"Who had a better chance?" said Alicia. "Who knew how so well as Brule? That's the real reason we didn't marry. He asked me to marry him after Crystal died. But I knew — If you want to know the truth, I was afraid. I was afraid the truth would come out sometime, and I — I would be caught in it too."

Oddly enough Rue believed that much. If Alicia had known or suspected that Brule murdered Crystal, she would have been afraid. Not for Brule; not because of the act itself; but for her own lovely white neck. Alicia loved herself; and as such people do, lived in a world of Alicia, hedged, guarded, marked by Alicia so other people and other suffering and other tragedy did not impinge upon Alicia herself. But murder — once discovered — would impinge. Would thrust through her hard wrappings of selfishness.

"Well?" said Alicia impatiently, as always curiously myopic when it came to detecting the reactions of other people.

"What is it that you say you know that could possibly cause my arrest?"

"Evidence," said Alicia. "Evidence they will have to accept as conclusive. And it isn't a question of my telling them. It's a question of" — her eyes flickered once — "of their finding it. I can prevent it. I will prevent it if — if you'll promise — what I ask."

How still it was in the library! With Crystal watching them and the mocking little smile on her painted lips. Rue took a long breath.

"I'll promise you nothing," she said. "You are — you are mad to suggest such a bargain, Alicia."

But as Alicia accepted it instantly and turned and went out of the room, Rue wondered if she hadn't been mad to refuse. She tried to shrug away the memory of the parting look in Alicia's eyes and failed.

As she tried to conquer the conviction of truth in what Alicia had said of Brule and of Steven. "Brule loves me," Alicia had said. And she'd also said, "Brule murdered Crystal." Once Alicia had accused Rue openly of having murdered Crystal; was that to shield Brule — and thus herself?

The trouble was Brule could have murdered Crystal.

It was after that fateful interview with Alicia that Rue saw Andy. And the memory of Alicia's words was stronger than even the thing she found hidden so carefully, with such diabolic simplicity and shrewdness, in her room. Although it was that that, actually, terrified her and reduced any lingering sense of unreality to sharp and poignant reality.

For it was a knife; a sharp, surgical knife, wiped free of fingerprints, rolled neatly in a red-and-white scarf belonging to Rue and tucked down into the cushions of the chaise longue in her room.

The room hadn't yet been searched by the police. If they had searched it, it would have been the first thing they found. Rue, returning to her room after seeing Alicia, going absently to the chaise longue, happened to lean back upon her hand so her fingers came in contact with the little roll.

She pulled it out and looked with utter, chill horror at the thing disclosed. The deliberate malevolence of it shook her as nothing else would have done.

"Conclusive evidence," Alicia had said.

It was then that Andy came. Came and asked to see her, and (this time) was permitted to do so. She put on a suede jacket with deep pockets and hid the knife in a pocket. Andy, familiar with the house, was waiting for her in Brule's little study on the second floor.

He, too, closed the door before he spoke.

"Rue, have you seen the chart for the day of Crystal's death?" he asked at once.

"Yes."

He didn't ask what entries there were. His face was white and strained, his eyes brilliant, and he was nervous, watching the door.

"Rue, you are not safe in this house. You can't stay here. I won't let you stay. Not another night."

"I can't leave."

"Yes, you can. I'll fix things. Listen, there's a woman, a dear old lady who's a patient of mine. She's — fond of me. She'll take you in and take care of you. It'll be safe there. . . . I'll fix it so we can get away without anyone knowing it; the police will stop us if they know. But once you are safe we can phone and tell them where you are. They can put a guard in her house for you; anything. But they can't compel you to stay in this house. It" — his voice broke a little — "it isn't safe here. Don't you understand that?"

Understand it? She understood too well.

He caught assent in her silence.

"Rue — will you come?"

She closed her eyes. The knife was like a weight in her pocket.

"Yes," she said. "Tell me how — and where."

CHAPTER XVIII

Andy knew exactly where and how. It was simple, he said.

"If it works," said Rue after listening.

"It will work," said Andy. "Listen, I'll repeat it. . . ."

"If they think I'm trying to escape," said Rue, feeling as if she were talking of someone else, "they'll arrest me. I mean, it — seems to prove guilt."

"Not at all. You'll be no worse off than you are now if they do stop you. But they aren't going to discover you've gone until you are safely there and telephone to them. They can't accuse you of attempting an escape if you tell them exactly where you are and your reasons for going. You can't be compelled to stay in this house."

Andy didn't know the most important reason. She put her hand in her pocket. He was watching her anxiously, yet listening, too, for the muffled murmur of voices in the dining room.

She said in a small voice: "Look, Andy," and showed him the knife.

"*Rue!* What —"

She told him; briefly.

"That settles it," said Andy. "Now you've got to go. . . . What a devil that woman is!"

"Alicia?"

"She hates you, Rue. But I didn't think she'd go so far as this. Well, give me the knife; I'll get rid of it somewhere. And I'll go right now and telephone to Mrs Brown. Don't bring any clothes; a bag would attract attention, and you'd never shake the police. You can have them send over anything you want after you're safely at her house."

He took her hands, held them briefly, said: "Don't fail me. I love you so, Rue. I can't let you stay here another night."

But after he'd gone his plan didn't sound so easy as when he told her of it. Yet escape from that house was just then for her the only sensible course. It was too dangerous to remain — where traps lay waiting for her. Traps like that knife.

And if she told the police, what would they do? As they had done about the powder in the glass in her room; which was, so far as Rue could see, exactly nothing.

She looked at the scarf she still held in her hand. It was like Alicia to select a scarf Rue had worn often enough for it to be promptly identified. And a knife that could have been the knife whose short wicked thrust had ended Rachel's life. And stopped her lips forever: so they could not reveal who had waited for her in the library, who had sent her for the charts, who, after that murderous, efficient thrust, had taken the charts (not knowing, yet, that the important chart was missing) and gone away so quietly that only a small current of air betrayed the passing.

It could have been that knife, keen because it was a surgical instrument, short, sharp — efficient as the murderous thrust had been efficient. Whether it was actually the knife the murderer had used, or a knife Alicia had discovered and selected, with that devilish simplicity, because it suited her purpose — in either case it ought to be given to the police.

And she didn't dare do that.

At any rate it was out of her possession now. But the sheer malevolence of the attempt chilled her. Well, Andy had offered her a refuge from more of such threats. She started upstairs, paused irresolutely to give the room, with its books, its smoldering coal fire, its deep, comfortable chairs, a look that lingered like a farewell. She might have been happy in that room. How happy she didn't dare permit herself to discover even in her too ready imagination.

Instinct told her that in all probability she would never return to the room and that house to live. When she left it now, it was almost certainly forever.

Alicia had won. Or was it that there had never been a contest; Alicia simply remained in the place she had always had.

There was no need to see Brule before she went away; it would be better not to see him. She looked at her watch; four o'clock. It was growing dark, and the rain that had threatened all that day was drawing nearer. There is nothing, she thought, looking out into the back lawn where soon she must venture, nothing so dreary, nothing so desolate as a cold November rain, with the sky black with smoke and fog.

No, she wouldn't see Brule again.

Besides every other reason there was one of concealment. Somehow, some way, uncannily, he would read in her eyes if in no other way her plan to leave his house.

Fifteen minutes more and she would get under way the little train of things Andy had told her to do. It was beginning to rain. A rain that would further his fatally simple plan. If it had been more difficult she would have refused.

She put one hand on the curtain beside her and leaned her face against the glass of the window to peer down into the rectangle of brown, wet lawn, hedged by the wall. She could barely see the door of the small conservatory, built onto Guy Cole's house and opening upon that same scrap of lawn.

She wondered when and under what circumstances she would see Brule again; whatever it was, it wouldn't be as his wife.

She thought rather dispassionately, now, of Alicia. Her acceptance of Alicia's story had nothing to do with Alicia's integrity or lack of it. Alicia would lie if it suited her purpose; Rue knew that. It was the truth that had convinced Rue. It stood out like peaks, recognizable, clear and sharp. Something that couldn't be avoided.

Yet, out of the rain, out of the silence of the room, a small, strange thought came and laid its hand on her heart. If Brule had made one small gesture of love — a word, even, or a look — the truth in what Alicia had said wouldn't have mattered. Would have lost its power. Would have been blunted on the shield that Rue would have possessed.

But Brule hadn't.

Then why are you waiting? she asked herself sharply. It's no good lingering here, hoping, waiting — wanting to see him again, when you know it's best not to.

She took a long breath and turned and went to the door. And at that moment the dining-room door opened, a wave of voices and motion came from it, and Lieutenant Angel, Brule, the little Funk and one or two other detectives came into the hall.

Brule saw her and came toward her.

"They want to talk to you again," he said.

Something intangible yet well marked, too, in their attitude, in their directness, perhaps, and in Brule's intent face, hinted that there was news. And there was.

They began first — Angel and one of the detectives (and, a little timidly, Funk, who peered out now and then from the shadow of Angel's shoulder) — to ask her again about the letters. Did she know anything at all of them?

"But I've told you I don't. So many times —"

"Yet, Mrs Hatterick, all those letters, according to the dates on the postmarks were written within the two months' time of your marriage.

None before that marriage took place. Doesn't that suggest anything to you? Or anyone?"

It suggested Alicia, but Alicia would have been afraid to write the letters and thus call attention to herself — the woman Brule had been in love with and the woman who, though Rue had forgotten it for a little, was actually one of Crystal's legatees.

So Alicia wouldn't have written those letters.

"No," said Rue.

Angel gave her a sad look and cleared his throat.

"There's no one — who might have had jealousy as a motive?" he inquired.

"Jealousy?" said Rue, still thinking of Alicia.

"I mean of you — on account of your marriage."

"A disappointed suitor," said Funk, popping out from the shadow to make things clear.

"Oh. No. No one."

"Rue —" began Brule, but Angel went on rather quickly as if not to give Brule a chance to tell Rue whatever it was that he wanted to tell her.

"You see," said Angel, "whoever wrote those letters — or at least whoever wrote seven of them — had access to the Town Club. Your husband is a member. And Doctor Crittenden is a member."

"But —"

This time Brule wouldn't be cut off.

"It's this way, Rue," he said swiftly. "The letters were typewritten, and the police have been searching for the typewriter on which they were written. I gather it's taken a lot of time and persistence, for they've even taken samples from the typewriters in Madge's school. However —"

"By great good luck," said Funk.

"This Mr — er — Funk was sent to the Town Club on another errand —"

"Investigating cloakroom thefts," said Funk.

"And while there discovered I was a member, and Andy, too, and got samples of the typing from the typewriters in the writing room. One of them corresponded to the typing of these letters."

"Exactly," said Funk with a note of dreamy satisfaction.

"But unfortunately," said Brule, "it rather limits the possibilities. I mean, visitors are seldom in the writing rooms — at least ladies never are. I didn't write the letters."

"We never said you did, Doctor Hatterick," said Angel.

"Andy wouldn't have written them for exactly the same reasons. Either of us stood to lose more, or at least as much, as anyone else."

"Does this fact suggest anything to you, Mrs Hatterick?" asked Angel.

It didn't. Twenty minutes later, with rain now slanting against the windows and the consciousness of a darkening gray sky and of Andy, perhaps, waiting, she still had no further replies to make to their repeated questions.

Brule came back to her after the others left.

"They've gone," he said, coming back into the library. "I watched Angel leave."

She paused, conscious of the things she ought to be doing. The interview with the police had made her late. It was important to Andy's plan for her to leave before it was dark.

Besides, face to face with him, she realized that there was after all, nothing she could say. Nothing that wouldn't seem reproachful; nothing that wouldn't appear to make demands she had no right to make.

She couldn't, even, tell him she was leaving.

"What's the matter?" said Brule. "You're worried about something."

She crumpled the red-and-white scarf in her hand and said a little crisply: "That's rather in the category of an understatement, isn't it, Brule?"

And just then Steven's studio door banged, and Steven himself came into the library.

He was disheveled and excited. He said, "There you are," glanced up and down the hall and closed the door after him.

"Look here," he said. "I — I'm in a spot. I — don't know why or — but I don't know what to do —"

"What's wrong with you, Steven? You look sick. What —"

"I am sick," said Steven and sat down in a chair and put his face in his hands and groaned.

There was a sharp instant of silence. Rue always thought that Brule guessed what was coming, for he put down his cigarette and went quickly to Steven and put his hand urgently, yet with the gentleness that had always characterized his treatment of Steven, on Steven's bent shoulder.

"Tell me, Steve," he said. "Is it the police?"

"It's the letters," said Steven. He dropped his hands and looked up. And said wretchedly: "I wrote them."

"Steven!" cried Rue in a smothered little gasp and stopped.

Brule didn't say anything for a moment. And Steven cried:

"And I think they're onto it. I wrote some of them at the Town Club. Times I'd be there waiting to lunch with you, I used a typewriter. Brule — what shall I do?"

Brule took a long breath then. He kept his hand on Steven's shoulder and said quietly:

"Why did you write them, Steve?"

"I — Brule, I was out of my head. I — I don't know why I did it. If I'd thought — if I'd had the sense to see what would be the result of it all . . . But I didn't. I only knew that I — I had got to know the truth."

Again there was a moment of silence while Brule looked at Steven and Steven at Brule. Brule said:

"You mean Alicia?"

Steven nodded.

"I thought you might have done it, Steve. Well

274

— you know, now?"

Steven said after a moment, speaking more quietly: "Look here, Brule. I've done you — and Rue — an irreparable injury. I know that now. But then, you see — I'd better tell you the truth."

"I think I understand," said Brule slowly.

"I'd better say it, though. Rue — ought to know." He turned to her, his eyes excited but pleading. "Rue, you see, after Crystal's death — well, it was only after that that I began to wonder if Alicia really loved me. If I hadn't been, in a way, a kind of cat's-paw for her. She — was so different after Crystal died. Well — little by little you see, I began to perceive that she was in love with Brule. That she had been in love with him for a long time; little things I hadn't noticed at the time began to — to take on color and significance. Then one day, here in this house, I heard her talking to Brule. She said —" He stopped and then went on, his manner grown simple and direct. "She said, Rue, that Crystal had been murdered and that she was afraid to marry Brule because sometime that — murder — would come out. And then where would she be? she said. I — there was more, but that was enough. It — opened my eyes, you see. And I — while it wasn't the shock it might have been, still it was a — a kind of shock. It — well, I didn't do anything about it; perhaps I was afraid to. But I kept thinking about it and wondering and trying to find a clear way out of it. And

275

Brule had married you, Rue, and Alicia seemed to want things to go on with me just as before. She kept putting off marriage, yet keeping me —"

He pushed aside Brule's steadying hand and got up and began to walk about the room, jerkily, stopping now and then to look anxiously at Rue and at Brule, as if there were something he had to convince them about.

Again the thought of time nudged at Rue. But she had to hear what Steven was saying. She had to know what Brule would say, after he'd listened.

Steven went on:

"That was the hellish thing about it. I mean, if she'd said she wanted our engagement to end, that she never intended to marry me — I could have taken that all right. Oh, I know you're both thinking, Why didn't he have it out with her, tell her he knew, tell her — Brule would have done it, but I — I couldn't. You see," said Steven, pausing in that restless walk to give them each that desperately troubled look, anxious of their belief in his words. "You see," said Steven simply, "I love her. I — that's the whole trouble, you see. I love her."

Brule's voice was still quiet.

"Had you — any definite evidence that Crystal was murdered?" he asked.

It brought Steven up short. He pushed his hands through his hair, stared at Brule and said: "Good God, no."

276

"Then why —"

"Why did I write the letters to the police? Why, to bring things to a head, of course. To clear it all up. To" — his hands groped into the air — "to bring it all out in the open so we could see where we stood."

Brule said a little grimly: "Well, if that was your intention, you succeeded." Steven just looked at him blankly and helplessly, and Brule said, more gently again:

"You mean you thought this would be a good way to" — rather helplessly in his turn he used Steven's word — "clear things up?" He stopped there, as if credulity had strained too far and Steven said eagerly:

"Yes! Yes, I did! I — when it occurred to me it seemed such a — a practical way to go about it —"

This was too much even for Brule, who said: "Practical? Good God!"

"Oh, I see now it wasn't! I mean, I didn't realize what it meant! I thought the police might just — oh, inquire a bit, stir things up. I couldn't go on any longer as it was, and I —" He stopped and again shoved his hands through his hair and said with a touch of tragedy: "But I didn't know it would be like this."

"No, I suppose you didn't," said Brule gravely. "Well, it's done now, Steve. Forget it."

"Forget it?"

"Certainly. Let the police go on worrying about it. That's their trouble."

"But, Brule, you don't seem to understand. I'm a murderer."

"You —" Brule strode to where Steven stood and caught him swiftly and savagely by the arm. "What do you mean, Steve? You can't mean —"

"I mean I've caused two murders. Two. If I hadn't written the letters," said Steven with the simple reasonableness of a child, "neither of those murders would have occurred. So I'm going to tell the police. All about it. The whole truth —"

"About Alicia — too?"

Steven hesitated, his troubled, dark eyes seeking Brule's.

"Alicia . . . But it's the truth, Brule. Alicia and you . . ."

There was another moment of silence. Then Brule said heavily:

"Oh yes, it's the truth all right. About — Alicia, I mean. And me."

CHAPTER XIX

The truth.

Well, she'd already known it. She hadn't needed confirmation. And Andy would be waiting, and she must leave that house — forever, it would be — before night. Before it was too dark to insure the success of Andy's plan.

Steven had moved. He had taken a step nearer Brule and put his hand, now, on Brule's shoulder. It was the last thing she would have expected Steven to do, yet it was like him, too.

For his hand was obviously a comforting one. He said, "Brule, I understand. Don't worry. I — I'm all right about it now. I've come through the worst of it — the jealousy and all that. It's all clear now. I — I've learned that you have to accept things. Alicia loves you. It's just one of those things; one of us had to lose. And — all those months when I didn't know — well, I understand that now, too. You've always been so good to me, Brule; you were always so strong and I was weak, and you — you understood everything. How could you have come to me and told me the truth when you knew how I loved her?"

Rue said brusquely: "I'm — going upstairs —"

"Wait, Rue," said Brule. "I want you to hear —"

"I've heard enough." She was at the door. The studio was empty, the side door unguarded.

But Brule caught her almost angrily by the wrist and whirled her back into the room.

"You will listen," he said. "You owe me that much. You've asked for the truth and you're going to get all of it."

She wrenched her wrist from his grasp.

"I've had the truth," she said and looked at him. His face wore its mask, but his eyes were dark and bright with anger. "I'm going," she said and caught herself on the verge of saying, ". . . away from your house. I'll never return. I'll make things easy for you. You can have your divorce. You can marry Alicia —" She didn't say any of it. She glanced at Steven, standing there so the light fell clearly upon his slender, haggard face, with its sensitive mouth, its high forehead, its look of introspection and the faint, intangible stamp of weakness.

It was only in his music that he had command; life itself and the emotions and problems engendered simply by living were too much for him. Yet was it that he comprehended too much rather than too little?

He said suddenly: "Rue, will you forgive me? It seemed the only way then. I — didn't know what I was letting you in for — I didn't know what I was doing." He said it simply. That probably was true too. He honestly, really didn't know what he was doing when he wrote the letters. And started the whole horrible train of events. As a pebble rolled out of place by the unthinking hands of a child may start a whole slide. But the slide has to be there, waiting, accumulated for some immediate, small release.

She put out her hand to him. It was a gesture of farewell, but neither of the men knew it. He took it in his own.

She said: "I know, Steven." And had gone from the room and was halfway up the stairs before the little phrase proved its familiarity. It was what he had said to her. "I know, Rue."

Meaning, I understand.

Poor Steven. But she wouldn't think of Brule. Not now. There were things to do.

No one was in the upper hall.

Her decision to leave was made. It was the sensible, indeed the only course to take. She told herself that, selecting and quietly donning a dark tweed coat. She pulled on a small brown hat and over it all her bright green rain cape with its concealing hood. Remember fare for the elevated, she told herself; there was a little change in the pocket of her coat; that was all right, then. Hat, coat, thin green rain cape with its hood; money for el fare and — oh yes, gloves.

All ready now. She must hurry; already the windows in the bedroom beyond were long gray rectangles and the shadows increasing in the room itself.

She didn't stop for a farewell look, but the room watched her leave — the room and the swan bed and the great gilded screen. The room where Crystal died and where Julie died and where the scent of roses was cloyingly sweet.

She was done with that room forever.

At the foot of the stairs the mail, just delivered, lay on a table, and her own name on a letter caught her glance. She took the letter, thrust it, too, in her pocket and went on without looking closely at it.

So far it had been easy; no one had looked at her, no one had stopped her. Perhaps it wouldn't be difficult.

She didn't know, and there was no way for her to know, then, of a conversation that was, perhaps, going on at that very moment. In a brightly lighted, official-looking room at police headquarters, over a table which was bare except for a stack of reports and a small brown bag.

"I'm going to make the arrest. She gave the woman poison in medicine likely; she gave it to the Garder girl in the tea. There's drugs enough in this bag —"

"You haven't questioned her about it; you've had it since —"

"Since you found it in the cupboard. I know. I didn't need to question her about it; I already knew it belonged to her; I know what's in it. Now the case is pretty complete, and I'm ready to make the arrest. I think it'll stick, and she'll break down when she sees this bag and knows we've had it all along. She'll confess."

Silence. Then, slowly:

"You may be right, Lieutenant. I'd feel better

if the bartender would talk."

"We'll make him talk."

Silence again. Then Angel's voice sharp with impatience:

"What's the matter? You're still not satisfied, Funk?"

"No, I'm not."

"You still think the bag of nurses' supplies and drugs indicates her innocence?"

"Well, Lieutenant, I still feel if she'd taken poison from that bag she'd have got rid of the bag damn quick. Or at least the medicines in it. I still feel she'd have had the sense to get rid of such evidence. . . . Look at the stuff, Lieutenant." Dirty little fingers clawed into the little bag, pawing over small bottles, neatly labeled, little boxes with R_x on them.

Silence again. Then a voice at the door: "Funk, you're wanted at the Town Club. That cloakroom business again. . . ."

By that time, probably, Rue was outside the house, safely through the hall and past the closed library door, and through Steven's studio and out the side door.

Cold air and rain touched her face. Her bright green cape was like a flag. A policeman, in uniform with a heavy caped mackintosh over it, was standing at the back gate. He turned, saw her, and Rue, her heart pounding, walked along the brick walk toward him.

"Is it — all right," she said, "if I walk up and down here?"

"Certainly, Mrs Hatterick," he said at once. His heavy face looked cold and impassive; he watched her stolidly.

She was approaching the difficult part of it; well, she told herself, it would either work or it wouldn't. She'd carry out the bit of acting Andy had suggested.

She walked up and down the strip of lawn, the second turn brought her near the hedge which divided their strip of lawn from Guy's; she hesitated, went through the little opening, and the policeman did not stop her. She went up the walk toward the door of Guy's conservatory, a small glassed room flung out from and adjoining his dining room. She hesitated there, too, perceptibly, as if in indecision, and that was the hardest thing to do because she felt perfectly certain it would give the policeman the time and a chance (if he needed it) to stop her.

But, incredibly, it worked as Andy had said it would work.

Apparently the policeman took it to mean, simply, that she'd had an impulse to enter that house (what would be more natural than to want to see their lawyer?), had paused to think again, and then had entered.

For she did so, and the door to the conservatory was not locked. That had been the second point of danger.

She closed the door behind her and peered through at the policeman. He was watching and had not moved, but she thought there was a kind of stiffness and alertness about that stolid figure. She removed the green cape swiftly and dropped it behind a bench. The air was moist and hot, laden with scent of wet earth and freesias.

Now hurry. Quick.

Hurry — because the policeman had moved. He was following her. No, he was going into the Hatterick house. To set another policeman on her trail? To get help? It didn't matter. She knew what to do.

She also knew the general plan of Guy's house. If anyone questioned her — but no one did. There were only a cook and butler on the premises; Guy was not yet at home from the office. The door leading to the dining room was not locked either. From that point on the coast was ridiculously clear. Through Guy's dining room and through the hall and out the front door, and there was no policeman in sight, and the corner of the house shielded her from her own street.

Into the hurrying groups of pedestrians. With the bright green cape for which, at first, they would look among all those pedestrians, left in the conservatory. Take the first taxi you see — there was one, cruising. She got into it.

Now for the Evanston elevated. She told the driver to go to the nearest el station.

Afterward she remembered that ride, hurrying, dodging other hurrying cars and taxis and trucks and the homeward flow of Loop workers.

She never knew what station he took her to; but they arrived at a lighted corner with the el thundering and clattering overhead, and she paid him and joined the flow of people surging up those long steep flights of stairs. Kept with them, in a line to pay her fare; stood with them, only one of all those milling people, their faces looking oddly white, like the papers they carried folded longitudinally. Struggled with those nearest her to board the first train that clattered, lighted and noisy, out of the night, and jerked to a stop before her and said in bright letters "Evanston and North Shore Local."

Soon she'd be with Andy — safe.

Rain slashed the windows.

It was still raining when she got out at the Anchor Street station (barely within the city limits); still raining steadily and drearily when, descending from the platform, she looked around and found, as Andy had predicted she would find somewhere near, a small, desolate-looking little drugstore. She went in. Sat at a table and ordered hot cocoa, and the shining white table reminded her of that other night, so short a time ago, when she'd sat in the bright din of another drugstore. With Andy.

When would he come?

Time passed and she finished the hot cocoa. Time passed and she heard newspapers hawked on the street outside and her own name, but wouldn't buy one and read it.

Time passed and she didn't once think of the

letter in her pocket.

It was nearly eight o'clock when Andy finally came. Came hurriedly, his coat collar turned up about his face, with barely a word of greeting, taking her swiftly out of the shabby but lighted little drugstore, down the street into the shadow of the stark elevated pillars where his car waited. Only it wasn't his car. It was one Rue had never seen — but it wasn't a new car.

It was old and battered and even in the dim light looked as if it wouldn't run for more than a mile or two. It might have come out of a junk heap.

Andy was holding the door open.

"Get in," he said.

As she did so a curiously irrelevant thought came to her mind. She wondered what Andy had done with the knife she'd given him. It was irrelevant and she dismissed it.

Andy got in the car beside her.

CHAPTER XX

The street stretched emptily ahead of them like a long tunnel, starkly outlined by the el columns which were shadow and substance intermixed, dotted bleakly at intervals with wavering, rain-blurred street lights.

Where there was light the steelwork of the elevated structure made an interlaced regular pattern of shadows. She thought of Steven's music; "Arabesque at Night."

And wondered, with again a curious irrelevancy, when she would see Steven again — if she would ever see Steven again.

She had no idea where she was. Warehouses seemed to line the sides of the tunnel. They turned and turned again, and she was completely at a loss. Even the guiding elevated columns were gone.

Andy said nothing; he was hunched forward peering into the rain ahead, trying to see through the wavering, dim light lane.

She could see only his white, strained-looking profile.

Well, it had all been as simple as he had told her it would be. No one knew she had gone, or if by this time they knew and had found the green cape, still she had completely escaped them. They couldn't possibly find her.

And she could telephone as soon as she was safe.

Safe? She was safe now. With Andy.

"How — far is it?" she asked above the wheezy rattle of the engine.

"H'm?" Andy came out of his abstraction with a jerk, said: "Oh — you mean to Mrs Black's. Not far. We'll go the back way, and come in again on Dempster Road. It's — safer that way." He glanced at her once, smiled briefly as if to reassure her and went back to his anxious scrutiny of the road ahead.

Not far. She drew a long, weary breath. She'd escaped the Hatterick house and the threats it had held for her. The difficult part of it had been accomplished. She settled her chin down into the collar of her coat and felt in her pocket for cigarettes. Perhaps her fingers actually touched the letter that was there.

She had cigarettes but no matches.

And Andy handed her a small advertising folder of matches, and when she had lighted her cigarette she returned the pack of matches to him. There can scarcely be a smaller or a more inconsequential act.

Yet it was in fact the last small link in a chain.

Neither of them spoke. The rain was making it increasingly difficult to see the road, and Andy, after several attempts to make an antiquated windshield wiper function, gave it up and bent forward over the wheel. They were leaving the straggling outskirts of town; she could see nothing of houses except now and then a light flickering off somewhere in the rainy darkness. But apparently they were on one of the west and north highways, for now and then a lighted filling station or a deserted vegetable stand loomed up along the road and was passed.

She said presently, idly, "Did you say Mrs Black? I thought you called her Mrs Brown. . . ."

Andy said abruptly: "Huh? Oh. Oh yes. I meant Mrs Brown. . . . Gosh, it's hard to see." He hesitated at what appeared to be a crossroad, looked along the intersecting expanse of wet black pavement leading into nothingness so far as Rue could see, appeared to decide against it and went on.

Probably they were in the country now; Andy himself seemed a little uncertain.

"Where are we?" said Rue.

"I — don't know exactly. That is, Morton Grove is over there somewhere. And Milwaukee ought to cross this road."

She knew and did not know the vicinity; it was vaguely north and west of Chicago and of the north shore suburbs. But it was a great, half-deserted section with muddy flats and open spaces, and a bewildering lacing of highways crossed and recrossed it.

There were roadhouses; there were filling stations. There were, now and then, small suburbs. But for the most part it was to Rue a blank and uncharted territory, always bewildering and that night, oddly, a little frightening. It was so very dark. And Andy said nothing.

They passed a filling station which was lighted at the roadside, but the building itself was dark. Closed, thought Rue, and it added to the desolation of the spot.

And they'd gone only about a quarter of a mile farther on when the car ran out of gas.

It chugged, wheezed, made another effort to move and stopped dead still.

Andy tried the starter, tried it again, swore and said incredulously:

"We're out of gas. We can't be. I had it filled — it must have leaked."

He got out of the car and went around to the tank and returned. He stood at the door, his face looking ghostly white and like the face of a stranger in the faint light from the dash.

"We are out of gas," he said and stared at her.

"There was a filling station back there," said Rue. "It was closed, but perhaps —"

"Yes. Yes, I suppose I can break in." He stared at her again and said: "Yes, of course. I must have gas. I've got to have gas. . . ."

It was rainy and dark, and they hadn't passed another car for a long time. She pulled her coat around her and said: "I'll go back with you."

He roused at that. He wouldn't have it; she'd get wet.

"I won't be long," he said. He looked at her again, eyes deeply shadowed and fixed, then he closed the door and disappeared into the murmurous darkness.

Rain slashed against the windows of the car.

It was very quiet except for the rain and very lonely. She could see no lights in any direction.

She settled herself to wait. It would take Andy, she supposed, about twenty minutes to walk back to the filling station, rouse someone or, as he said, break into the place, get some gasoline and trudge back through the rain to the car.

Well, if no car came along in the meantime, then there was no one to molest her. Consequently the sense of uneasiness that nagged at her had no meaning.

She reached for another cigarette and again had no matches. But in reaching into her pocket her fingers encountered the letter, and, because she had nothing else to do, she pulled it out, opened it and read it by the small light on the dashboard.

Read it — and knew why she was afraid.

It was a letter from Elizabeth Donney. And it enclosed another letter. Both were brief. She read Elizabeth's first.

DEAR RUE:

The girls told me you were here, and we were speculating about whether or not Julie could have been having some kind of love affair. I think she had had, because this note was in a book in her room. I think it was from him, whoever he is, and that she'd gone to meet him

*the afternoon she was murdered. It's written,
but I don't know the writing and it's not signed.
I'm sending it to you instead of to the police;
if it doesn't really mean anything I'd rather
nobody else knew. I'd hate Julie's little love affair in the papers, poor kid. She had so little.
Telephone if you want to see me.*

ELIZABETH

Rue read that first. Then she unfolded the enclosed note.

Rain drummed steadily upon the *top* of the
car, sounding like footsteps sloshing through the
wet.

"My sweet," said the note in heavy, markedly
backhand writing.

MY SWEET:

*Be sure you meet me this afternoon: in the
restaurant on Rush Street at four. Did I tell
you how long I've loved you? How, in the hospital, I've tried to find you, made excuses to
talk to you. Among all the nurses and their
white uniforms, I know the square little set of
your shoulders and the knot of smooth brown
hair under your perky little cap. Don't fail me
this afternoon.*

It was not signed. It needed no signature.
She did not even reread it. There was no need
to.

". . . the knot of smooth brown hair under

293

your perky little cap. . . ." Only, that other time, it had been gold hair. Her own. "Among all the nurses in the hospital . . ."

She broke off. She felt completely, utterly detached from her body, yet she knew there was danger.

It was her first clear thought.

Another one, racing, followed it; perhaps it came first and subconsciously roused her to danger, sounded the small clear tocsin of warning.

Andy hadn't wanted her to talk to Julie, because if Julie and she got together something would come out. Something that was hidden because — why, because it was the medicine. The medicine she herself had given Crystal. She hadn't prepared it, and *Julie hadn't prepared it*, for if so Julie would have made a note of it on the chart, and there was no such note. She hadn't prepared it, and Julie hadn't, yet the medicine was ready and waiting in a glass at seven, and Andy had been with Crystal at six o'clock.

He could have sent Julie out of the room on an errand. There were a dozen ways he could have accomplished a moment or two over the table of medicines. Just at that time, when Julie left and Rue came on duty, so Rue, naturally, would assume Julie had prepared the medicine.

She didn't pursue it further.

For every conscious thought and feeling she had was submerged in one only, and that was a blind, compelling instinct of escape. She was out of the car, into that murmurous, wet darkness

294

with rain on the top of the car which sounded like footsteps sloshing along toward her. She could see little. Lights reflecting eerily on wet pavement ahead, the light outside the filling station winking uncertainly through the rain and making a blurred halo around the gasoline pumps. Andy was back there somewhere in that dark wilderness between her and the area of light.

Yet the light outside the filling station was the only light to be seen.

She wanted Brule; she must find Brule; that was blind, unreasoning instinct too.

There would be a telephone in the filling station. The small, low building itself had looked as if it were closed. Andy had said: "I'll rouse somebody or break in." If somebody were there, she would be safe.

How could she travel that black, treacherous area between her and the light of the filling station and in doing so avoid Andy?

By listening, by watching for him, by knowing that he would be coming and, when she saw him (as see him she must against the light which would be behind him), by deserting the paved highway and taking refuge in the uncharted blackness at the side of the road. Perhaps there would be a hedge, a wall, anything she could crouch behind so there would be no betraying shadow.

She couldn't wait to consider any plan. Telephone, Brule, filling station — hide when you hear a footstep or see anything move against the light. Her conscious thought probably ran like that.

She must have left the car almost instantly, for she was all at once in a completely black, wet world, with rain on her face now and her own footsteps barely audible through the murmur of the rain upon pavement all around her.

It was incredibly lonely.

Had Andy really gone to the filling station?

That stopped her sharply, her heart giving a great terrified leap. But, answering it, all at once rectangles of light sprang up ahead and were the outlines of windows. He had roused someone, then — or he had broken in in order to get the key to the gasoline pump.

She must have begun, then, to run. As much space as she could cover before he started back to the car with the gasoline can would in that race for time count for her.

What would he do when he found she'd left the car? First start the car, then probably call to her — perhaps drive ahead on the road a way. He'd be uncertain, perplexed. She could count on time for him to arrive at the conclusion that her escape was intentional — thus that she knew the whole horrible and dangerous truth. It would be then that he'd think of the telephone in the filling station.

Rain, wet pavement, blackness; her own breath coming in painful gasps, she was perceptibly nearer the area of light. Gasoline tanks loomed scarlet and shining with rain. Then she became aware that the rectangles that were windows had vanished. When? Surely not more than a moment ago; she would have noticed. But it meant he was coming.

She left the pavement; stumbling in the darkness, half falling down a kind of embankment. She paused to listen, and it was well she did, because Andy was coming along the road. She could hear his footsteps plainly, and he was making a curiously irregular progress — first walking very rapidly, with almost feverish eagerness for a few steps and then going very much slower, almost stopping altogether, and suddenly, decisively, quickening his pace again.

What had been his plan? Perhaps he had none. Perhaps that hesitancy, that abstracted silence, that anxious seeking for roads, indicated his dreadful indecision. Indecision only as to means; from the beginning he had realized the threat her very existence offered him. "Come with me," he had said the night the thing began. Come away with me he had meant, so I can watch you, so I can keep the police from asking you certain things. So you will not talk to Julie; so you will not remember what you must not be permitted to remember.

Dark as it was, she had a horrible moment of certainty that he would see her, huddling there below him; that he would feel her presence, that her very thoughts would be lines guiding him to her.

But he didn't. He went on, running for a few

steps, and then stopped, until she thought she could bear the silence no longer and would scream — and then realized that his footsteps had blended at last with the drumming rain.

At last she crept out of the ditch and, finally, to the highway again.

Afraid, even then, that she had been deceived by some sound of the rain; that it hadn't actually been Andy who passed her there on the road.

But it was. The lighted area of the gasoline tanks was bare and empty. Away back along the black path she had come was a blur of lights outlining an object that was the car, and a tiny red dot that was its rear light.

The shabby car. That looked as if it had come from a junk heap.

She must cross the area of light quickly. She did so, flashing like a hunted small animal for cover.

The door of the little white building was closed but not locked. He'd broken in, for the bolt hung by one staple. It meant no one was there.

Would there be a telephone?

She didn't dare turn on lights as Andy had done. But the light from outside came faintly through the little window, and square in the path of it was the counter and telephone.

She grasped it, and her hands were so cold or so unsteady she couldn't, for a moment, dial correctly. She forced her fingers to steadiness; she could barely see the slots in the dial.

But she did dial her own number, and after a long time a voice came over the wire — and it was Brule.

"Brule —" She didn't know she sobbed.

"Rue — Rue, good God, is it you? Where are you? Rue —"

"Brule, come for me. Come — hurry. It's Andy. . . . Come —"

"Rue, where are you? What do you mean? We've been looking —"

"Listen." She must make him understand. "Brule, listen. Andy killed her. Julie. And Crystal. He — he's out there now, on the road. He'll be looking for me. I'm in the filling station, telephoning. Brule, come for me —"

"*Where* are you, Rue? Answer . . . tell me exactly . . . you must tell me. Ask the filling station attendant —"

"There's no one here. It's closed —"

"Closed — Rue, I've got to know where you are —"

"It's north and west of Chicago — near Morton Grove, I think. I don't know what road we're on. There are no houses —" She couldn't speak lucidly; she was sobbing and couldn't stop it.

Brule's voice came sharply.

"Rue, listen — is he near you?"

"Not now. He's at the car. It's a horrible old car —"

"How far away?"

"About a half a mile —"

Someone was talking to Brule — and Brule

was answering; someone was beside him talking, and she could hear their voices but not what they said. Then Brule said urgently:

"What's the number of the telephone you're using? Quick —"

She couldn't see the numbers in the little plate. She couldn't turn on the light. She'd given Andy back the little pack of matches.

"I can't — I can't see it, Brule," she cried brokenly.

"Stop that, Rue. You're hysterical. Listen. I will come. Understand. Tell me the number."

"But I can't see it — I can't turn on the light. I —"

"Can you hide from him? Do you mean he knows that you know?"

"Yes — yes —" She was sobbing again. She forced herself to reply slowly and distinctly:

"I'll try to hide. It's dark. Oh, Brule, come."

There was another quick colloquy beside the telephone.

Brule said tersely: "When you leave the telephone, don't hang up the receiver. Leave it hanging. We can get the address. Do you understand?"

"Y— Yes —"

"And listen, Rue — Is he coming?"

"Not yet."

"Tell me. Quick. The afternoon Julie died, what did Andy do with his overcoat — when he came into the room, I mean — did he have it with him?"

"Yes." She could see it again, in a queer flash,

against the darkness of the little filling station, with its smell of oil and gasoline, and the heavy drumming of rain on its low roof.

"It was on a chair. He put it on a chair."

"It's that. You're right; it's the cloakroom theft business!" It didn't sound sensible, but it was what she heard Brule say — not to her, but to someone near him. Brule said quickly and sharply into the telephone:

"Hide, Rue. Get away from him and hide. They've got the evidence — the bartender'll talk now too. Everything's all right if you can hold out till I come."

Andy was coming. She couldn't see out toward the black stretch of highway. She couldn't hear, for the sound of the rain drowned more distant sounds. But she knew he was coming.

"It's one of the western highways," she cried desperately. "It intersects Milwaukee, but it's before you reach the intersection. Brule —"

The drumming of the rain on the roof took on rhythm — became louder — was the wheezing throb of the engine of a car. Headlights glanced against her, searching her out through the window as a car swung jerkily into the paved square and stopped at the door, which was open.

CHAPTER XXI

She was never able to remember the next moment or two; she'd had no consciousness of leaving the telephone, of any movement or conscious and lucid thought at all. But sometime in that blank interval she found the back door and tore her fingers on some kind of bolt and was outside the ghastly little trap of walls and into the rain and darkness again.

It gave her for an instant a promise. But only an instant, for there was no place to hide, no shelter except darkness, and the lights of the car could seek through that.

She ran — and had no direction; she stopped, gasping for breath, trying to plan, to think. She couldn't. There were no outbuildings, there was no hedge. She stumbled through the rain, instinctively trying to put as much distance as possible between her and the lights behind her. And then she found the shrub.

A little shrub with thorns. It loomed, a small blotch of deeper darkness, beside her and caught at her coat. And Andy called behind her somewhere: "Rue . . . Rue . . ."

Rain blurred the voice. She couldn't tell where he was — far away or near.

She crouched down beside that thorny little shrub. Rain drowned the sound of his footsteps.

She was too near the filling station.

But his voice came again, nearer, so she could distinguish the queer pleading in it: "Rue — don't be afraid. Rue, where are you? . . . Rue, I won't hurt you. . . ."

And it was so much nearer that she didn't dare move; didn't dare seek a better hiding place.

Rain and darkness; time must be passing, though it seemed to stand still. There were sounds; her own heart beating heavily, loudly. She thought he'd gone once and was about to move cramped muscles when she heard him. Quite near:

"Rue, where have you gone? I won't hurt you. Don't be afraid. . . ." It was queer, not quite intelligible. A monotonous murmur.

It stopped. And she became aware that he was trying new tactics, making a short little rush in this direction and that.

"I know you're here, Rue. You hadn't time to go far. You're here somewhere. You'd be afraid to go into the fields — and leave the station and — There you are." He chuckled deeply. He'd seen her, he'd caught a glimpse of the soldier shadow in all that blackness. But he hadn't, though once he passed so near she thought he'd touched her.

Time stood still but must be passing.

He began to range further from the filling station. He must have passed the pitifully sparse little shrub a hundred times. Its very smallness, she realized suddenly, helped conceal its presence and her own.

Unless he blundered into it . . . She wondered suddenly if she'd left the telephone receiver hanging, still connected so they could trace the number. She couldn't remember.

She realized all at once that for a long time she'd heard no sounds. Had he gone? Or was it a trick? She waited, cramped, breathing lightly. She was right to wait, for his voice said, clearly through the rain, almost at her side: "Ah — caught you that time," and he chuckled again and made a little rush — which took him to one side of the shrub and away from her again.

So she was in a way prepared for it when he said loudly, almost shouting from somewhere near the filling station: "Rue — all right, Rue. You've won. I'm leaving. Do you understand? You can come out now from wherever you are — I'm leaving. . . ."

For an instant she believed it. Believed it, too, when the car started up and moved away — slowly, into the highway — believed it, yet some instinct told her not to move. So she crouched there, still and cramped but able to draw long breaths — and the car all at once swerved and turned and swept its light back and forth over the vacant, flat area, piercing the gloom not brightly but clearly enough so her own scurrying, hurrying figure would have been caught by those swerving fingers of light. And they fell upon the shrub — fell and lingered, and she could see its outline and her own, humped and solid, and the sparse grass so near her face.

It lingered, and she thought she was seen; then it swept on.

But he came back. Came back slowly, deliberately got out of the car.

She heard the door bang. Heard nothing for a while and then his footsteps. His voice even, murmuring as if the nightmare of the thing had touched him too. Saying: "It's only a shrub. Too little. . . . Rue, where are you? Rue, I've got to find you. Rue, I don't want to do it. I never wanted to — not even with Crystal. I couldn't help it. It was other people — not me; it was Crystal. I didn't want to; she made me; she insisted; there was no other way to get rid of her: it would have — Rue — Rue."

He touched the shrub. She felt it waver. And he swore and bent, and his fingers came out of the darkness and touched her face, and Rue screamed.

Against the rain — against the darkness. A darkness that became for Rue all at once entirely black, an engulfing current on which she drifted lost even to terror.

All black except it was pierced with sounds — sounds, lights, voices, men running, and above and through it all the steady throb and racing of engines — car engines, many of them, with great strong lights turning the whole bare little space into lighted tumult.

Someone was holding her, but it wasn't Andy. Somebody . . .

"Rue — are you all right now? Had he hurt you —"

It couldn't be Brule, and it was. Where had she been? How had all that turmoil happened without her knowing it was about to happen?

"I — fainted; he found me. He's here —" She thought she was speaking with the utmost intelligibility, and Brule didn't hear a word of it, for he put his face beside her own, and his cheek was hard and cool, and he said: "Oh, my God . . ." as if it were a groan.

The lights confused her; there were men shouting; gathering in a group. Brule was swiftly touching her; demanding; making her tell him she wasn't hurt. She tried to reply.

It was all confused, too, when he took her to a waiting car. He put her in it and got in beside her and shouted to someone outside.

"I'm going back to the house," he said. "You'll find us there. I'm taking Mrs Hatterick."

But he wouldn't let her talk; during all that swift trip, swooping through rain, through darkness, through at last lighted streets, he wouldn't let her talk.

They were at the house and the door was flung open; there were lights, people, confusion there too. But only for a moment. Then she was in the little guest room; a maid was there, and Madge, and Brule was giving swift orders.

Somebody (Madge? And was it possible there

were tear streaks on the child's round cheeks?) helped her undress; got her into a warm woolen dressing gown. Brule himself brought in a little white tub, and somebody poured hot water in it, and Brule had a homely little can in his hand labeled "Mustard."

"Your feet go in this," he said and knelt and pulled off her slippers himself.

"Ouch."

"I know it's hot. Keep them there —"

"Brule, I've got to know — everything —"

"Keep your feet in; all right." He looked up at her and said: "I suppose you've got to. It was Andy. Sit still. I'll tell you." He tested the water with his hand and plunged her feet deeper into it. "It's all very simple ready. It developed, however, just tonight; after you — had gone. It was one of those — those stubborn little ways truth has of convincing us of her indestructibility. In other words," said Brule simply, "malachite."

"Mal—"

"Malachite and Funk being dragged from the thing here to investigate cloakroom thefts at the Town Club. He —"

"What is malachite? Brule, that water's boiling."

"No, it isn't. Keep still. Malachite's a dry stain, that's a powder. They'd sifted it over things in the cloakroom; there'd been a series of petty thefts, and they were trying to detect the thief and stop it without resorting to the police. They thought some of the staff — a waiter or a page boy — was doing it. Anyway, the stuff was on Andy's coat. He must have arranged to meet Julie —"

"Yes, there's a letter — I don't know what I did with it," she said, bewildered. "I had it —"

"Look in her coat," said Brule. Madge found the coat and said: "Is this it?" over a crumpled, soggy piece of paper.

It was. Brule read it.

"Andy wrote that?"

"Yes." There were questions and answers unspoken; put aside.

Brule went on:

"When Andy met Julie she must have touched him, put her — hands on his arm."

"Malachite —"

"Oh, that. It sticks to your hands, you see, and, when your hands perspire or are washed, turns green. Becomes a dye. It's an old trick; forgotten with more modern methods. Remembered, luckily, by the old porter at the club. It isn't too efficacious, as he found for his pains, for he'd scattered it so liberally that instead of catching his thief he immediately got complaints of club members — several, at any rate, who had lunched there the morning he essayed his little trap, and found themselves with unexpected streaks of green dye on their hands. They — five or six of them — were told the truth. Among the five or six was Andy. He'd accidentally avoided it himself by putting on gloves as he left the club. The porter did not use malachite again after his unsuccessful attempt; we wouldn't have known of it if they hadn't had to call in the police, finally. And no one came forward to tell us because that detail of the green stains was kept out of the newspapers. And the porter also remembered that Andy had lunched there the day of Julie's murder; Andy himself told the police he'd lunched at some little restaurant on Michigan; they wasted a lot of time trying to check that story. But the lie, when they discovered it, was significant; Andy had learned of the malachite; he'd heard about the stain on Julie's hands. He knew his own danger. Later the maid, Rachel, shaking up the cushion of the chair where Andy had put his coat when she cleaned the room for the first time since the murder, got the dye on her hands too. We figure Julie knew something of how Andy gave Crystal poison —"

"I know," said Rue in a small voice and told him.

He listened, asking no questions.

"I thought it must be something of the kind. Something that would be obvious only if you and Julie pooled your stories. It was so simple, that matter of the medicine; once you and Julie had occasion to be suspicious, he didn't dare permit you to meet and talk of that night and of exactly how and when Crystal's medicine was prepared. Julie — poor Julie — torn between suspicion and — Andy's charm."

Brule paused. "Andy's charm," he repeated

thoughtfully. "Too much charm, too much of the wrong kind of ambition — and too little courage. . . . Well . . ." He put his hand in the water and turned briskly to Madge.

"Give me more hot water, Madge," he said and resumed: "It's a direct trail, then. From Andy to Julie to the house; he had the extra key, the missing key; Crystal — must have given it to him. He let Julie into the house and didn't call anyone. He figured she'd die before anyone could reach her; before she could reach you. Perhaps she insisted, dazedly, on seeing you. So he brought her directly from the little restaurant here, thinking there would be no danger. If Gross had been ten — even five minutes — later, Julie wouldn't have reached you at all. As it was she only mumbled things he'd said to her. Repeating — dazed."

Someone knocked hard on the door. Madge went, and it was Guy Cole.

"The bartender's identified him," he said. "They promised to let the fellow off if he told the truth; he says he's sure it was Andy. How are you, Rue? I want to talk to you —"

"Later," said Brule. "Close the door, Madge."

"Wait a minute, I've not finished," protested Guy. "He had a pack of matches in his pocket; advertising, you know; and they'd come from that little restaurant, and Andy said, at first, that he'd never so much as seen the place. So that was that. Rue, what's the story —"

"I said later," said Brule. "Get out."

"Oh, all right," said Guy reluctantly. "But after all —"

Madge closed the door.

The little table which had held a thermos and a glass caught Rue's eyes. She said: "But the poison in the glass — in the house — would he dare?"

"Let the police worry about that if they want to," said Brule, pouring more steaming water into the little tub. "I think he was scared; the whole business is one actuated by the extremest cowardice. Andy was always a coward. He could get into the home because he had a key. But he had to get the police out. And he probably figured he'd be safer if he got me out too; so he put in a phony telephone call, that's the way we've figured it, anyway. But I think it's right. More mustard, Madge."

Rue's feet were scarlet.

She made a tentative effort to withdraw them which was instantly foiled, and said: "It isn't possible he actually entered the house — just to put poison in the glass as a threat."

"Not impossible, for it happened; perhaps he intended something else — and lost his nerve."

She thought of certain moments in the nightmare just past — that curious look of anxiety and terrible indecision.

"Did he really intend to . . . ?" she was whispering.

Brule looked at her sharply and said: "No. Certainly not. He — didn't know what he was

311

going to do. Forget it. All of it."

"Brule, why did he kill Crystal?" began Rue and remembered Madge.

Brule glanced at her, too, and Madge came to Rue.

"Rue, I — I rolled the knife (that Alicia found in Father's instrument case) in your scarf and put it in your room. It — it was a beastly thing to do. I — there isn't any excuse." She gulped. Her face flushed and paled. "I — you can't forgive me. I was — crazy."

"She was told to do it," said Brule. "It doesn't make it more forgivable, though."

Madge's dark eyes sought into Rue's with the appeal of a small child's.

"Will you — ever — forgive me?" she said. "I didn't realize —"

In the warmth and safety of that room Rue could have forgiven anything. She put out her hand toward Madge. Madge said unsteadily: "I didn't realize; I was — scared. She said, Alicia said —"

Brule, watching Rue, said: "Run away, Madge. I think Rue won't be — unforgiving." Madge put back her dark mane of hair and went away. And Brule said slowly:

"Are you, Rue? Unforgiving?"

There were things yet unspoken, hovering in the warm little room.

Brule said: "I want you to know the whole thing, Rue. You see, all along I knew that Andy had a motive for wanting to be rid of Crystal.

312

That was it; he had to get rid of her. Crystal — Crystal had always loved attention; I didn't know that, in Andy's case, she was serious until it was too late. He — was equally culpable, I suppose. Flattered, pleased — frightened only when he began to perceive the iron strength Crystal had when she wanted anything — her utterly ruthless tenacity. . . . And I had my share of guilt in it; I let it go on even when I saw how things were, but I thought she'd get over it. She had got over other — affairs. I don't know what Andy has told you; or what Alicia has told you. But my great fault was in letting things go on until they reached the point they reached. That is," said Brule slowly, "the point where Crystal was determined to divorce me and marry Andy, and he, knowing that his career depended upon me, knowing which side his bread was buttered on, was equally determined not to. Crystal, you see, had used enough of her capital so that Andy wouldn't have been riding on velvet, so to speak. Crystal had dipped into it with both hands; she gave money to Alicia, she gave it to Andy —"

"Andy!"

"Oh yes. Crystal — had a kind of empress complex about money. It kept me going sometimes to pay the bills. . . . Besides, it gave her an extra claim upon Andy. An extra obligation. But except for this house and the bequest she left Alicia there wasn't really much property remaining; her will gave all she had to me — years ago when it was made, it was considerable.

313

When she died there was very little. In short, if Andy had consented to her divorcing me he would have found himself married to a woman he didn't want, a woman twenty years older than he, a woman with extravagant tastes, with little money herself, and Andy's whole career blasted. So he thought. I don't know what I would have done, really; kept Andy on in my office, I suppose. I was so tired of — all of it. I didn't care much what happened. But he didn't know that. And he was always a little afraid of me. I suppose during her illness he'd realized how her death would simplify things for him. But she didn't die. Therefore —"

"Alicia," said Rue without knowing she was going to say it. He caught her up quickly.

"I couldn't defend myself before Steven," he said. "And you wouldn't listen to what I could say. But I couldn't rob Steven of his last illusions of Alicia. I couldn't tell him —"

"Tell him what, Brule?"

Brule turned swiftly to her. He was kneeling at her feet; he took her hand and looked earnestly, almost pleadingly as Madge had done, into her eyes.

"Rue, will you try to understand? Alicia — was there, you see. Always there when I was lonely; always entertaining, always agreeable, a friend of the family's. Gradually, I don't quite know how, I began — to accept Alicia. I didn't love her; I don't think she ever loved me really, for Alicia doesn't love, she merely seeks a pleas-

ant and comfortable life for Alicia. We were together a lot. Once Crystal got suspicious and
began to ask questions, and Alicia roped in
Steven as easily as — as she'd pull in a trusting
dog on a leash. Alicia didn't want to lose Crystal's very remunerative friendship. That settled
Crystal; Crystal didn't want me herself, but she
was vain and she was considerably older than I
and conscious of it — she didn't want Alicia, a
younger woman, to take me away. But with
Alicia and Steven engaged, everything was all
right. I — I don't know what I felt during that
time; mainly, it seems to me, I was tired — and
in a trap of my own making. Well, at any rate,
Alicia kept strengthening that intangible thing
that existed between us; when Crystal died I felt
in duty bound to ask Alicia to marry me. Besides, it would have pleased Madge. And Alicia
refused. I believe Alicia more than half believed
I had murdered Crystal myself — for love of
Alicia. And I thought —" He bent his head suddenly and placed it upon Rue's hands.

"Rue, here's where the forgiving comes in.
You see, I thought that if I married somebody
else it would end the — the entangling affair
with Alicia. It was never — you'll have to believe
me — what you'd really call an affair."

"Steven . . ." whispered Rue.

His face turned on her hands.

"Steven," he said. "I couldn't go to him and
say: 'Look here, you must break your engagement with Alicia because she has led me to be-

lieve she's in love with me.' And to tell the truth, Rue, I didn't care very much. About anything. I was tired and I'd worked like a dog for years, and I — everywhere was disappointment and weariness and sham, and I — I couldn't see anything that I'd gained. All those years of hard work, and I had reached a stalemate. I had absolutely nothing that was of value to me. Except Madge. And she was, then, her mother's child. I'd been too ambitious. I . . ." He stopped.

And simply turned his head on her hands and kissed them.

"I want you, Rue."

There were tears on Rue's cheeks.

Brule looked up; his eyes sought into her own deeply, searchingly, half afraid. She'd never known Brule to be uncertain.

Then he saw the tears.

After a moment he touched her wet cheeks gently with his fingers.

And took her slowly in his arms and kissed her mouth.

"I love you . . ." he said.

Rue's heart sang madly: I've always loved you. I've always — always — always loved . . .

She caught back the words. Presently she moved her feet cautiously. He felt the motion, turned, caught both slender ankles and pushed them back in the hot water again. He got to his feet and rang for Gross and ordered a number of things, while Rue sat in a kind of bewitched silence, and, when they came, mysteriously mixed something hot and smelling of lemons in a tall glass.

"Drink it."

She did. Because his arm held her; because he held the glass and watched lingeringly while she drank.

She was drowsy; the room was warm; Brule held her in his arms and talked:

". . . We'll go on a trip. Have you ever been to France, Rue? We'll sit in golden sunshine beside a sea as blue as your eyes. When we've tired of that we'll go on . . . and on . . ."

"Home . . ." said Rue.

"Home. I'll get a house in the country on a river. There'll be flowers and sunshine and blue sky — and you, Rue. . . ."

The phrase repeated itself goldenly, following her into dreams.